QUINTET

QUINTET

Douglas Arthur Brown

KEY PORTER BOOKS

Library and Archives Canada Cataloguing in Publication

Brown, Douglas Arthur,
    Quintet / Douglas Arthur Brown.

ISBN 978-1-55263-997-9

    I. Title.

PS8553.R684967Q55 2008   C813'.54   C2007-905705-5

ONTARIO ARTS COUNCIL
CONSEIL DES ARTS DE L'ONTARIO

The publisher gratefully acknowledges the support of the Canada Council for the Arts and the Ontario Arts Council for its publishing program. We acknowledge the support of the Government of Ontario through the Ontario Media Development Corporation's Ontario Book Initiative.

We acknowledge the financial support of the Government of Canada through the Book Publishing Industry Development Program (BPIDP) for our publishing activities.

Key Porter Books Limited
Six Adelaide Street East, Tenth Floor
Toronto, Ontario
Canada M5C 1H6

www.keyporter.com

Text design: Marijke Friesen
Electronic formatting: Alison Carr

Printed and bound in Canada

08 09 10 11 12 5 4 3 2 1

Denne bog er tilegnet
Per Bundvad

This book is dedicated to the memory of
Per Bundvad

Row, brothers, row, the stream runs fast,
The rapids are near, and the daylight's past.

THOMAS MOORE

Cameron

AUGUST, HALIFAX

MOM AND DAD ARE DEAD. There, I've said it. I couldn't bring myself to actually think those words at the wake and funeral. It wasn't so bad when old friends kept referring to the folks' deaths as hard luck or a blow. But every time we were told that it was a disaster or a freak accident the collar tightened around a big lump in my throat. And I couldn't help noticing that everyone who entered glanced quickly at the two caskets, relieved, I'm sure, that they were closed.

Now here's the funny thing, dear brothers. I didn't even know the folks were on vacation. Nobody told me anything. I was watching the news on television and a reporter was standing in front of the site where the train derailed in Florida. He was looking all serious and there was a swarm of mosquitoes buzzing around his head while he delivered the gruesome details. He pointed to a lopsided barge in the background that had rammed the bridge as the train crossed it, recounted how the locomotive caught fire and the dining and sleeping cars fell into the alligator-infested waters below. The camera zoomed in for a close-up of his face as he said that most of the fifty-five people who died were a group of seniors from Canada. Then he flashed a big smile as he signed off, an enormous mosquito perched just above his eyebrow, sucking him dry.

I headed for the kitchen to fetch a fresh beer. That was when the call came. Beth, calling on behalf of our Big Brother. I got a weird déjà vu feeling as she recounted the story I'd just heard on the news. Only she added another detail. The folks were among the seniors who perished. The Big B, she said, was in Florida, identifying the remains.

Everything was murky in the coming days. Thank God for Beth, picking each of us up at the airport and making excuses for the Big B, who was *busy* attending to the details of the funeral. She stocked the fridge at the folks' house with enough food to last us a month. Me, I felt like we were kids again, raiding the fridge. Not that we ate much of it. It was always one of mom's big taboos. "Sweet Jumping American Moses, if you want a piece of watermelon, ask for it." She'd be on her hands and knees, scooping up all the pieces that splattered over the floor when I dropped it. On my foot. Lost a toenail that time.

Then the wake. Greeting an endless parade of mourners at the funeral parlour, friends and neighbours who had known the three of us as kids, but were still awkward when they gazed into the same set of eyes on three identical faces. When they reached the Big B at the end of the line, warm smiles sprouted on their faces. The Big B helped them shake off the bewilderment of confronting us three.

So it was a relief to get away from all that sorrow and grab a few beers after the wake. You were squeezed between Rory and me, Adrian, your shoulders leaning into ours like those golden retrievers that press themselves against your leg when they sit beside you. That was the first time we'd talked in years. It was a momentous occasion, the three of us together in the same city.

Of course, in those first moments we had to warm up to each other again, cautiously circling like flies above a picnic table. Chit-chat about lost luggage between Copenhagen and Halifax, the cost of season tickets to see the Blue Jays play at the Rogers Centre in Toronto. Admiring my flashy Ray Bans. Finally, we landed in the sugar bowl.

"You broke your arm, Rory," I said.

"I did? How old were we?"

"Three, four at the most."

"Mom said you had a cast and all the kids in the neighbour-hood signed it. Adrian was jealous and thought he should have one as well."

"Really?"

"According to mom, you asked me to jump on the cast, Adrian, to see how strong it was. And I happily obliged. It snapped in two."

"Are you serious?"

"Why would mom lie?"

"Not that, you dolt. I can't believe you actually broke my arm."

"That's when we all got our own bedrooms," I said, lifting my glass. "To the folks."

"To the folks."

I'm sure that if anybody had looked closely they'd have glimpsed pain in our eyes, even though we made a good effort, wielding our temporary high spirits like shields as we drank, protecting our private grief.

Around the tavern we caught sidelong glances from the other tables, regulars who always scrutinize anyone new to their turf. When we stared back, they didn't even bother to turn away, dangling their nosiness like fishhooks. But we never took the bait.

It was the first time since arriving home we'd had a chance to catch up with what's been going on in our lives, only we couldn't seem to get past reminiscing about the folks.

"Then there was the egg timer," Adrian said, stretching out the syllables, pausing to take a deep swallow from his beer. "Whenever we started bickering, dad set that friggin' timer to half an hour. If either of you were arguing with me we weren't allowed to talk to each other again until it went off."

"I never started the arguments. It was always you or Cameron. Mostly you, Cameron," Rory countered.

"Bite me."

That was the moment I had my *epiphany*. Of course, it might have been a stroke, seeing how rare it is for me to ever exhibit a spark of genius. I flagged down the waitress and borrowed her pen. I started scribbling on a napkin, the greasy pen slipping between my fingers.

"We should write all this down," I said. "Stop looking at me like that."

Bending forward, Adrian tried to get a peek at the napkin. "Write what down?"

"Stuff. What we've been talking about. Catch up."

"That's a lot of catching up, Cameron."

"Exactly, Rory."

"So you want us to write a diary?"

"Don't poof out on me, Adrian. We'll call it a journal. And share it. I get it for four months, mail it to you, and you mail it to Rory when you're finished. That way we each get to write something once a year. For the love of God, stop looking at me like that."

I could see a big "but" forming on your lips, Rory, and cut you off.

"It has to have a sturdy cover," I continued, the pen tapping madly now, keeping beat with my knee banging the underside of the table. "You know, so it won't get bent in the mail. And it has to have a dark cover."

"Dark?"

"To hide the coffee stains. In case you write in it while you're cooking one of those *fabulous* meals at your restaurant, Adrian."

"And it should be red," I said, turning to Rory. "Your favourite colour. Actually, it's the only colour you like. How could you spend four years at an art school and then decide you'll only paint in one colour for the next twenty years? You're a mystery, Rory, you really are."

"What about Talbot?"

"What about him?" I snapped.

WHAT IN THE HELL was I thinking? I must have stared at these empty pages a dozen times before I picked up a pen. And when I did, I had nothing to say, scratching out what I wrote, which is why the first three pages are missing. I just couldn't get into the flow of things. I kept ripping out a page and starting over, which is why I finally decided to smoke a joint. Now there's no stopping me.

Let's see, what to write? Well, next year we turn forty. Damn, that's hard to believe. Right now I'm enjoying the first day of our thirty-ninth year, and I take some comfort in knowing that by the time you get this journal, you'll both be closer to forty than I am today. How's that for anti-aging logic?

I digress. God, I love the way that word rolls off my tongue. I usually find words like that fruity. No offence, Adrian.

Which reminds me of the time I took you out for a bite to eat after a hockey game. Just you and me. Cameron and Adrian. You were *oohing* and *aahing* over the menu, giving loads of attitude to the waitress, and when she finally suggested something, you shook your head in that wimp way you had and told her you wanted something more substantial. Christ! Only the babes use words like *substantial*. I wanted to kill you. I should've known then you were queer. I mean gay. No, I mean queer. I saw a program once, a bunch of queens, and they were calling each other sister, so I guess if it's okay for them it's okay for the likes of me to call my brother queer. Because frankly, Adrian, you were never very gay growing up. Moody, as I remember. Except when you smiled.

Now don't get your noses out of joint, boys. You know how it is, a few tokes always make me bitchy, saying things I don't necessarily mean or remember. I've never written in a journal before. It may require a few more attempts to temper my writing, to find a style that won't offend either of you. Granted, it may take awhile before we find our stride, but I'm sure we'll start to produce some serious steam along the way. It shouldn't be any different from when we get together, as infrequent as that has been in recent years. Did you ever notice that since growing up, we're always reserved for the first hour or two when we're in a room together before we let our guard down and relax?

Writing in this journal shouldn't be any different. We always survive those first awkward hours together, don't we? I mean, aren't we supposed to be able to read each other's minds and finish each other's sentences, like all good stereotypical triplets? Of course, that would have to be another family, another set of triplets, wouldn't it, since we defy all the conventional wisdom on how triplets should behave. But we've beaten the odds before, so get writing, no matter how stilted, or in your case, Rory, how Victorian, the first few attempts may read.

And no skipping. I don't want it coming back to me all the time with some lame excuse on your part, Rory, because you were too busy mounting a new exhibition. Or yours, Adrian, because you couldn't recover from the trauma of a soufflé that failed to rise. I always have something to say, but this is *our* journal, not just mine. This is the route. It starts with me in Halifax. It goes on to Adrian in Copenhagen, and then to you, Rory, in Toronto.

Now I know this is going to come up, so let's get it out of the way right now. I don't want to include the Big B. He doesn't count. I mean he counts as family. He is our Big Brother. But we all know it wouldn't work, he wouldn't go for it, and even if he did it wouldn't last. He's too judgmental. During the funeral I got the feeling that he didn't approve of the way we mourned. I can just hear him rattling on to Beth. Rory was too philosophical about the deaths, Cameron asked too many goddamn questions, and Adrian treated the whole thing lightly, as if it were no more than the death of a couple of goldfish. Then again, and I'm going to cut the Big B a little slack here, maybe he thought we cried too much, gazing at us, seeing us as one, our faces merging into one massive waterfall of tears.

Anyway, he's too old. There are ten years between him and us. That's a lot of years. We three go back a long way. Ever since we were roommates in mom's womb. The Big B is another unit. Another generation. And he's a prick. He got the house in Cape Breton, the family home in Sydney, didn't he? Our house. Even though he has that farm in Bras d'Or.

That's probably why I caught him looking so smug during the wake, standing there in his skinny body, his cold grey eyes revealing a sparkle I'd never seen. Gloating. Batting those long eyelashes of his in self-satisfaction when he didn't think anyone was looking at him. But I was looking at him, stretching to my, *our*, full six-foot frame, looking down at our much shorter, much older brother.

I've been keeping a close eye on the Big B lately, and watching my back whenever I'm around him. Why? Let's just say that the Big B has given me good reason to be wary, something I never got around to mentioning to either of you when we were home. It wasn't the time or the place. I'm sure you're dying of curiosity, Rory, but you'll just have to wait until I'm ready to write about what happened between the Big B and myself.

Speaking of the prick, he'd look a lot younger if he shaved off his beard. It's too grey and it makes him look old. And he has those puffy cheeks. You'd think a skinny guy like him would have our high cheekbones, not a chipmunk's face. I'm wondering if I was the only one staring at the Big B, or if he looked around the room at the wake and saw three identical sets of eyes looking back at him.

Mom used to say we did that when we were young. She'd be reading the newspaper, the three of us playing on the floor, each doing our own thing, me louder than you two, naturally. Looking up from her paper, she'd meet all of our eyes in that instant, as if we synchronized our stare to meet the sweep of her gaze. None of us was aware that the other two were also looking at her. Then we'd quietly return our attention to the comic books, or the toys on the floor, without a word said. Sometimes I snuck a second glance at mom. She'd sit there with that goofy look she got on her face in those first few seconds after she pulled the quilt up to her chin to take a nap on the chesterfield.

I'VE NEVER BEEN on a train. Love them, but have never ridden the rails, as they say. When we were home I snuck away for a couple of hours between the afternoon and evening wake. Took a stroll along Charlotte Street, something I haven't done for years. First stop was that old pawnshop at the lower end of the street where we used to trade in comic books. That place reminded me of Doctor Who's time machine. From the outside it looked like a little hole in the wall, narrow, squeezed in between two bigger shops, but when you stepped inside it was packed floor to ceiling and must have been at least fifty feet deep. Buddy used to wheeze behind the counter, and it felt like he was boring a hole into the backs of our heads as we went through the stack of comics. Rory and I looking for the latest *Silver Surfer,* cringing while you went through every *Betty and Veronica* you could lay your hands on, Adrian, although you did toss *Little Lotta* on the next pile and buy up all the *Daredevil* comics. Okay, sometimes Rory and I lowered our standards, Rory grabbing for *Richie Rich* and me for *Spooky the Tuff Little Ghost*.

Meanwhile, Buddy was sorting our old comics behind the counter, dividing them into two piles, those he wanted to keep and those he put in the trash. He never gave us back the trashed comics. So what do you think happened to the rejects? Me, I think he took them home with him, a little unreported commission from the guy who actually owned the place.

There were at least a dozen of those bowl-shaped mirrors around the shop so that Buddy could see what was going on in every corner. If you positioned yourself just right in front of one of those mirrors you could see your reflection bounced to the other ones, on and on, as if there were a hundred of you standing there, like the lady holding the box of Moirs' Pot of Gold chocolates. Customers watched themselves disappear into infinity, waving into the mirrors or sticking out their tongues. Of course, it was no big deal for us, we were used to seeing ourselves reflected anytime we looked at each other.

Anyway, the pawnshop isn't there anymore. Instead, it's a hobby shop, selling model trains. I'm remembering the set we got one Christmas when we were about ten. Actually, to avoid any squabbles between us, the folks bought three sets. It got pretty stale watching the trains make that same loop over and over on three separate tracks, so we hooked up all three sets with intersecting tracks and set the trains on a collision course. Bam! Rory's locomotive lost its cowcatcher, Adrian's smashed its headlight to smithereens, and my engine hopped the tracks and the metal wheels gouged the floor, leaving a ten-foot-long groove in the hardwood. It was another opportunity for dad to spout his familiar Chinese proverb before he exploded. "Consider thrice before you act!" You know, for years I thought he was saying "Consider Christ before you act." He always had that little problem with "th." Next day, the Salvation Army received more anonymous gifts from the Hines brothers.

As I stood outside the shop, I watched some kid put the finishing touches on a display in the window. He had a black dye job going on in his curly hair, fingernails to match, and something metallic that looked like a booger on the side of his nose. Weird thing was, this goth store clerk was wearing a Lacoste polo shirt. Just didn't look right, didn't match the rest of his *ensemble*. The little choo-choo train was making its laps around the track, passing over a bridge. Below it was one of those tinfoil pie plates filled with water. It was a pretty dull display, if you ask me. Kid stuff. I was more interested in the sleek locomotives displayed on the posters hanging in the window.

The kid smiled and nodded to me. There was a gap the size of a canyon between his two front teeth and I nodded back, about to step inside, when I noticed he was holding a shoebox. Out came half a dozen plastic alligators, in a variety of shapes, which he placed in the pie pan. Dull just got promoted to morbid. He was making fun of the train accident. I couldn't look this sick puppy in the eye and dropped my gaze to his shirt. The alligator logo on the polo shirt looked like it was snapping at me.

Jesus H. Christ.

BACK TO THE JOURNAL. Now, Rory, I know that you and the wife have one of those "we don't keep any secrets from each other" things going on. Don't get me wrong. I'm not insinuating Janet is anything like the Big B. She's not. Your missus is a classy lady. I've only met her a few times, but she makes an impression. You can't help remembering those dark good looks. I like her. And I don't know whom you're shacking up with these days, Adrian, over there in Denmark, but if experience is any indication, it could be any Tom's Harry Dick.

My point is, I think the journal should be for our eyes only. I just wouldn't feel comfortable knowing that someone outside the triad was peeking over our shoulders while we wrote.

I'm putting this journal in the mail today. I have to get a good night's sleep because tomorrow our choir is performing at Pier 21 for the cruise ships. There are four ships in port, thousands of tourists wandering around downtown Halifax.

I'm impressed. Aren't you impressed? I didn't need the full four months to finish my entry after all. I have a couple of weeks to spare.

This is Cameron, signing off in D flat. Remember. Maximum four months. And write. Write *something*.

Adrian

SEPTEMBER, COPENHAGEN

A GAY PRIEST is presiding over a burial, and he suddenly has a crisis of faith. He can't decide if God is Divine or simply fabulous.

AUTUMN ARRIVES ABRUPTLY in Copenhagen, not like the leisurely onset we enjoyed growing up in Sydney. There are no warnings in Denmark, not like the flare of colours on the leaves of the maple trees around Cape Breton, followed by the long sleep of winter to follow.

I often emerge from my winter somnolence a season out of beat to greet a wasted spring long fled.

Like a wasp in winter, awakened by the teasing promise of a sunny day, called forth to greet the spring while the chill winds of February temporarily part their drapes of bitter cold. The wasp bastes its wings, and at the moment of virgin flight, the sun sets and February snickers as the eager and premature wasp perishes within a shroud of frost.

I am like that wasp, only it is autumn and not winter. All the inhibited energy that nourished me through a lazy and indifferent spring and summer siesta wants to break free. Around me, the people who populate my days grumble and pull their collars around their necks, guarding against the bite of the night as darkness uncoils day by day like a long black snake. Already, some of my staff at the restaurant are sniffling with premature colds, dragging their feet around the kitchen.

But autumn has always been a time of renewal for me. I look forward to this season to get busy with life. As if the darkening days are horse blinders, forcing me to go forth, onward, not to be distracted by the lethargy along the sidelines. I grasp it and sally forth to take a chance, to try new ideas. Like this journal, allowing me to find the courage within its pages to remember and finish what I need to say. Before the winter settles in and I forget. Before the wasp closes its wings, deaf to the world around it.

I DON'T THINK I ever mentioned it, but the restaurant I own in Copenhagen is called The Little Supper. We often serve exotic meat and fish dishes. Now get this, last week the frozen carcass of a seven-foot American alligator arrived at the back door, and it required the assistance of the entire kitchen staff to carry it into the cooler from the delivery truck. After reading about your weird experience at the train store, Cameron, I was inclined to donate the beast to the food bank. This particular alligator had an elongated and armoured body with a muscular flat tail, and the rounded snout was long, with nostrils at the end to allow for breathing while the body was underwater.

Alligators don't chew their food before swallowing, and it isn't unusual for one to shake its prey in its mouth, to dislodge a piece small enough to swallow. It allows the carrion to rot so that the meat falls away from the bone. This alligator was almost an adult and the short legs bore five toes on the front feet, but only four on the back, and I estimated its weight at two or three hundred kilos.

The meat from an alligator has a delicate, light-grained quality about it, high in protein and low in calories and fat, unless you fry it. The tail is the favoured meat and my chefs decided to barbecue the tail in three-quarter-inch-thick steaks. It was seasoned with rosemary and black and cayenne peppers, and then tenderized in diluted coconut milk for several hours. Once marinated, the meat was patted dry, re-seasoned and brushed with olive oil, and placed on the gas grill for ten minutes on each side, then served on a bed of saffron rice. After getting over my initial repulsion at the sight of the alligator I tasted it.

What can I say? It tasted Divine.

I THINK I AM GOING to enjoy this journal. For once, I'll be able to say what I want, when I want, without one of you interrupting me or finishing —

— *We don't do that.*

Mind you, it took me a long time to be comfortable without either of you around all the time. When I left Sydney to study culinary arts in Montreal, I took the train. The first eight hours were a horror. It was a rail liner that inched along the milk run, stopping at every station on its route through Nova Scotia.

— Why have I left? I thought. Why did they let me go? And most important, How are they going to survive without all my pranks now that I am gone?

I think it was during the train trip to Montreal when I decided never again to become attached to a place, thinking, in part, that it was also Cape Breton I missed. And it was then, I believe, on that long, slow trip, that I lost what you consider my laughter, Cameron. But I didn't lose it. It was just my ability to titter on cue at your bidding that vanished.

It was definitely the dope you were smoking that made you write that about me, claiming that I was a gloomy child. The dope interfered with your short-term memory. Because, as usual, I cracked jokes all the time when I was home, despite the grief of the funeral. We all laughed. Except Talbot, who never expresses amusement in our presence.

As you can read, I am living up to the demands that you've placed upon us, Cameron. I am writing something. I am giving you both something of my life. Uninterrupted.

Maybe you'll be surprised to discover, as these pages unfold, that I too have memories. At the moment, you seem to prefer to remember me as a gloomy child, Cameron, indecisive and fey.

There was also time at the tavern that night for me to notice a few things before the familiar whirlwind engulfed us. You wear contact lenses now, Rory. We couldn't see the green specks you have in your brown eyes, specks that Cameron and I don't carry. Our eyes are still strong. Our hair is still thick, no balding at the crown, although you still keep your hair short, Cameron, very short. We three have some salt and peppering at the sideburns. We aren't overweight, nice necks, although our Adam's apples are pointy.

Maybe we crowed too loudly in the tavern after the wake, not quite comfortable sitting there in our black suits, our shoulders a little too broad, our waists a little too slim for the long belts, and maybe it is this you find unsettling, Cameron, choosing instead to recall a memory of me, of us, less cheerful, more reserved.

Because I will say it again. We did laugh that night, many, many times. Throwing our heads back in gales of exuberance, tears rolling down our faces, down your tanned face, Rory, salty and refreshing, not hot and fierce like our tears of mourning in the days leading up to the wake and during the hours after the funeral. My God, I needed you to laugh at my jokes. Every time I try to tell a knock-knock joke to a Dane, he always says, *Come in*.

AT THE LITTLE SUPPER our specialty is aphrodisiacs. For example, the alligator, with its long phallic tail, has always enjoyed the reputation of instilling vigour in men and lust in women.

My partners and I chose the name because *petit souper* was a popular eighteenth-century custom in France, where seating at dinner tables was kept intimate and hearty dishes were prepared to increase the erotic sensibilities of the guests. It is even rumoured that Richelieu invited his friends and their mistresses to these cozy meals, and once all were assembled, they dined together in the nude.

— *Yup, that's our Adrian, Rory. Sex on the brain. All the time. Food and sex.*

YES, SEX.

Bumping into someone from my past at the tavern in Sydney, where he was playing pool across the room. Only he didn't meet my stare. But he knew who I was.

I walked up to him and extended my hand.

— I wasn't sure it was you, he said. He leaned the cue against the table and shook my hand. Quickly.

This is a man who doesn't like to shake hands.

And as a teenager, I remember, he didn't like to be hugged.

I glanced back at our table, at you, Rory, then at you, Cameron. Thinking to myself, How could he not know it was me? There were three of me sitting over there.

— I heard about the accident, he said.

I waited.

— I mean, about your loss. He looked over at our table. You and your brothers, he added.

I grinned. Thinking again, If you weren't sure it was me, how can you be sure they're my brothers?

— Do you still play? he asked.

— No.

— That's too bad, he said. You were a wicked drummer.

We had played in the school band together. That he remembered.

— Are you married? he asks.

In case I misunderstood. In case I thought he was coming onto me. Again.

— Widowed, I said. And you?

— Two kids.

Then.

— Wife and kids are out of town. Can I buy you a beer?

— No, I said.

— You look good, Adrian.

— So do you, Joseph.

He extended his hand.

I took it. Then I leaned in and gave him a hug, briefly pressing my hips against his waist. He started to lean into the hug, but I pulled away from him.

— How's your father? I asked.

— He's dead.

He didn't look away from me. He was remembering other things about me now.

— I am sorry about your father, I said.

— You didn't like my father. He smiled.

— No, I said. Reflecting his smile. It was mutual.

— I've got to finish the game, he said. They're waiting for their turn.

I glanced over at the bar. Two guys in baseball caps were watching us, their pool cues resting between their legs.

— I didn't think three people could play pool, I said.

— We're not playing together, he says. They're just waiting for me to finish my game. Most of us play by ourselves.

And that is why I was smiling when I came back to our table, Rory. Three guys playing with themselves. That's funny.

Only I kept the joke to myself.

SEX AND JOSEPH.

We three must have been around seventeen and in grade eleven. Joseph had just moved to Sydney. His family came from the other end of the province, close to Yarmouth. His father was a gynecologist and his mother was a teacher. He quickly became popular with the other kids in the school band.

Joseph played the cello. I was the percussionist. I managed the timpani, side, snare and bass drums, the cymbals, triangle, tam-tam, tubular bells, xylophone, glockenspiel, and gong, the marimba, vibraphone, and wood block. It was the essential difference between us two: he played, and I managed.

Joseph started to date one of the girls in the band. Her name was Susan.

— *Susan?*

Yes, Cameron, I knew your ex-wife before you did.

In fact, she was my best friend that year in school, even though she was a year younger than me. Joseph and I used to walk her home every day after band practice. When we went to parties I called on Joseph because his house was on the route to any other part of the city. Together we called on Susan.

At the parties they always found five or ten minutes to neck.

On the way home Susan always had a last cigarette, and she always handed me her smoke a block from her house, in case her father was out for a walk with the dog. My job was to puff on the cigarette, keep it lit, so she could get one last drag.

Joseph would also light a cigarette as we approached his house, and as we got closer hand me his butt for much the same reason as Susan had. We usually sat on his doorstep and talked about the party for half an hour while I kept lighting cigarettes so he could sneak a few drags.

He managed to get ten or eleven quick puffs during the half-hour before the light went on over the front step, which was his cue to come in for the night. I still had several blocks to walk alone.

One Friday Joseph asked me to pick up the butts from the front walk before I left. His father didn't like seeing cigarettes in front of the house on Saturday mornings. I picked up the butts every Friday and stuffed them into my jacket pocket before I started on the last leg of the walk home.

Once, the pocket of my jacket started smouldering. I took it off and beat it against the sidewalk to put out the fire. But I still continued to pick up Joseph's butts every Friday night from the sidewalk.

At the end of the year I started to buy cigarettes of my own and Joseph started to bum my cigarettes. He convinced me to switch to Player's, his brand.

Twice a month, on every other Saturday, Joseph had to babysit his younger sisters and Susan and I kept him company.

As usual, I walked Susan home because her curfew was at midnight. And as usual I kissed her goodnight. Only this one time, there was something different about the kiss. It wasn't a quick peck on the lips. But the kiss did feel strangely familiar. Susan parted my lips with her tongue, exploring my mouth without hesitancy, running her tongue over my teeth as if she had kissed this same mouth a hundred times before.

— *That was my mouth, Adrian.*

Yes, but she didn't tell me about you at the time, Cameron. Instead, she apologized and quickly ran into the house, embarrassed for kissing a face she knew, but an unfamiliar mouth.

I returned to Joseph's house and waited with him the last hour until his parents came home.

Then, out of the blue.

— Have you ever played strip poker? he asked.

— No, but I have had sex. He was twenty-one.

29

— Did you kiss?

— Yes.

— I don't like kissing, he said.

— Maybe you haven't learned how, I said. Let me show you.

— Is that better? he asked, after a few attempts.

— Yes.

— You're a better kisser than Susan.

Susan sniggered when I told her. Then dumped him.

— She broke off with me, Joseph said. There's someone else.

— Who?

— She wouldn't tell me. Said I wasn't a good kisser.

Then.

— I need more practice.

— All right.

Another night.

— What do two guys do in bed? he asked.

I showed him.

I left for Montreal in September and promised to write to him. Joseph promised, too. I wrote three times, but he didn't write back.

Christmas rolled around and on my first night home, Joseph and I were babysitting again.

— Why didn't you answer my letters? I asked.

— Nothing to write about, he said. I can't get your buckle open.

I wrote Joseph a letter that spring. I was explicit, writing about different guys I had met in Montreal.

He didn't write back. I flew home for summer vacation in June. Luckily, he answered the telephone when I called.

— My parents read your letter, he said. My father is going to tell your parents everything if he catches me with you, he added. About the letter. About us.

I had to see him.

It was arranged through Susan. She left us alone in her living room while her parents were outside in the garden.

From the other side of the room Joseph didn't say anything. I almost asked him to repeat what he didn't say.

I approached him with open arms.

— I want to give you a hug, I said.

— What good is that to me now? he asked. Before I could close the distance between us.

He told me not to call him again.

— It's over, he said.

But he called me the next day.

— My parents know you're home, he said. Stay away from me. And another thing. I'm not gay.

Over the next couple of weeks I started to see his father's car everywhere I walked in Sydney. Sometimes it was a coincidence, but other times I felt like I was being stalked. It was no big deal. Let Joseph deal with it.

Then one day, a few weeks later, I was walking home from town. I passed Joseph's house. His father followed behind me in his car. From the window of my bedroom I could see that he was parked across from our house.

He stayed there for an hour with the motor running. Not once did he look up to my window. I was rattled.

Fortunately, Joseph's mother and Talbot taught at the same school. After the incident with Joseph's father, I borrowed dad's car and scribbled a note, which I left in Talbot's mailbox, explaining some of what had happened. I told him about the letter I'd sent to Joseph. I told Talbot to talk to Joseph's mother before his father could talk to mom and dad. It was the first time I had ever asked anything of Talbot, and even then, I couldn't do it face to face.

Talbot wrote me a short reply. He would take care of everything. He urged me to return to Montreal for the rest of the summer. Out of sight, out of mind. This wasn't an option, he insisted. Go back to Montreal.

I took his advice and returned to Montreal for the rest of the summer. And all the next summers.

Since then I have become principled about what I write in letters, before I sign my name. For years I have composed two versions of every letter I have written. One copy is sent and the other is indexed. I am very careful about mailing the appropriate version to the right person. The others, the inappropriate variants, are retained in my drawer. This is the single most important lesson I learned from the experience of the letter I wrote to Joseph. Keep something for yourself. Don't give it all away.

It is probably the reason why I don't write many letters. Why I haven't written letters to us over the years.

It is the same with hugs. Squeeze too hard and you fall away from the embrace all dizzy and tired. I haven't asked for a hug in years. And I must admit, the quality of the hugs I have received has improved.

SEX, JOSEPH, AND FOOD.

Deciding to stay on at the tavern a little longer that evening after the wake. When you both left, I accepted Joseph's offer to play a game of foosball, and have a nightcap at his house.

— You're kidding me. You were married to a guy? Joseph asks.

He fluffed the pillows, made himself comfortable on his bed. I don't think he realized I would be getting dressed in a few minutes to leave.

— Yes. We were married in Denmark. Exchanged our vows at City Hall.

— I don't think I could do that, he said.

— What? Divorce your wife? Get the kids every second weekend?

— No, man. Marry a guy.

— That's right. You're not gay, I reminded him, laughing.

— Hell, no. He sat up on the bed, flexed his biceps. Made a show of it and winked at me.

— You just have sex with men, Joseph.

— I have sex with you, Adrian.

He thought he had offended me and there was a flash of pain in his eyes. As if I had doubted some absurd claim of fidelity from him.

Still.

— You've never had sex with other men, Joseph?

— No.

— That's a pity. I brightened before he got offended again. He leaned in and kissed me. He was a very good kisser.

I would stay a little longer.

Joseph lay back on the pillows with his arms folded behind his head.

— Tell me about him.

— His name was Claes.

— And?

— That's all I want to say, Joseph.

— Do you think you will ever get married again, Adrian?

— Probably not.

I kneaded his thighs with the palms of my hands. They were soft. He was distracted.

— How did he die, Adrian?

— In his sleep.

I massaged deeper.

— Have you met anyone else? The muscles twitched in his thighs. Cripes, that's none of my business, is it? He's only been dead a few months, right?

— Jesus, I'm not celibate, if that's what you're asking.

— I'm sorry, Adrian. It's none of my business. I didn't mean to pry. He reached over the side of the bed for his shorts. I'm starved, he said. Let's get a pizza. Then I'll drive you home.

There was nothing left to say. We'd moved on. Joseph had finished my sentence for me.

— *But I've still got a few questions, Adrian.*

— *Me, too.*

Rory

JANUARY, TORONTO

I THINK I'VE FOUND something to write about and it came to me while I was staring at a blank canvas. Not exactly blank. I'd already prepared the surface, laying down a layer of fire I'd subdue later with glaze, which is how I always approach a new work, setting it ablaze, then standing back for a few moments, waiting for its heat to reach me, warm and inviting. If I'm not attentive in applying these first brush strokes, the fire will scorch me, and I'll have to put it out, start over again.

Somehow, I couldn't get the fire started at all, it felt wrong. I couldn't hear the familiar crackle that motivates me in the beginning of a new painting. It was reminiscent of something else, and it gave me something to write about.

But first I need to clarify one detail. You were wrong about Tally getting the house, Cameron. The will clearly states income from the property, when sold, will be divided among the four of us. Mom and Dad simply added a condition. I'm sure it was written into the will years ago.

Yes, the wording of the clause was complicated, but in essence they wanted to make sure we all owned our own homes at some point. At the time of the train accident, Tally didn't. I was as surprised as you were to discover he's only been renting that farm in Bras d'Or all these years. That's why he's taken up residence in the family home. If he chooses to vacate the house, then it'll be sold. That's the condition and there's nothing we can do about it. Personally, I don't care one way or the other. I, like both of you, have my own house and in a nice neighbour-hood of Toronto.

Anyway, I was standing in front of my canvas and it wouldn't ignite, as if it were damp. And dampness made me imagine water, water that was still, and it made me think of Mom and Dad. So what I want to write about is the accident, because it was the one topic that kept falling off the edge of the table when we went out for drinks after the wake. I was evasive, wasn't I?

Every time one of you brought up the deaths, I changed the subject. Why? What was so horrible about talking about the accident? I asked myself this later. Unless it was the accident itself. It was a horrible misfortune. You even told us the story was on Danish television, Adrian.

When I returned to Toronto after the funeral, the old woman sitting next to me on the plane mentioned it. She was leafing through a copy of *Maclean's* and there was a picture from the train derailment in Florida.

A few minutes after I got settled in my seat she put the magazine away and turned her attention to me. She wanted to have a word.

"Did you hear about those Canadian pensioners who died in the train crash while vacationing in Florida?" she asked and, without waiting for an answer, continued. "They took the train because they were afraid of flying. Imagine. The irony." She punctuated this last word, giving it a hard emphasis so it sounded brittle.

"It was a terrible accident."

She shrugged her shoulders and became haughty. "People die every day. You take your chances," she said, or something along those lines. "You're not afraid of flying, are you?"

"No, I'm not afraid of flying. But it was a terrible accident," I said again, louder this time, so she could hear me. "Some of the passengers were enjoying lunch in the dinner car when the train derailed. It was one of the cars that broke free and slid off the bridge into the water below. Some of the passengers drowned, first."

"First?" my travelling partner questioned, her curiosity piqued.

"Yes, before they were eaten. The water was full of alligators, attracted by all the disturbance in the water."

"They were probably more interested in getting a free meal," she said, unsympathetically, I might add. "You know, all that thrashing of life."

"One end of the car was above water and some of the passengers crawled up to that end. Waiting, hoping, as it slowly sank into the mud. They thought they were safe. But they weren't. They were eaten alive, ripped from the car and devoured by massive jaws. My mother was one of the lucky ones. She drowned, first."

My listener's dry lips parted slightly in a suppressed gasp, cracking her lipstick.

"Why, that's horrible," she said. "You poor dear. What a tragedy!"

I scoffed. I'd humbled the old crow and she, people like her, don't like to be humbled. They're like Tally, and like to bully others to their point of view.

CAMERON, SOMETHING YOU WROTE struck a note, about the ten years between Tally and us, because I'd completely forgotten he was born on Christmas Day. Janet has a calendar in which she keeps important dates. I don't have a head for details, but I admire it in other people, like Janet. She records all dates, mostly family events, birthdays, anniversaries, and other such occasions. It's how I was able to confirm Tally's birthday. She didn't get this information from me. I'd never be able to figure it out. She ended up asking our mother.

How could I forget he was born on Christmas? Surely there were birthday parties to mark the occasions when we were growing up, but sadly the only parties I can recollect are our own. And of them, only one in any particular detail. The others, those Dad recorded with his movie camera, are vague. Mom and Dad cut out all festivities after we reached nine years of age because they said when we turned ten we were too old for kiddie parties. And it was our tenth birthday I'll never forget.

We were swimming at the Mira River, just below the old green iron bridge. It was a popular spot, teenagers jumping off the side of the bridge into the river thirty feet below. Mom and Dad had spread out a blanket on a little piece of shoreline and we three were floating in rubber inner tubes under the bridge. It was our birthday and late in the season to be swimming, but we were in the middle of an Indian summer. Tally was with us that day and he was the only one allowed to jump off the bridge.

None of us, with the exception of Tally, was a good swimmer, so that's why we were using the inner tubes. The two of you paddled to shore to dry off and claim your birthday cake. Mom always cooked three small ones for our birthday, one for each of us so there was never any bickering over who got the biggest piece.

I stayed in the water, watching Tally jump from the bridge. I felt a light tingling on my feet, but ignored it, using my arms to propel me to the middle of the river. Suddenly the tingling turned into stabbing pain, as if someone had lit matches on my legs. I looked down to discover I was in the middle of a smack of jellyfish. There were dozens of them, each with deep purple centres, undulating around me, and I became tangled within their long tentacles. The pain was excruciating and I started to wail, thrashing the water and losing my hold on the inner tube. I slid out from underneath it and fell below the surface of the water. The next thing I knew, Tally was beside me, under the water, grabbing me by the waist and pulling me to the surface.

When he got his footing, he carried me in to the shore. I was crying and writhing in his arms. There was nothing Mom or Dad could do to calm me down. Tally laid me on the blanket and sat beside me, pulling the tentacles from my legs and chest. Through my tears I noticed his torso and the side of his face had erupted in red welts from the stingers.

I stopped crying, realizing I wasn't hurting. I had been more scared of drowning than anything else. My skin was red in spots, but it didn't hurt anymore, although one stinger had penetrated the skin and left a thread-like scar on my leg. I offered my birthday cake to Tally. But he was looking beyond me at Mom and Dad.

I'll never forget the look on his face at that moment, sitting there, his welts getting bigger by the minute, which resulted in a frantic trip to outpatients when, a few minutes later, he started to wheeze. But there wasn't any pain in his eyes. Instead, they were full of hostility and directed at Mom and Dad. Like he was blaming them for what happened. I mean, what did he expect them to do? Jump in and save me? Neither of them was wearing a bathing suit.

Mom spruced up on our birthday, the front of her dress protected by an apron, even when we sat down to eat. Never a hair out of place, and if our birthday fell on her rinse-and-cut day at the hairdresser's, we had to wait until she got home to celebrate.

She tried to get Dad to put on a suit coat for our birthday dinners. He didn't like that and it never became a tradition. Which suited me fine because I always found he looked stern dressed up, especially in the home movies. I don't know why he kept his hair cut in that style. The other kids used to make fun of him. No sideburns, the back of his head sporting short bristles, the hair cut too far up his neck, revealing the bump he had on the back of his head. It didn't suit his long ears. Or his eyes, narrow with big droopy eyelids. I don't think Mom liked his haircut either. She used to cut our hair with the kit she ordered through the Eaton's catalogue. Dad wanted to take us to the Lebanese barber he went to, but she wouldn't hear of it. You were afraid of that electric razor, Adrian. When she turned it

on, you could see a blue spark under the plastic casing. It terrified you. She'd give you a quick slap on the back of the head to
make you stop crying. You'd sob for the rest of the haircut.

I always received the first gift on our birthday because I was
the first-born. The second one was for Cameron, who came
forty-five minutes later, and the last present was for you,
Adrian, born twelve minutes after Cameron. Everyone used to
call you the baby, because you were born last.

As I thought about our birthdays, I was also trying to figure
out the last time I actually saw either of you before the funeral.
According to Janet's calendar, it's been seven years since I've
been in Cape Breton or in the same room with both of you at the
same time.

Doesn't it strike you both as odd? I mean, we never had any
falling-out to cause this drifting apart. Seven years is a long time
without face-to-face contact. I managed to keep in better touch
with Mom and Dad, even Tally, though you mustn't construe this
as an act of favouritism on my part. Tally was always dropping
into the house when I came to Sydney. I'd visit him a couple of
times at his farm on those trips. Really, he didn't have to come
into town, but he'd show up at the house anyway with a box of
tools, and then disappear into the basement to tighten a screw on
the furnace or something. Dad always stood in the kitchen, a
bemused grin on his face.

"Funny how everything gets fixed whenever one of you boys
are home," he'd say. "Even things I didn't know were broken.
You should come home more often." Then he'd wink at me. I
suppose Tally wanted us to know he kept an eye on them. Or
maybe he had other motives, letting us know, with toolbox in
hand, he didn't think we did our part as good sons.

Tally attends a convention here in Toronto every couple of years so I've maintained contact with him in that way as well. Having tasted Janet's culinary delights once, he has never turned down a dinner invitation since. Sometimes Beth is with him. Janet enjoys her company on those visits.

Through Tally and our parents I've received snippets of news about both of you. I've always asked after you. And I suppose I felt sufficiently apprised of what was happening. I realize now this picture I have of you both is terribly distorted, or at the least incomplete.

Janet says the conclusions we draw are from the impressions we take, and not from the impressions we're given. Whatever you both chose to reveal of your lives to Tally, and to Mom and Dad, was filtered before they passed anything on to me.

It's like the fable about the five blind men. You know the one. Each man feels a different part of the elephant and determines it to be something entirely different from the others, based on the limited information at hand. None of them can describe the entire elephant.

Janet says we distort the process further by being selective in the questions we choose to ask of people. Everything is tilted toward getting the answer we want. And when all the information is passed on to a third person, the process starts over again. This is her definition of a rumour. 'Course, this also works the other way. What rumours have you heard about me lately? Ha ha!

I don't want you to get the impression Janet is opinionated. On the contrary, she's circumspect about what she says in public, she never wants to insult anyone. If I want to learn more about what she thinks, then I wait until she's preparing dinner, because we have some of our most interesting conversations while she's in the kitchen. I'll ask a question and she'll usually give a quick answer, but if she's in the middle of a task, like cracking half a dozen eggs and separating the whites from the yolks, she'll elaborate, just long enough to finish the task at hand. I find it fascinating to watch her talk and think through what she's saying, often focusing her gaze midway across the kitchen, somewhere between where I'm sitting at the table and the counter where she's working, fixing her attention on an invisible point in the air, all the while considering other points of view, the pros and cons of a situation.

I didn't ask her why we've lost our closeness as brothers. Janet would say it's a question for me to ponder, it'd be too easy for her to slip into judgment, which she abhors. So why've we drifted apart? Do you suppose it's because the onus has always been on us to visit Mom and Dad, not each other? They never saw my house and I know they never visited Denmark, Adrian. And I assume they never set foot in your house in Halifax, Cameron. So if we wanted to see them, we went home, picking up news about each other's lives from them, and from Tally. And as I've already pointed out, this kind of intelligence is incomplete, only half the truth at the best of times.

Going home to catch up was a routine, our duty you might say, though I never felt obligated. It was just the way things worked out. Our parents' home, our home, was the meeting place. It was there we learned of each other through what they told us, as if the house were a repository for family business. We came to depend on the news it divulged on our collective lives, rather than making the effort to learn for ourselves. This is why I've had more contact with Tally than with either of you, why I feel more a part of his life. He's never moved away. He was part of the comfortable, effortless routine. Yes, I think this accounts for the drifting apart, this I can accept.

I'VE BEEN THINKING about the last family reunion, Mom and Dad's thirtieth wedding anniversary. My God, that's twenty years ago! I found some pictures. There's a date on the back of one of them, our hair is long and shaggy, except for you, Cameron, your hair is short as usual. It's a dreadful snapshot, none of us is looking at the camera. Mom and Dad are sitting in the front, Dad resting his arms on his knees, his wrists too long for the cuffs on his sports jacket, and the legs of his pants about an inch too short. I can see Tally's going to look more and more like Dad when he gets older. When I was younger, I thought Dad was a tall man. But he wasn't, he was just skinny, like Tally.

Mom has her black purse with the gold handle on her lap, a pair of gloves crossed on top. Her church gloves, long and white. Sometimes the tips got smeared with rouge, from putting her fingers to her cheek, her classic pose as she listened to other adults. It's a wonder she didn't rub the skin off, the way she attacked her face with powder.

'Course, she was usually angry when I saw her doing this, summoned as I was to her dressing table before they went out to play bridge. She was irritable before they left the house because we wouldn't settle down, or more often because you were bouncing off the walls, Cameron, causing grief for the babysitter downstairs. She'd snarl at me as she rubbed powder into her cheeks, her voice lowered so the babysitter wouldn't hear.

"For the love of God, be good, won't you," she'd plead. "Give your father and me a couple hours of peace, won't you." For some reason, she always summoned me to her room before they went out, even if it was one of you who was acting up. Then she'd wave her hand, dismissing me from the bedroom, and bite into a crinkled Kleenex, removing the excess lipstick from her mouth.

I think your ex-wife took the picture with one of those cheap cameras you could buy at K-Mart and then had the shot copied, Cameron. Susan was always snapping pictures. It irritated me. You must've spent a small fortune on developing them. Her purse was always stuffed with at least two or three rolls of film.

Tally often ran into Susan at the shopping centre when you were still living with Mom and Dad. Always in the same spot, planted in front of the one-hour developing booth. I can see her standing there now, tall and lanky with her long, straight brown hair hanging midway down her back, the bangs cut low across her forehead. She's wearing big glasses that seem to cover half her face. She's all legs, wearing those short-shorts cut just below her arse. 'Course, they're great legs, I'll give her that, and she does have some nice curves at the hips and in the bosom, as Mom would say.

Susan often struck up a conversation with Tally, and when he glanced at your daughter in the stroller, Cameron, the baby was always sucking on a bottle, usually a bottle of Kool-Aid, Tally claimed. Tally is never one to disguise what he's thinking, he wears it on his face, and Susan, who was quick to complain about the high cost of milk and juice, didn't miss this. She never did have her priorities in order. Photo albums were more important than nutrition.

I'll be frank. I never did warm up to your relationship, Cameron. You were both too immature to get married. Tally was more blunt, insisting you got drunk on a Friday, married

Susan on Saturday, knocked her up on Sunday, and sobered up on Monday. By then it was too late.

But you do have a beautiful daughter, Cameron. Before Mom died, she sent me some nice shots taken with a 35-millimetre camera. Mary Anne must be at least nineteen by now. Did she finish up at the special high school where you sent her?

By the way, Susan looked us up last year. I didn't see her, but Janet was in the Gallery one day and ran into her. Janet was surprised to meet her there, but it appeared Susan was just as surprised, first at seeing Janet and then at discovering the Gallery was ours. Didn't you ever mention the Gallery in all those years together, Cameron? Janet and I are proud of it. How could you not mention the Gallery when discussing me? Once. Not even once?

Apparently Susan came inside to get out of the rain. But my name is on the sign outside, so I disregard the coincidence. I never discovered her true intentions because the conversation Janet had with her was brief. Janet, ever the diplomat, extended a dinner invitation, but Susan, surprisingly, turned it down. I say surprisingly because we all know Janet is a fabulous cook.

Susan was passing through the city but she didn't say where she was headed. She lives in Vancouver now, doesn't she?

Janet said Susan was looking well. In case you don't know, Susan's made an effort about her appearance and has slimmed down.

Janet found the brief exchange pleasant and enjoyed Susan's relaxed smile. This surprised me because I don't think Susan ever had a carefree smile. There was always a grey cloud hovering above you as a couple, Cameron. I never knew when one or the other of you would explode. Those episodes are best forgotten, I'm sure, and I apologize if I'm causing you any embarrassment.

Janet asked Susan if she'd a chance to look at any of the works while she was waiting out the rain. There was nothing of my own work on display. I'd just shipped my canvases from the permanent collection we keep on hand to Calgary for a retrospective of twentieth-century Canadian expressionism. Janet was surprised when Susan said yes, she had looked at a few of the works and recognized one piece. She knew the artist and he was a friend.

Has Susan come up in the world, Cameron? Does she really have friends in the art world? The friend in question, Jimmy something-or-other, was part of a group show of British Columbia sculptors I'd put together for the Gallery. I only had one of his pieces on display, an eight-inch obelisk fashioned in teak. He's a minor name, but there's potential, I admit, otherwise he wouldn't be invited to exhibit.

I don't know how much to believe, Cameron. Susan might've glanced at the name beside the sculpture and claimed immediate familiarity with the artist. Then spouted this fib just to have something to say to impress Janet. On more than one occasion you yourself have alleged Susan was a liar.

MY THOUGHTS KEEP returning to something I wrote earlier. I mentioned this arrangement we had, of our visiting the family home and not the other way around. I don't want you ever to assume it was a duty, at least not on my part. I've always been meaning to spend more time out east. Janet and I have discussed buying property there. Several other artists have bought and restored old farms or weatherworn houses in various Nova Scotia fishing villages. They always want an opinion from me, as if I'm an expert on rustic coastal living. My advice is always the same. I tell them to imagine living in their little paradises during the long, cold winters, snowed in for days at a time.

It's surprising I don't make more of an effort to visit Nova Scotia. It was never my intention to leave. I bet this surprises you. I know you both consider me cosmopolitan, hardly the small-town type. But it's true. I wanted to stay. I wanted to stay on the coast. I was seriously considering the College of Art and Design in Halifax at the time. Do you know where it is, Cameron? It's worth a visit if you get the chance.

Then, in our senior year of high school, Tally was appointed guidance counsellor. 'Course, you had transferred to the Vocational School by then, Cameron. I wasn't too thrilled about this appointment. Though it could've been worse. He might've ended up as one of our teachers, Adrian, if a position was vacant.

Fortunately, we were counselled in groups. Tally was seated when we assembled in the library, wearing a new polyester suit. All the other male teachers in the school wore old sports jackets and slacks, careful not to draw attention to themselves or wise-cracks from the students. Tally looked like he was dressed for a wedding. The library was cold, it was winter and there was ice on the windows. The end of Tally's nose was red, he was shivering, but he tried to look composed. And stern. He had his hands folded in front of him on the desk.

He put out a pad of paper and a pencil for each of us, and I was impressed with the stack of university calendars on the middle of the table. When he spoke, he addressed a point just above the top of our heads, so we were spared direct eye contact.

He had rehearsed what he was going to say. A few of the kids from the previous session had already warned us about his odd lecture, insisting we choose a university at least fifteen hundred miles from Cape Breton, urging us to break free from our mothers' apron strings and face a competitive future.

He took a few moments to look around the room, trying to browbeat everyone. We'd been assembled no more than five minutes and a third of the group had abandoned any idea of going to university. Coming home on the occasional weekend was the arrangement the rest of us wanted. We could take our laundry home and stock up on food for the coming week.

We were instructed to look at the calendars for the next hour. I wanted to be an artist and go to an art school. I'd heard about an alternative to the College of Art and Design. It was a school in Ontario with much the same kind of uninspired name, the Ontario College of Art. I thumbed through the calendars, but there was none for the Ontario college.

When the session was over, Tally asked us if we'd made our choices. This was his third session of the day and our silence didn't deter him. He warned us no one would be dismissed without choosing at least one possibility from the table, and waved a piece of paper we had to sign. In less than a minute almost everyone signed the paper, jotting down any college that came to mind from those we had thumbed, just to get out of the room. Tally glanced at the number of names on the paper and then did a head count, pointing out he was missing one signature, directing his observation to the atlas just above my head.

I refused to meet his challenge and he kept staring at me with a blankness that was meant to suggest to the other kids he didn't know who I was, as if I was a complete stranger. Some of the other kids knew he was my brother, I'd told them in advance. For a split second I felt as if Tally's blank stare was asking me what my excuse was, for being a student at his presentation, for being his brother, for being a part of his family. And it made me angry.

I could feel the other kids' unease, they wanted to get out of the room, so I finally told him the university I was interested in wasn't among the catalogues. For a split second we made eye contact. Tally feared a revolution. I was going to disobey him and choose a university close to home, maybe even the junior college in Sydney or the one in Truro where he got his licence, coming home every other weekend with a load of laundry. This anticipation passed between us in a flash. I gave him the name of the college I was interested in, and I detected a blush of approval at the corners of his lips.

I'd chosen a school about fifteen-hundred miles from Cape Breton.

I'd done his bidding, had set an example for the others. What's worse, I'd committed myself.

I spent four years at OCA. I arrived with my high school art teacher's advice to try everything, and a couple of art history books I'd borrowed from her but hadn't returned. I enjoyed Toronto more than the school, hanging out on Queen Street, partying.

I took everything that was compulsory at school before I settled back into the two things I liked best, painting and art history. I had some good instructors, and I ended up liking the school. But I never came home for weekends, and after the first year I stopped coming home for Christmas. Once or twice during my first year, I thought about transferring to the school in Halifax, but Tally's rule was tattooed in my head.

If I hadn't taken him seriously back then, I could've studied in Halifax, on the coast I never intended to abandon. So Tally was the reason I moved away. I don't regret it, I've done well, exceptionally well, as you both know. But I hold it against him all the same, though I never mention it to him. It's a good thing he's not part of this journal. Otherwise, I'd never have got this off my chest.

MY GOD, is it April already? Have I had our journal the allotted four months? I'll have to be economical with my time. I've been busy preparing for a small touring exhibit arriving at the Gallery next month. Three women from Rimouski have chronicled their ancestors' voyage up the St. Lawrence. They've built a dory, by hand, then dismantled it and divided the framework between them, using the dissected sections of the dory as their canvas. The entire exhibit is mounted on platforms sitting in three six-by-six wading pools five inches deep. When the tour is over, they plan on reassembling the dory and setting sail for Rimouski from Quebec City.

Most of the exhibits at the Gallery are touring shows these days. I still try to build an exhibit from scratch once a year, like the sculptor's show I mentioned, but I just don't have the energy anymore. When we bought the Gallery seven years ago, I created three shows a year, all of them good, but I wasn't painting as much as I wanted. Still, it's been a good investment for Janet, putting money into the pockets of artists rather than Revenue Canada.

We've just returned from a week in Bermuda. I got a great tan. Janet avoids the sun, but with her wonderful bronzed skin tone, she doesn't need it.

I don't have time to respond to everything you've both written. As Adrian pointed out, it's not one of the conditions you put on the journal, Cameron. But I do want to say I was sorry to hear about your friend Claes, Adrian. I suppose in the eyes of Danish law, you're a widower. What's to keep you in Denmark now?

I'd like to visit Scandinavia, but Janet doesn't like the continent. She spent a summer in Austria years ago and has mixed feelings about her European experience. As to this guy you ran into at the pub, Adrian, I don't even remember you leaving the table, or staying out all night. How did you slip away without us noticing?

I'm glad to hear you're still singing, Cameron, it'd be a shame to waste such a beautiful voice. Do you think your choir will record a CD? Let me know, I'd love to get it. I don't know what's going on between you and Tally, but I hope you've worked it out by now. Let us know.

Until next time.

Cameron

JUNE, HALIFAX

HOLY MACKEREL was I surprised to find a notice in my mailbox today that I had a parcel waiting at the post office. A registered parcel. What could it be? I haven't had a registered letter for years. I did send away once for a couple of porn magazines in the States, but that was long before you could rent Candy Melons doing Old MacDonald's farm, pigs and all, at the local video store.

You remember those advertisements in the back of the detective magazines dad used to read, don't you? There was always a little picture with a black star covering the model's privates. Or a black dot on the guy's *bells* so it looked like the girl was taking a chomp from a lump of coal. God, we've come a

53

long way since then. Well, I sent in the little microscopic order form. Months later, long after I had forgotten, this card came in the mail saying I had to pick up my parcel from Canada Customs. Yeah right, I said to myself. March down to Customs and run into Mr. Ferguson. You remember him. The Fergusons moved into the Smythe house a couple of doors up the block while we were in high school. Mr. Ferguson worked for Customs and was, what was it dad used to call him? Right, a Black Baptist. The guy never smiled. His wife played bridge with our mom. There was no way I was going to visit Customs and chance running into our good Christian neighbour.

But get this. Mr. and Mrs. Ferguson had a daughter. She was a year older than us and used to hang out at the rink after the games. I got into the habit of walking her home, seeing she was a neighbour and all. They always used their back door, so I walked her around the side of the house. It was pitch black, and she'd take my hand so I wouldn't fall on anything in the yard. There was never a light on in the house when she went inside. She said her parents were always in bed by nine.

We'd pass a door going down into their basement and then hold hands for a couple of minutes. As soon as I started groping, she'd skedaddle up the back steps and disappear into the porch.

I thought that was as far as I was ever going to get with Miss Ferguson, and I made up my mind that I wouldn't waste any more of my time walking her home. But this one Friday, she stopped at the door going down into the basement. She took a key out of her pocket and unlocked the door and beckoned me to follow. We were very quiet, but I wasn't worried, because I knew the parents were asleep. She turned on a light and before I knew it she had her tongue buried in my throat.

In the meantime, my eyes were rolling in their sockets and I was all hot and sweaty. My eye caught this stack of magazines on the floor, up against the wall. There must have been three or four hundred of them. She told me they're what her father confiscated through the years at Customs. I thought they were supposed to burn stuff like that, I said to her. She just smiled. She handed me a stack to take home and I could see from the covers I had some heavy-duty reading ahead of me. Thanks to old Mr. Ferguson and family.

The very next Friday I was looking forward to some more tongue, but Miss Ferguson didn't show up at the rink. The family had moved! Just like that. From the one Friday to the next. Gone. Never met a girl like her again. And I never saw magazines like the stack she gave me again, either. Even today you can't get your hands on that kind of stuff, not legally.

Anyway, today I was looking at this letter from the post office and I was wondering who would send me a parcel. Even after I picked it up and read your return address on the label, Rory, I still didn't know what it was.

Bingo! The journal. No offence, brothers, but the whole idea was an impulse on my part. I never expected to see it again. I didn't think either of you'd take it seriously, and from what you've been *emoting* in these pages, you've taken it very seriously. Surprise of surprises.

Feeling the new weight your ink gave the journal started me shaking. The whole experience was almost holy. Suddenly all of life's big philosophical questions begin to parade through my head. The questions that have weighed heavily upon me all these years. Only, because of the journal I was holding in my hands, they weren't questions anymore. They were statements, facts. There is a God after all. Hell will freeze over one sunny day. Hallelujah. I lit a joint and sat back to contemplate. I mean, I was touched, here you were, my brothers, my blood, taking something I suggested seriously.

My God, Virginia, there is a Santa Claus. The journal I held in my hands was proof.

I read everything you both wrote in one sitting. Which is tonight, because I just had to write something too. And because the adrenalin is pumping, I have clarity. All these questions suddenly have answers. I know now that a falling tree does make a sound when it falls in an empty forest. I have awoken.

IT'S 31°C AND THE HOUSE feels like it's covered in Saran Wrap. There's no air and I'm sitting here on a plastic chair in my Calvin Klein jockeys. When I shift my weight, the skin on my back rips away from the clammy chair. It's the same sensation as tearing a Band-Aid off all those tiny hairs on your arm.

I'm in one foul mood today. My van is in the shop for repairs and I have to take either a bus or a taxi across town to pick it up. The taxi will cost an arm and a leg and the buses here don't have air conditioning.

And the smell! Sweet Mother of Christ. I forgot to put the garbage out on the street before I went to bed last night. It got as far as the back porch, and seeing that the thermometer didn't dip below 25°C during the night, the kitchen smells like dog breath.

They say the weather should break tomorrow. It reminds me of your weather up there in Toronto, Rory. Last time I was in the big city you could cut the air with a knife. I remember when the weather finally broke after four days, the skies exploded in lightning and thunder like I'd never seen before. Someone told me that was normal Toronto weather. Unbearable heat, the humidity building and building for days, and then wham, the Gods let loose. Then it starts all over again. How can you bear it? Of course. How silly of me. You've got your summer house up on Georgian Bay. Must be the humidity in my head making me all forgetful and worried for you.

You're probably there now, aren't you, Rory? Sitting around the patio while the Missus catches a little sun on your private wharf. The Big B told me that what you affectionately call a cottage would put any bungalow on Cape Breton to shame. In fact, he said you could fit ten bungalows inside your cottage. What I want to know is, who's minding the gallery while you're away? Surely you don't close it for the entire summer? According to the Big B, Janet doesn't take any real vacation. She goes up to the cottage on the weekends, returning to the city on Sunday evenings to rest before embarking on another week of boob jobs. The Big B said you use the summer to work on new pieces, Rory. Funny, though, when I asked him if you had a studio at the cottage he couldn't remember seeing it. Maybe I misunderstood him, maybe he said that you use the summer to get ideas for new pieces.

You asked me why I never mentioned the gallery to Susan? I'm sure it popped up once or twice in conversation. I did tell her you were once a famous Canadian painter and Janet is one of Canada's foremost plastic surgeons. If I'd known how important the gallery was to your ego, I'd have made a point of mentioning it more in my social circles. I could have had some flash cards made up with a checklist on what to talk about when your name came up. Made sure I plugged the gallery, performed some free PR for you.

This humidity is killing me.

Speaking of Susan, let's get a few things straight. She was never fat, she wasn't even heavy. She was, and is, a gorgeous babe. Nor was it Susan who took the picture at the folks' wedding anniversary. I hadn't presented her to the family yet. And how would Susan, or I for that matter, know anything about Janet's culinary skills? We've never broken bread with you. Yes, Susan does have a friend who's an artist. Only she was being modest, the friend is her fiancé. Nor has Susan ever told a lie in her life. And lastly, seeing as you're interested in knowing, Susan is living in Vancouver now, together with our daughter, Mary Anne, who's almost a senior in high school, as she likes to remind me. I think it's essential to have all the facts before you start trashing someone you've never taken the time to get to know. It's more fun that way, you get my drift?

Goddamn it, this pen keeps slipping out of my fingers. I'm going to take another shower. My third today. It'll probably break my flow, so in case I don't get back to this journal for a while, I just want to say something to you, Adrian, before I forget. My condolences. That's about it. I don't see why I should cry crocodile tears for your friend Claes, seeing that he didn't warrant a mention from you all these years. You had to wait until he was dead before you told us about him.

I'M SORRY, Adrian. That wasn't fair. I can understand why you never talked about Claes. We never asked. I'm glad you've told us about him now. Why don't you slip in a photo the next time you get the journal.

POST SHOWER. Only it's late afternoon now. While I was showering, the skies finally broke. It rained for two hours and cleared. I took the plunge and called for a taxi, picked up my van, and then drove home with all the windows open. Despite the rain, it's still 25°C, but the wind whistling through the van felt cool.

I took a spin down to the Historic Properties on the waterfront, bought myself an ice cream cone, and I'm sitting here, cross-legged, with our journal on my lap. It appears half of Halifax is on promenade. I'm wearing my dark shades that allow for some discreet eye movement as I people-watch.

I'm not so pissed off anymore. I'm almost feeling, how should I put this, tranquil?

Yeah, tranquil. You dig?

And it's not because of any medication. Although I'm hoping to score some good dope while I'm down here. Besides, I'm in no rush to get home. It's summer. Time to party. And you should get a look at the babes. All the best babes in Canada are in Halifax. I should know, I've been "relocated" all over this country and compared them.

After I finished Vocational School, the Big B set me up with an unemployment program at Manpower that lasted a year, and they ended up shuttling me from Sudbury to Oshawa and to Windsor before finally exiling me to Winnipeg. It was a long year and I suffered from constant jet lag.

While I was in Windsor, I had to meet with an employment counsellor. Relocation, she offered. All expenses paid. I suggested *she* relocate. But this babe behind the desk isn't amused. I wasn't amused either. I've been relocated three times, I reminded her, all within the year. I'm getting too old to relocate, I joked. I've got roots in Windsor, I told her, although I'd only been there three months. She said people had to go where the jobs were. It was one of the conditions of the program. I told her to get me a job with the airlines or the moving companies or the landlords, because those were the real growth industries. Those are the people doing all the hiring, I told her, they need all the extra hands they can get to shuffle all the unemployed Cape Breton cattle around this big corral they call Canada.

She told me I had to go where the jobs were. Those are the stipulations of the unemployment program I'd signed on to. I was hearing an echo. I told her I wouldn't take a job if it didn't match all of the qualifications I'd mastered in carpentry over the past several months. She said times were tough. Had I considered upgrading my skills, taking a government-sponsored course? I reminded her that I was on a government-sponsored program. I asked her if she'd read my *dossier*. She said she had. Then why hadn't she noticed that I'd upgraded my skills three times in nine months?

Couldn't she read from the paper in front of her nose that I was the proverbial jack of all trades? Of course, I hadn't had time to use any of my new skills because they kept relocating me.

Sorry, she said, there's been a job reform. My program had been discontinued. Change of policy, she says. Then she perked up. Told me with the new rules she could send me out of province. A clean slate.

There was a pause as she looked at her computer screen, the first computer I'd ever seen up close. Well, she said, scratching the side of her head with a pencil, what have you done the last year? Was this babe stunned? She was my friggin' caseworker. Unfortunately, we can't sponsor any courses in your current field, she said. It has been declared redundant. If you'll reconsider, we can relocate you to Manitoba, where there's plenty of work in your field. You have to be flexible, sir, she said. Flexible, I grunted. According to the program, she said, you're even eligible for upgrading. You can take a word-processing course, she said, patting the computer as if it were a dog. In the entire time I'd been sitting there, she hadn't entered any information on her keyboard. I don't think she even knew how to use the machine. Or you can return to Nova Scotia, she said, almost in a whisper, as if it were a fate worse than death. I signed the papers. I was heading to Winnipeg.

I told her she had something on her chest. When she looked down I gave the end of her nose a flick with my finger. I'd always wanted to do that. Next time I'd try a tit-twister.

THERE ARE A LOT of poofs cruising here on the wharf, Adrian. Didn't you tell me you got picked up one sultry summer night for loitering in Montreal? I'm sure it was awhile before you dared to drop your shorts again.

Oh-oh. I'm getting bitchy again, aren't I? And that doesn't really fit with my character. It's all you gays who are supposed to be bitches. I think the good fairies sprinkled some of their fag powder over my cradle when I was a kid. Maybe it was dark and they didn't see that your cradle was on the other side of the room, Adrian. They started to shake their wimpy wands and hit me first before they realized their mistake, before they moved on to you. That's why I'm the bitchy one.

Mind you, I'm the one with the prettiest singing voice, but I've got to give credit where credit's due. I think you'd agree with me, Rory, there isn't an ounce of bitchiness in Adrian. So I guess you can count your lucky stars, Adrian, be thankful the good fairies screwed up and sprinkled a lot of powder on the floor before they got to you. Probably landed on the dog. You remember Sampson? He loved to hump any leg within sight. That's it! It was Sampson who got hit with a good douse of fag powder.

People are beginning to stare. I've been having a good grin at your expense, Adrian. You always did make me tickle. Come on now, give us a smile. Don't go acting all flustered. If you were here beside me, I'd have you on the boardwalk in another two minutes, splitting your gut. It's what I like about you, Adrian. You could always take a good razing, a good joke. So maybe you weren't so gloomy after all as a kid. I've just been remembering the wrong things, like you said. You sparkled a lot, come to think of it. You twinkled for the whole family even if you did get us into a lot of shit.

Like grade four. Ms. Black was at the front of the class, standing in front of the table with the one-thousand-piece jigsaw puzzle she'd been working on all year, while we're all supposed to be quietly reading. Once she'd started on that puzzle nothing could distract her.

She was wearing a dress and her back was to the class. Next thing I knew you were passing me a note, Adrian, daring me to crawl over to get a look under her dress. I wriggled out of my seat and snaked across the floor. The entire class was holding their breath. I was inches away from her and rolled over onto my back and eased myself between her legs for a quick peeka-boo. There wasn't too much light under her dress so I only got to glimpse her calves. The temperature in the classroom had risen twenty degrees. I made it back to my desk.

Rory's turn. He almost chickened out when he looked across

at Bonnie Burchell, who had tears streaming down her face. He was afraid she was going to start wailing. But you beamed the back of his head with a spitball and he was off. I didn't think Rory could move that fast. He was across the floor, under her legs, and back in his seat in less than a minute.

Finally, it was your go, Adrian. You probably figured that one of us would've been caught before you had to take up your own dare. George Sanders pissed his pants, but we didn't hear about that until later. Anyway, you made it to the table and wiggled under Ms. Black and decided to linger, crossing your arms under your head, all relaxed. And that was when she moved and knocked into you.

The principal appeared and out came the strap. Bonnie Burchell was blubbering and pointed at Rory and me. So the three of us were lined up, and because we're triplets we each got three whacks with the strap. On each hand. Next day, we were put in different classes. I was the one who stayed behind with Ms. Black. When she returned the next day she started a new fashion trend for the other teachers. Slacks.

STILL THE SAME DAY, boys. Only it's night now. I'm up here in the attic of this big, empty house. I don't come up here too often, heights give me a nosebleed. I wanted to find some family pictures. But they're gone. No trace. Maybe Susan has them. Next time I talk to her I'll ask her to have a look. Ask her to send a couple of them to me.

It's raining again, heavy. Heat lightning in the distance, some muffled thunder coming from somewhere. It's cooled down since the afternoon, but I'm sitting here without a stitch.

I got all muggy looking through the trunks up here. Nothing I hate more than clammy shorts. Gives me crotch rot. I cooled down once I stripped off my clothes. Now I'm sitting in this little alcove with dust on my butt, a cup of tea, half a joint, and looking at a picture I did find. Not the one you mentioned, Rory. Another anniversary snapshot, a couple of years earlier.

There's the skinny Big B on the left, standing too far to the edge of the shot so his left shoulder and leg are cut out of the picture. His hair isn't long, it doesn't reflect the times. On the other hand, Rory, you look like something out of that movie *Hair*, which you got plenty of, hanging down over your shoulders. You're wearing a piss-yellow shirt and a piss-yellow tie with a big smirk across your face and two little red dots in your eyes from the flash.

I'm standing next to you with my crewcut. Nice thing about a crewcut, it never really goes out of style, does it? I have one now. The shirt I'm wearing is supposed to be chocolate brown. It looks like the colour of poop. I've even got the collar button closed. What a virgin. Pimples all over my cheeks. How come I got the pimples and you didn't? We all have the same DNA. Of course, the meds I was taking in those years took their toll on my silky cheeks, all four of them, my ass was pretty bumpy too.

And then the baby, little Adrian. You're the only one with a twinkle in your eyes. The rest of us are all making attempts, only it looks like I'm grunting on a fart and the Big B's got crabs in his shorts, his lips are all pulled thin and blue. Rory, well, I've already described you, psychedelic. You're wearing a lumberman's jacket, Adrian, and those bibbed overalls all the rage back then.

Oh yes, there's one little detail I missed in the picture. The stitches above my right eye, cutting into my eyebrow. Four stitches. Three things happened that day, I remember. One was the anniversary, the second was getting expelled from high school for good, and the third was dad kicking me out of the house, which is why we don't have any picture of the folks from this anniversary.

Mom was all teary and puffy, clutching her purse, didn't want to have her picture taken. Dad's ears were scarlet, they always looked twitchy when he was mad, and his narrow eyes were barely slits. The veins on the backs of his long hands were throbbing. Those veins always spooked me as a kid. Do you remember all of this? I think we're the only family that ever had a family portrait with the walls of a hospital as the backdrop, because that's where the picture was taken.

You were all waiting at home for me. The deal was, we'd go down to the photographer and have our pictures taken before we'd go out to eat. Only there was no Cameron. Dad got a call from the principal at the high school, saying I'd been in a fight. I'd taken a swing at the vice-principal, who, in defending himself, had slit open my forehead with the ring on his pinky finger. I was at outpatients now and I'd been officially expelled. The good news was that the vice-principal wouldn't press charges. Is this all coming back to you yet?

So there I was at City Hospital, my head all tingly from the stitches, but I was in no pain because I was wired on lithium, as I was in those years. Should have remembered to take my dose before I went to school that day, things might've turned out different. You all came rushing into the waiting room, dad screaming like a banshee, mom lagging a good ten feet behind him, behind all of us, as if to say, I don't belong to this crazy bunch. I thought dad was going to hit me in front of everyone. But he didn't.

To make a long story short, this was the last straw. Three suspensions in the first three months, followed by this. Expulsion. And on mom's special day, to boot. Dad was through giving me chances. I could fend for myself now, seeing that I was such a hothead and know-it-all.

But he wanted a picture. He shoved us all up against the wall, took one shot, and left with mom and you two in tow. That left the Big B and me. He didn't say a word. He drove me to his farm. The first thing the Big B did was to make me empty my pockets. He told me to get some sleep. It was four o'clock in the afternoon. He practically shoved me into his bedroom, closed the door, and left to join you all at the restaurant. Funny thing is, I stayed in the bedroom. I was there when he got home that evening.

He told me that everything was settled. I was going home in the morning. I was starting at the Vocational School on Monday. I was going to take a trade. Like all the other dropouts and delinquents and morons and haloperidol junkies, I was going to the Vocational School.

All of which I did, but none of which stopped me from continuing to date the vice-principal's daughter behind his back. I used to sneak her into the house on Friday nights while the folks were out playing bridge. Did you know that?

I liked the Vocational School. The instructors are afraid of most of us, which meant they kept out of our way. Nobody ever flunked. I got straight A's, despite sleeping through the rare classes I attended during the three years I spent there.

The rest is history, isn't it? The aforementioned vice-principal's daughter is Susan. On the day I graduated from the Vocational School he dropped dead and Susan and I got drunk. She to mourn, and me to celebrate. It was a Friday. I married her on Saturday and knocked her up on Sunday, after her old man's funeral. Susan was prego. But I didn't sober up on Monday. The Big B got that part of the story wrong.

Susan and I moved in with the folks. You were both gone by then, graduating before me because I had to repeat that grade in junior high.

I couldn't get any work, so on the Big B's advice, I enrolled in a course. It was a four-month course in basic carpentry. It was a lot like the shit I learned at the Vocational School, but this time I was paying attention, because I had a wife now and a little one on the way.

Our daughter, Mary Anne, was born in March the following spring. I took one look at her, kissed Susan on the chin, and made it as far as the hallway before I threw up. The baby had no pupils and was blind.

Enter the Big B. He suggested we put the baby up for adoption because of her birth defect. I mentioned it to Susan and she kicked me in my *bells*. Enter the Big B again, the next day. There was an unemployment program in Ontario, they would pay to relocate me. I could learn more carpentry skills. Was I interested? Couldn't I use the money I'd earn to help with the new situation? I'd only be gone nine months. I could earn a bundle in that time. It would give Susan and me a chance for a new start. In the meantime, he'd work on Susan. Get her to see things his way, the right way, regarding the adoption issue. Susan rang his bells too, I'm told. I wasn't around when it happened.

I took the offer and flew to Sudbury within a few days. Susan stayed on with the folks. She and the baby. She wouldn't leave, said they were her only family now and someone had to take responsibility. Enter the Big B, again, a year later. It was the Big B who gave her the airfare to join me in Winnipeg.

STILL HOT AND STUFFY in the house, even though it's only 22°c today. I tried to find that story about the blind men and the elephant you mentioned, Rory. I looked through every book of fairy tales in the attic. Couldn't find it anywhere in Mother Goose. Sure you didn't make it up? It doesn't matter. I did find another fairy tale though.

Once upon a time there were three goats and they were triplets. They were looking for some grass to smoke so they could get high. The three goats came to a stream. On the other side there was a lot of grass.

There was a small bridge over the stream and under it there was an ogre. The goats were afraid to cross the bridge because of the ogre. Every time he heard somebody on the bridge he sent them packing. The three goats decided that the oldest goat would try to get past the ogre.

"Who's on my bridge?" roared the ogre.

The oldest goat spoke in a deep voice, "It's only me, an old goat," he said.

"You're trespassing," roared the ogre. "Get away from here."

"If you let me pass this one time, I'll move away," the old goat promised.

"Good," the ogre said. "Now get out of my sight." The old goat heads for the grass on the other side of the bridge.

The youngest goat decided to go next.

"Who's on my bridge?" roared the ogre.

The youngest goat spoke in a raspy voice, "It's only me, the young goat."

"You're trespassing," roared the ogre. "Get away from here."

"If you let me pass this one time, I'll move away," the youngest goat promised.

"Good," the ogre said. "Now get out of my sight."

The young goat headed for the grass on the other side of the bridge. It was now the middle-aged goat's turn.

"Who's on my bridge?" roared the ogre.

The middle-aged goat spoke in a clear voice, "It's me, the middle-aged goat."

"You're trespassing," roared the ogre. "Get away from here."

"Screw you!" the middle-aged goat said and charged the ogre. But the ogre moved to the side and the middle-aged goat rushed past him and didn't stop until he met up with his brothers in the field.

"They won't be back," the ogre said. "I'll see to that."

Adrian

SEPTEMBER, COPENHAGEN

A GUY GOES into a bar and orders a bottle of schnapps.

— What's eating you? the bartender asks.

— I just found out my brother is gay and is marrying my best friend.

The guy returns the next day and orders two bottles of schnapps.

— More troubles? the bartender asks.

The man sighs and shakes his head. —I got a call from my son last night and he's gay too.

On the third day the guy orders three bottles of schnapps.

— Doesn't anyone in your family like women? the bartender asks.

— Apparently my wife does.

WHEN WE THREE left home, you wanted to go to art school, Rory, and, well, you wanted to run away for a while, Cameron, and that was a purpose in itself. As for me, I wanted to become a chef. I had worked the summer after graduation at the Keltic Lodge in Ingonish. At first I was assigned to the waiting staff, but my supervisor said I was too cozy with the guests, so he put me in the kitchens. There's little time for chit-chat when you're filling dozens of orders during a shift, so I put all my energy into cooking, which I loved.

According to Talbot's frivolous rule about choosing a school or college, Montreal fell short of his fifteen-hundred-mile limit. But there was no hesitation on my part. I was bound for La Belle Province.

— *You were always pushing Talbot's buttons, Adrian.*

— *Way to go. Pissing off the Big B like that.*

Of course, Montreal had other things to offer besides food.

— *Slut. What would the folks think?*

I never actually sat down and told mom and dad that I was gay, because I was sure they knew. Long before I had intended to tell them, maybe even before I knew myself. Once I was talking to mom on the phone. The bathhouses in Toronto were raided in the early eighties and there was a protest in the streets of Toronto.

— I covered my eyes, Adrian, she said.

— Why?

— I saw those parades on television. I saw all those young men marching through the streets. Afraid to see you at the front of the parade. Waving a flag. Defiant.

— It's not right, she continued. Publishing the names of those men in the newspapers. That was their business, nobody else's.

That's all that was said.

But I had learned two things. That mom approved of whatever I did in private. Behind closed doors. And she thought I was defiant. Even though I hadn't travelled to protest in the streets of Toronto, I reached around and stroked my backbone anyway. Proudly.

— WHO TAUGHT YOU *this*? Joseph had asked once, when we were rolling around on his couch.

— Something I picked up, I answered.

A few years earlier, actually. A man of twenty-one, and myself, a young man of fifteen. Saturday afternoons in his apartment on a small residential side street, a few blocks from our house. He was a volunteer at our high school who occasionally tuned the band instruments, inviting me home for tea on a Saturday afternoon, after discovering we walked the same route. A man with a pointed jaw and strawberry blond hair.

— I'm home every second Saturday of the month, he said. I work on the other Saturdays.

We were sitting on a blanket in his living room. There was no furniture, only plastic crates, some filled with records and the others overturned with sheets to serve as tables. A few big cushions, a stereo, and beside it a small fridge with a hot plate on top. His mattress was on the bedroom floor.

— Watch me, he said. Watch what I do.

I watched and later he watched me. Only it took longer on him, the muscles in my mouth ached.

— You'll get your revenge, he said. When you get control.

Which didn't take many Saturdays to master. These became my private Saturdays and lasted for two years. Before he left Sydney, he told me something.

— There are a lot of bad men out there, he said.

— You aren't one of them.

— No. But I've met a few, he cautioned.

— Where? I asked.

— In public toilets, alleys, in the back of trucks, he said. At bars. Bathhouses. They weren't all bad.

— Bathhouses? I asked.

He smiled. — Maybe if you travel, he said. There are bathhouses in Toronto. In Montreal. Vancouver.

— What else? I asked.

— About bad men?

— No. What else should I know?

— I'll teach you everything I know.

Most of it I liked. Not all of it. But almost all of it. He told me about the bad men because he was sick.

Down below, he said.

I couldn't see anything down there when I looked.

— Gonorrhea, he said. It'll clear up. Give me a couple of weeks. We'll make up for lost time.

— Where did you catch it?

— From a bad man.

He moved away, before we could catch up but after he taught me everything he knew.

He taught me much about sex between men, which I passed on to Joseph a few years later. But he wasn't able to teach me how to be comfortable as a gay man. This I knew for myself. It was my instinct. And I knew that outside of the Saturday apartment and the bad-men places in other cities, he wasn't comfortable about being gay.

It happened like this. Once, after making out, we decided to

74

walk downtown to get something to eat. Outside the restaurant, on the busy street, a car came by, filled with men.

— Faggot, they shouted.

At him.

I'd never been called a faggot, a sissy, or a fruit. I think he had. He didn't turn his head to look at the men in the car. He was walking close to the curb. One of the men spit on him. It landed on his cheek. The saliva and phlegm rolled down his neck and under the collar of his white T-shirt.

— They spit on me, he said.

Yes, someone in the car had spit on him. Big deal. The city was full of yahoos. I was hungry. My eyes caught the last of the spit disappear from his neck. He didn't wipe it away. His neck was crimson, the colour rising quickly to his face.

— They spit on me, he repeated.

Imploringly.

The spit reminded me of come. It gave me an erection. There. On the street.

We didn't eat that afternoon. We walked home.

Separately.

I DIDN'T MEAN to offend either of you by not mentioning Claes when we were home for the funeral. He passed away four months before mom and dad were killed. Four months after I buried him, I returned to Cape Breton, joining the two of you and Talbot, to bury mom and dad.

Claes didn't have any family when he died. He was an orphan, and I buried him on my own. There was a family when mom and dad died. Four sons.

I never mentioned Claes when I was with us because you had never met him, and as the only correspondence we've had in recent years was through Christmas cards and what mom and dad passed on in their infrequent letters, I didn't feel a need to talk about Claes and have his memory compete with our grief. Not then.

— *So tell us now, Adrian. Let us in. We won't interrupt.*

When I close my eyes and try to picture Claes, it is still difficult to fit all of him in my mind's eye. At first, I see his hair, a thick head of hair, straight, although it tended to feather around his ears and at the back of his neck.

He was probably born with the white blond hair typical of many Danish boys, but it had darkened with age, a blend of blond and light brown. In the front, he let it grow down over his high forehead. When he stepped out of a swimming pool, he shook his head vigorously, running his fingers through his hair, brushing it up off his forehead. It changed his looks, he became very aristocratic, perfectly suited to a tuxedo, which is something he never wore.

— It suits you, I told him. Often.

Claes liked to swim, three or four times a week, forty-five minutes of laps in the pool. He didn't have a long torso or long limbs. I was surprised when he told me that he was five-foot-ten, only two inches shorter than we three. He didn't have the muscled slenderness of swimmers, but there were muscles there all the same. He could heave a crate of heavy melons like they were marshmallows. Claes was a chef.

When I send you a photo of him, you might think that he brooded. When he was at ease, which was most of the time, he looked serious, but never worried or stressed. His face reflected confidence and the shadows around his eyes and chin made him look a little angry.

It kept people on their guard. He had the kind of face that people never second-guessed, just in case there was a simmering temper below the surface, which there never was. Still, when we played cards, you never knew if he was bluffing.

Claes had a fair complexion and he never let himself tan.

— Why? I asked.

— Tanning will fade my tattoos.

He had several, on his earlobe, arm, shoulder, and hip.

When I first met Claes, I thought he had a deep purple birthmark on his earlobe, but it was the tattoo of a small seashell. He caught me staring at it and, when I met his gaze, there was delight in his warm eyes, his lips pulling back to reveal a toothy smile.

I remember him showing me the outline of the starfish tattoo he had on his shoulder. One of the arms was crooked.

— I laughed, he said. You don't laugh when you get a tattoo.

They were all connected with the sea, the starfish on his left shoulder, an octopus above his tailbone, a seahorse, its tail wrapped around the biceps on his left arm, and the shell on his earlobe.

— It is like making love in an aquarium, I said.

A COUPLE OF WEEKS after I came home from my first year in Montreal, I decided to get a tattoo. There was a tattooist in North Sydney and I asked Susan to come along for moral support. We hitchhiked and our short ride was in the back of a half-ton truck that weaved from side to side. We sat on bales of hay that kept shifting. At one point Susan reached out and touched the window of an oncoming car as it passed too close to the centre line.

We interpreted the clouds as we rode.

— It looks like Captain Crunch's hat, Susan said, pointing to a tri-cornered nimbus, identical to the cartoon character's hat on the cereal box.

We were dropped off downtown just as the clouds burst, and Susan herded me into a church. I wanted to wait outside under the eaves, but Susan dragged me inside to one of the pews and sat down.

— Did you know Cameron and I go to church? she asked.

— Cameron?

— Yes, Cameron.

— What does he do in church?

— Listens.

— To what? The minister?

— No. He just sits with his eyes closed and listens.

— Spooky, I said.

— That's our Cameron.

When the rain ended we headed for the tattoo parlour.

— Do you know what you want? she asked.

— Not exactly.

— I want a flower.

— Let me guess. A rose?

— No. An iris. A beautiful blue iris on my shoulder. And I want to go first, she said. In case I chicken out.

— Deal.

It didn't take very long, and Susan's shoulder was swollen.

— Well? I asked.

— Some iris, she said. It feels like a thorny rose attacked me. Your turn.

Cluck. Cluck.

I fled the parlour, flapping my arms.

AFTER WORKING in Montreal kitchens for almost ten years, I was bored. I needed a change. I'd always been part of a team of chefs and this had satisfied me. Now I felt I had the ambition and experience to run my own kitchen. I had some capital and decided to create my own small restaurant.

Maybe even in Cape Breton.

Talbot was against the idea when I came home to scout locations, catching up with me on the last day of my trip. Unemployment was high on the island, the steel workers and miners didn't eat snails, and the checkout girls at the supermarkets couldn't identify an avocado.

— *They sell avocados in Sydney now? The only vegetables I remember were carrots, iceberg salad, and canned peas.*

I hadn't mentioned my idea to Talbot. Mom or dad must have passed on the information. Next thing I knew, he was lecturing me.

Cape Breton wasn't Montreal. Everyone wore a baseball cap. People's taste in Sydney was limited to meat and potatoes.

I had been more interested in Louisbourg or Baddeck, both with a high volume of seasonal visitors.

As to our parents, they were ambivalent. Or so Talbot claimed.

Why would Adrian leave Montreal, they asked, a city he loves, and return to Cape Breton?

Cape Breton wasn't Montreal. There were limitations. Men like me couldn't buy the fancy clothes I liked to wear in any of the shops in Sydney. People would talk. I couldn't hire staff like that boy Joseph. People didn't want to be served by sissies.

And the roughnecks had guns in Louisbourg.

I told him roughnecks had guns in Montreal.

Not hunting rifles. Not shells that left a gaping hole in your stomach.

No, as far as I knew, there were no rifles for shooting queers in Montreal.

— *Attaboy, Adrian. You tell him.*

Talbot had insisted on driving me to the airport, his sermon conveyed on the short walk from the parking lot to the terminal. It was blustery and most of his homo homily was lost to the wind.

There was a light drizzle in the air and it annoyed him. Talbot doesn't like the rain or the wind, it smothers him, and as we walked toward the terminal that day he whisked away the drizzle with the tips of his fingers as if they were spiderwebs above a door, punctuating each swipe with his lecture.

I was just like Cameron and Rory. Worrying mom and dad at every turn. They married too young. Cameron's house was too big. Always needed repairs. A money pit. Rory was buying a gallery. Who was paying for that?

When we were finally inside the airport, his hair was flat and his eyes puffy. He had all the symptoms of an allergy and sniffled while I checked in at the counter.

I had barely gotten a word in edgewise from the moment I set foot in his car. What was the point? The only thing he said that stuck in my head, like a gob of spit on my cheek, was the word *sissies*. At the gate I extended my hand.

It stopped his rant and he looked at my outstretched hand in surprise, then smiled. A first for Talbot. When he leaned in to shake my hand, I kissed his cheek.

He turned on his heel and left before he could see the smirk lighting up my face, a short wave of disgust above his head as he walked away. As if I were just another cobweb.

I DECIDED TO TAKE a vacation overseas. I spent six weeks in southern Europe, flew to Lisbon, continued through the Algarve, crossed the border into Spain, a week in Seville, days in Granada, and backtracked to Venice for the last week of my sojourn.

Odd routes, with no aim other than moving through villages, countryside, and cities virgin to my wanderings. In Venice I told someone in a club, late at night, that I was a chef. Although the young Italian didn't invite me home to his flat that night, he did tell me I should visit the Venice Culinary Expo.

— There are chefs from all over the world, he said. You might find another *Americano*. Feel at home.

I found Claes. Gulping beer at one of the stands set up in the middle of the exhibition hall, taking me in at the same instant, sitting at the next table, alone, sipping a tepid cappuccino and watching him. As it turned out, we were staying at the same small hotel.

Venice is bisected by the Grand Canal, and on either side there are three neighbourhoods. Our shared hotel was on the border of two, San Polo and Santa Croce, on the upper sweep of the Grand Canal where tightly packed streets and squares reveal a less hurried pace than that found close to San Marco and its thousands of summer tourists crossing the great square every day.

The hotel looked shabby from the outside, its large wooden

door splintered and the paint long faded. But inside, the narrow stone staircase that wound itself up to the four floors was spotless, and a decorative door jutted into the stairwell on each landing. All of the rooms had been recently renovated and there was still carpenters' dust on the windowsill overlooking the small courtyard below my window.

On my first full day in Venice, arriving early in the morning, I tossed my knapsack on the bed and walked the streets of the quarter, crossing the Grand Canal at two of its three spectacular bridges, and climbed dozens of small bridges along the smaller canals. Although I visited a few clubs I was back in my room before midnight, blisters on my feet from a new pair of sandals I had bought in Monte Gordo, Portugal. I soaked my feet in the bidet, and inhaled the faint aroma of late-blooming wisteria that wafted up to my room from the courtyard below.

I awoke fresh the next morning, welcomed by the peal of church bells from somewhere close, and headed for the expo. On my third morning, over breakfast, Claes introduced himself and asked if he might join me at my empty table, our conversation quickly turning to our professions and food. He was toying with the idea of refurbishing his bistro in Copenhagen. He wanted to serve French and Italian cuisine, and he told me the name he had chosen for the place, The Little Supper, and that he was collecting ideas for aphrodisiac meals.

I spoke easily about my theories on food, especially French cuisine, interrupted often by his questions.

— Is this a job interview? I asked.

He smiled and asked if I'd consider visiting Copenhagen, spending some time in the kitchen of his bistro. Perhaps there was a future in Scandinavia for me, he suggested.

We spent the next three days sightseeing. He left for Denmark and I returned to Canada. A week later I accepted his invitation to visit him. I flew to Copenhagen and he drove me immediately to the bistro.

I was infatuated.

With the restaurant. The city. Claes.

I HADN'T REALLY SETTLED in Montreal, despite the years I had spent there. Maybe I was remembering my oath from the train trip that had delivered me to Montreal, not to get attached to a place.

In truth, I really didn't give Montreal a chance. I worked in restaurants that catered to English-speaking customers and hung around with other anglophiles, using my French sparingly although I was fluent, usually at the clubs, picking up somebody for the night. I should have learned about Montreal through the eyes of my French friends, but I never took the time.

Mom and dad didn't seem too upset about my moving to Denmark.

— It's not exactly down the block, is it? mom said. I guess it doesn't matter. Montreal or Copenhagen. It's still away. You loved Montreal, she said. I guess you'll love Denmark. And I guess you'll have to learn *Dutch*.

— Danish, I corrected.

— Whatever.

— Even the animals speak Danish, I said.

— They do?

— Take the pigs. They say *øf øf* and not *oink oink*. The dogs bark *vov vov* and not *woof woof*. And the ducks. Even the ducks.

They say *rap rap* and not *quack quack*.

Mom was speechless, but dad wouldn't let me have the last word. He patted me on the shoulder on his way out of the kitchen.

— Well, Adrian. You'll have to take the time and learn a third language. The one the animals really speak.

WITHIN A MONTH of settling into Claes' apartment, I enrolled in a Danish language course and became a partner in The Little Supper. The sprawling seven-room apartment was on a street overlooking a plaza where the open-air market is held every workday morning. I was living in the centre of the city, surrounded by magnificent parks.

Every June, there is a country-wide celebration called the Night of Saint John, when bonfires are lit all over the country and witches are burnt in effigy. Claes and I used to stroll along the shores of Amager, an island in the south of Copenhagen, moving in and out among the dozens of fires. The sky was smoky and pungent, and hundreds of Danes serenaded each other, huddled in tight groups as the embers burned intensely on the pyres.

The celebration coincides with the beginning of summer and the start of the mesmerizing twilight nights, another comfort I welcome each year. The sun fails to dip completely below the horizon during these few brief weeks, resulting in rich seablue skies at midnight set against the verdigris spires, delicate apertures along the city's skyline.

There's a small courtyard behind The Little Supper and Claes and I often sat there until one or two in the morning after a long shift, our weary bodies fortified by fiery Danish schnapps and those majestic midsummer skies.

I have mentioned that many of the dishes we serve at The Little Supper are aphrodisiacs. Like me, Claes loved to eat. He also loved novels, French novels in particular. He had a small library in the apartment and it included the books of the Marquis de Sade. In *Les 120 Journées de Sodome*, the Marquis wrote of a meal that included bisque, dozens of hors d'oeuvres and entrees, poultry, roasts, hot and cold pastries, and Greek, German, and Italian wines.

In his *Mémoires*, Casanova writes on the topic of erotic foods, and the topic recurs in the writings of Restif de la Bretonne, Crebillon Fils, and André de Nerciat. So I am told. I have never read the novels. I am not a fan of reading in general. But Claes loved to read and to read aloud.

He often read to me before we slept. Short passages, no more than two or three pages, long enough to sate the moment, gentle segues between lovemaking and sleep.

Most often his selections were passages about food from novels not about food. I never knew the plots in those stories, the characters or even the settings, but I retained the titles and the names of the authors, for reference, I suppose, inspiration for the future.

It was a habit. Memorize the titles and authors, jot down the page number the next morning. Claes' passages were my recipe cards, although I never had occasion to use them. Early on, we discovered that almost all foods have an aphrodisiac quality attributed to them. We could put anything on our menu and call it love food.

WE DECIDED TO BUY a house. Claes wanted us to be able to walk outside into our own backyard. We found one in the east end of the city, Østerbro, along the man-made lakes in Copenhagen. It was a neighbourhood of small working-class houses, row after row, which was why they were called potato houses, reminding me of the company houses built in the mining towns of Cape Breton.

For most of the nineteenth century, living conditions for the mushrooming working class in Copenhagen were abysmal. Open sewers contributed to a severe outbreak of cholera that killed more than five thousand people. The housing project in Østerbro was supposed to change all that, but the houses were still too expensive for the labourers to afford. Instead, office workers and managers moved in. Today, it is an expensive neighbourhood of artists, architects, lawyers, and other professionals.

The first day in our new house, Claes planted a garden.

— Hug me.

And afterwards.

— Hug me again.

— Like this? I asked.

— Yes, he said. Some people just squeeze. There's a difference, you know.

— Yes, I said. There is a difference.

Joseph hadn't understood the nature of hugs. He knew nothing about reassurance. All the times that I let Claes hug me I was telling him with my body it was okay, we could get beyond this point together. Or alone. Hugs have nothing to do with how we feel at the moment, they're a signal for the changes ahead. They rouse us from the inertia we have reached and shift us into new time.

— I don't want you to feel lonely, Claes often said.

Then he always gave me a hug. Sometimes it was inappropriate because he said it when he found me alone but not feeling lonely.

CLAES WAS A HEMOPHILIAC and suffered from terrible nosebleeds. He had contracted the HIV virus from a blood transfusion before we met. He didn't find out that he was positive until he was having routine blood work during an insurance checkup, when they tested for syphilis and the virus.

— I might have been positive for years. They didn't test blood for the virus back then, he said.

By the time I met Claes we were both practising safe sex. I took his diagnosis in stride. A few years earlier he might have been devastated by the sentence and I might have fled out of fear. Because the unending rounds of wakes and funerals in the late eighties eroded the courage of the dying and the surviving. But the cocktails were available now and Claes wasn't showing any symptoms of full-blown AIDS. We no longer considered ourselves victims.

Claes had a motto. Eat right, exercise regularly, and die anyway.

It was while we were planning a trip to the arctic town of Akureyri in Iceland, to help christen a bistro one of our former sous-chefs had opened, that Claes was stricken with pneumonia. We were both surprised by the sudden illness. Claes had escaped the flu that had ravished Copenhagen the winter before and confined me to bed for a week, and we couldn't recall that he had ever been the victim of a cold in the two years since we moved into our house.

VICTIM OF A COLD. What an odd way to put it. The closest I had come to victimhood was in Montreal. I had never met any of the bad men my lover in Sydney had warned me against. Other types, yes, even before I left Cape Breton, far worse in fact, but not gay bad men. Yet they fuelled my imagination for a few years after he said it. I wanted to look into their faces and catalogue them for my fantasies. Montreal provided that opportunity, strolling through one of its parks famous for cruising.

I didn't know exactly where the cruising areas were located and I felt conspicuous crossing the large greens, despite the protection of the groves and darkness. It is a frigid October evening and after twenty minutes my nose was running and my fingers were blue. I felt stupid and headed for the park exit.

Just outside the gates a car was parked and the driver noded at me. I don't know why I did it, a polite reflex perhaps, but I nodded back at him and smiled. A few moments later as I walked down the deserted boulevard, the same car sidled up beside me, and the driver rolled down his window.

— Need a lift? he asked.

— No, I answered. Smiling again.

The car rolled a few feet ahead of me. He got out, opening the back door.

It was an unmarked police car.

— Get in, he said. Flashing his badge.

I climbed into the back seat and he slipped in beside me, closing the door. I don't recall wondering whether I should get into the car or feeling any sense of dread or danger. My heart wasn't pounding. The car reeked of aftershave.

— You looking for a little action tonight?

— No, I answered. I am looking straight ahead of me.

— Just out for a late-night stroll?

— I'm meeting some friends.

— This neighbourhood is full of queers, he said. In fact, the whole fucking city is queer. Even the broads. He put his hand on my knee. Look at me, he barked.

I turned and faced him. There was no expression on his face. He had a bushy moustache, the face was broad, the neck thick.

— Did I do anything wrong? I asked, turning away from his heavy breath.

He has my face between his fingers, twisting it toward him, squishing my cheeks like a peach.

— I told you to look at me, he said.

He kept holding my face. I looked at him, searching his eyes for some clue as how to respond.

— Open your mouth, he said.

He inserted a finger in my mouth, probing the insides of my cheeks and gums.

I gagged and my body leaned forward.

— I didn't tell you to move, he said. Open your mouth. Wide.

He put two fingers in my mouth, rougher this time.

— You like that? he asked. He started to probe my mouth, inserting his fingers deeper with each stroke.

— Clean my fingers, he said.

I closed my lips around the fingers.

— That's it, he said. Suck those fingers. Use your tongue. Clean them. Take them all the way in your mouth. Down to my knuckles.

The nicotine on his fingers mixed with my saliva.

— Put your head back, he said. I want to go deep.

I eased down on the seat a few inches and feel the fingers sliding along the back of my tongue.

— You got a nipple down there? he asked.

The tip of a finger touched my tonsil.

— You want me to squeeze that nipple?

There were tiny beads of sweat on his brow. He wiped them away with the back of his free hand. He was still pressing his fingers down my throat, his tongue between his teeth, trying to get a third and fourth finger in my mouth. I was having difficulty getting air and choked, thought I was going to retch. I could feel my heart pounding, but I was not afraid. I was angry and grossed out by this pig.

He withdrew his hand, his fingers wet. His face was red. He continued to look at me in the same expressionless manner for about a minute. Then he spat in my face.

— Get out, he said.

I slid out of the car and he shut the door after me. I saw him strike a match and roll down the window, the smoke wafting into the crisp air.

I wiped away his spit, the odour strong and sour. I walked up to the window and looked down at him.

I told you to beat it, he said.

I smiled at him and put my finger to my lips, sliding it along my tongue.

— Didn't get enough, you little faggot? I heard him unclasp his belt, his greedy eyes on the foreplay with my tongue.

I forced my finger down my throat and emptied the bile from my stomach on his face.

He started to vomit. I ran as fast as I could, whooping at the night, jumping up to give a stop sign a quick high-five as I disappeared into the protection of the park, closing the gate behind me to keep out all the bad men.

— He's making that up, Cameron.

— Are you kidding? Adrian could always outrun us. Outrun anybody.

— He could've been arrested.

— I'm proud of you, Adrian. The bells between your legs must have been clanging like crazy that night.

WHEN CLAES DIED, it was because of complications from the pneumonia that had settled in his lungs. There was, no phlegm, diarrhea, or other bodily fluids to require gloves or masks. Still, at the hospital, everyone wore gloves, masks, and paper coats when they entered his room.

For Claes' protection, a nurse suggested I wear the same props when I visited. Her tone was insistent, almost bullying me with her instructions. I told the nurse it was unfair. She took it as a challenge and I quickly sweetened my tone.

— Unfair, because Claes will never know what it is like to gaze on your pretty face, I said.

I gave her the benefit of the doubt. Like Claes, I'd never seen her face, hidden, as always, behind a mask. Still, her eyes came alive then, and we talked more often after that. I caught her once, running her fingers through his thick hair while she took his temperature, absentmindedly parting it to the side.

At his funeral, I didn't recognize some of the nurses offering condolences until I distinguished a voice or style of glasses on their noses. Only then did I know who was talking to me.

I wasn't at Claes' side when he died. I arrived about an hour later. The duty nurse accompanied me to his room and squeezed my hand at the door. She followed behind me and went to the window and opened the blind. The afternoon sunlight bathed the room, washing away the hard, shadowy outlines of the furniture. All of the machinery had been removed, the heart monitor, drips, and respirator.

I hadn't seen Claes' face without tubes covering his nose and mouth in weeks, or glimpsed his long neck, buried to the chin in sheets, or his ears, sunken into the pillows.

My impulse was to quietly remove my clothes and slip in beside him, careful not to wake him from the deep sleep needed after one of his marathon shifts at the restaurant.

It was a difficult impulse to suppress, because Claes was like the unspoiled snowdrifts of my childhood. It was his quiet spirit that always aroused me.

I sat beside him, reaching under the sheet to find his hand, mildly surprised at the warmth of his palm against my icy grasp, smiling despite myself, because Claes always said the touch of my cold hands could rouse the dead, and I gave his hand a good squeeze.

I was confused then by an odd sensation, a perception of wholeness and of nearness when I looked at him. For months I'd been vaguely aware of Claes' presence retreating from me. At first the fatigue of the infections and then the pneumonia occasioned a lack of participation from him or of interest in the life of the moment, the day-to-day routines of our lives. But there were two things he wanted, a tattoo and to marry me.

— If you marry me, the state won't be able to take anything from you after I die, he said.

It was a fitting sentiment for a relationship that had never been tarnished by sentimentality. I wouldn't deny his request.

In the last weeks, at the hospital, seeking him with my eyes when I entered the room felt like gazing across a vast distance, the four or five steps to cross the room an agonizing trek. Then, in those last weeks, his features started to disappear beneath the respirator tubes. When I returned home those nights, I looked through our photo albums for clues to help me piece together his face into someone I knew.

I held his hand, stroking his thick hair as I sat beside him on his deathbed and thinking, you have come back to me, all of you.

The duty nurse quietly re-entered the room. She told me that some of the nurses would like to send flowers or make a donation to a charity.

— Which would I prefer? Then, what would Claes have wanted?

— A charity, I told her. The Hemophilia Society.

She pressed something into my hand, wrapped in tissue. She watched me as I unwrapped it, perhaps fearful that I would become angry. It was a lock of Claes' hair. She was immediately apologetic, telling me that she had never done anything like that before, that it was unprofessional. I kissed her, hugging her close as she wept into my shoulder, pressing the lock of hair to my nose, seeking his scent.

CLAES HAD NO APPETITE in those last months. Mine was insatiable. I took to fasting in the afternoons. There's an irony in hunger. It can fill your stomach. It displaced the other emptiness I experienced in those months. Hunger gave me hope. It was the one void I could replenish every day.

I sat around the house on the days I didn't visit the hospital, with Claes' black lab lying at my feet. His only movement was to roll over, following the path of a sunbeam as it crossed the floor. He looked like a woolly black slug.

Sometimes I joined him on the floor. I hugged him so that it produced a little grunt from his throat. If the afternoon was late, the sun strong, he gave up his stomach for a rub.

During the last three months of his life, Claes didn't come home. I was angry at the dog because he didn't seem to notice. One evening, out of spite, I didn't feed the dog. I wanted to give him something to miss. I watched him walk from me to the kitchen and back again. Over and over. Occasionally resting his head on the edge of the sofa where I sat. Not daring to look in my eyes. Followed by a little dance in the middle of the floor. A wagging of the tail and a short bark. I gave him something to miss that night.

After the funeral I found myself on the floor beside the dog, sharing his sunbeam. Like old times. I gave the dog a hug, squeezing just enough to produce the familiar grunt. But I'd forgotten everything I had learned about hugs. There was no happy grunt from the dog. Just a rolling growl.

Rory

JANUARY, TORONTO

I WANT TO THANK both of you for the cards and flowers you sent to Janet. She was touched by the overwhelming presence of the Hines brothers in her room. The nurses had to bring in a special table for your large bouquet, Adrian. According to Janet, when you send flowers overseas the receiver doesn't necessarily get the arrangement you order from the catalogue, as seasons and local flowers differ from country to country. Personally, I think you failed to realize how strong the Danish crown is, compared to the Canadian dollar.

And Cameron, I must say I experienced a tinge of jealousy because the flowers you sent just happen to be Janet's favourites. She was delighted. It brought a blush of pink to her cheeks. I only wish I'd considered such a detail. Well, next time. No, there isn't going to be a next time. The doctors are confident they removed all the cancer, and Janet should be up and about in another week or so. She's still feeling a little too tender to write, but thanking you both is her priority when she's on her feet again.

She's pleased with the results of the surgery. Before the operation she advised her surgeon on how he was to proceed and she even made a series of contingency plans in the event of complications beyond what was foreseeable, using one of her medical markers to draw game plans across her own chest.

When I arrived this afternoon there was a celebration going on in her room. Several of Toronto's finest plastic surgeons had descended to wish her well. Janet's oldest colleague and my biggest patron, Dr. Ivan Kolerus, struggled to remove the cork from the champagne bottle. Kolerus is your man for rhinoplasty, or the proverbial nose job. He slits the inside of the nostrils to isolate soft tissue from the cartilage and bone. The hump or excess bone is extracted and the remainder is reshaped. It's rumoured Kolerus got his first experience on his own nose, a bulbous onion.

Janet's partner, Dr. Diana Riis, sat on the edge of the bed, gingerly picking at a box of truffles. Janet and Diana have been in practice together for ten years. Diana gave Janet a pair of tiny diamond studs, and she was sporting them with pride. They're the ladies to see for big tits. Though Janet insists I say breast augmentation.

Last but not least, Dr. Aktky shook my hand rigorously and gave me the once-over, subtly inspecting his own handiwork on my face. Yes, dear brothers, I've succumbed to the plastic fantastic world and allowed Dr. Aktky to perform a blepharoplasty on me, getting rid of the bags under my eyes, which fortunately neither of you seem to possess. For two weeks I looked like I had been poked in the face with broom handles, but I'm happy with the results. My face looks less tired. I could've opted for a shot of Botox around the eyes, but the thought of living bacteria swimming around inside my skin didn't appeal to me.

THE LAST OF THE GOOD DOCTORS left at six. Janet and I ate dinner together in her room and she was asleep before I finished my coffee. The sheets were bunched close around her neck, which is unusual because Janet doesn't like anything tight at her throat. I gently pulled them away, revealing her beautiful long neck. She looked less fragile in the bed and she stretched her legs in her sleep.

I've got a slight throbbing in my temples, champagne does that to me. I think I'll make it an early night. Which is just as well. Ivan Kolerus wants to stop by the Gallery in the morning at seven-thirty before his early rounds at the hospital. I'll have to get there around seven because he's viewing three *Red on Red* panels from one of the earliest series. Kolerus owns at least two pieces from each series I've produced.

The panels he's got his eye on haven't been unpacked since the exhibition last year, so I better be at the Gallery by six-thirty. The crates are buried deep in storage. If Tally were more of an early-morning person, I'd ask him to help me. He hasn't dropped by the Gallery on this trip. He's out for the evening. I don't know when he'll be back. He has a key, so I'll just write him a note and suggest he meet me there later tomorrow, before we go to the hospital.

I haven't seen much of him on this trip. He was reluctant to accept my invitation to stay over this time because of Janet, but

I was persistent. Nonetheless, with the Gallery, the hospital, and his conference, we've only spent one full evening together and that was last night.

Tally is almost completely grey now. Do you think we'll be grey by the time we're fifty? Still, there's not a wrinkle on his face. It suits him, the white hair. I was just shocked to notice, all at once, the change. I wonder what Beth thinks about it. She's in Montreal at a conference of her own and Tally is meeting her there the day after tomorrow. Then they're going to Florida for a week before returning home. The flowers he gave to Janet were signed with both their names, a first for Tally. He's always so circumspect about his relationship with Beth. I don't understand why. We've all known her for years, it's hard to think of Tally without Beth.

It feels like she's been around forever, and I mean that in a good way, it's comforting. As standoffish and distant as Tally can come across, Beth is just the opposite. Her face holds no secrets, she's always relaxed around Tally, and I've always felt you could ask her anything. Janet assures me Tally is embarrassed by Beth's weight. I had to think about that for a couple of minutes when Janet brought it up. Beth? Overweight? I just don't see her that way. Though Mom often described Beth as big boned or of generous proportions. I always considered Tally skinny, but I never thought of Beth as fat. Even now, I wouldn't call her hefty or big. She's curvaceous.

And stylish. Her dresses never looked like anything Mom wore, fashionable as they were for a small city, bought off the rack even if they were from the better stores in Sydney. I helped Mom get ready one night for bridge, not because I volunteered, I just happened to pass her bedroom and she decided to commandeer me to help her zip up. She smoothed the sides of the material at her hips and stomach, trying to erase folds invisible to my young eyes, complaining all the while.

"I paid a fortune for this dress," she said. "You'd think a woman could buy something that fit in the hips, chest, *and* the small of the back." She was frantic with her hands, pulling at the material. It bunched up in the back, but I didn't say anything.

"Beth doesn't have those problems." I cocked my ears. Mom rarely mentioned Beth. "That girl could slip a potato sack over her head and it would still fall nicely on those big bones. I don't know where she gets the time to do all that sewing."

It was Beth's secret, she made all her own clothes, tailoring everything to her shape and taste, and it fit everywhere at once.

"Why do you think Beth and Tally aren't married?"

Mom stopped yanking at the dress and looked at me blankly for a moment, as if she'd never considered the question.

"I suppose they think that things are good the way they are now." Dismissing my presence momentarily, she returned to looking at the dress in the mirror.

"I did ask him once, though," she said, addressing my reflection, "and he said that if it's not broken, don't fix it." So Mom had considered it after all. "Your brother can be flippant at times."

Janet made a comment once, claiming Beth had a habit of twirling the thin gold-plated engagement ring on her finger, a habit she had acquired to pass the time over the many years since Talbot gave it to her. Standing in line at the bank, the doctor's office, or in the checkout aisles at the supermarket, the worn band stemming Beth's mild impatience with anything she couldn't hurry along.

So I put the same question to Talbot I had put to Mom all

those years ago during his brief visit and he promptly told me it was none of my business.

Tally's wall. But did I detect a crack in that wall?

The muscles in his lips were moving. If I could lip-read, I'd say a *besides* was perched there, waiting to fall out. So I waited, listening.

Besides. Had I ever really asked myself why Janet and I had married? *Or.* Why we stayed together? *Because.* These are frivolous questions. *Therefore.* Ask him something he could answer. *But remember.* He wouldn't ever ask why I painted the same picture, again and again. *When.* He knew I wouldn't answer. *Besides.* I couldn't answer.

Up until this point I did want to ask him an important question. Not about Beth. I wanted to ask Tally about some pictures. Family pictures. He sent each of us a handful of the photos from the family albums after the funeral, which was considerate of him. There were pictures of Mom and Dad together and singularly, pictures of relatives remembered and forgotten, family friends, pictures of me with you, Adrian, or you, Cameron, and pictures of all three of us. But there were no pictures of Tally. But after our brusque tête-à-tête I decided not to ask Tally why he kept all the pictures of himself. He had once again exhibited his knack for deflecting unwanted questions, for refusing surrender of his self. Perhaps photographs are like questions for Tally. Unwanted. Unavailable. Unanswered.

Like the high school friend you mentioned, Adrian. Is that why Tally kept all the pictures of himself? So we wouldn't get too close, memorizing details about him he didn't want revealed? Or remembered? But even without the photos, we know the colour of his eyes. They're grey. Icy grey.

TALLY'S GONE! Just like that. Not a word. Instead, a little note on the fridge. Beth's conference had wrapped up early and he'd taken an evening flight to Montreal. He's lucky I noticed the note in the first place. I mightn't have seen it until tomorrow, or even later as I'm not in the habit of reading my fridge. It's really too bad. I was looking forward to previewing the new exhibition for Tally at the Gallery and then, after a quick visit to Janet, driving him to the airport for our traditional couple of hours over one warm beer before his flight.

I only noticed the damn note because I got up a few minutes ago to get a glass of juice. Another effect of champagne, thirst. I've a sneaking suspicion I won't be able to get back to sleep now. It's two-thirty in the morning and raining. Or as we say out east, it's spilling.

I wonder where the expression comes from. Are we supposed to imagine some gigantic pitcher in the sky, tilted by an unseen hand, spilling its contents over the earth?

I'm sure we Maritimers aren't unique in using the phrase. I'm going to Vancouver in two weeks, so I'll make a note to ask Father Sears, a curator I know out there. His speciality, other than art and Faith, is etymology, and he enjoys quoting the sources of words and expressions. His gaze bores into your skin while he talks, owing to a set of bulging eyes on a rather tiny face with a flat nose, upturned at the tip.

At our first meeting, he was showing me where he wanted to hang my paintings in the church, quickly dismissing an alcove I found inviting. Until five years ago, St. Agnes was one of several boarded-up churches in Vancouver. Father Sears was behind the drive to convert it into a public gallery and he's been the curator ever since.

I'm the first non–Western Canadian to receive a showing in the gallery, and naturally I was flattered by the invitation. However, I was curious about his insistence the exhibition open on Ash Wednesday and run until the last three days of the Easter week.

"It's not at all odd, Mr. Hines. I specifically wanted your *Red on Red* series because in the colours of church decoration, red, along with being the colour of martyrs, is also the colour for Ash Wednesday, the last three days of the Holy Week and Whit Sunday.

"Unfortunately, my budget doesn't allow for the exhibition to extend to Whit Sunday. But two out of three is satisfactory."

"What else can you tell me about the colour red, Father?" I ventured, cautiously. I didn't want him to misunderstand me and think I was asking for a critique of my work.

"I'll be brief," he stated, not missing a single opportunity to parade his encyclopedic knowledge. "In metals it's represented by iron, the metal of war. In precious stones, by the ruby, and in the planets, by Mars. In heraldry, red is engraved by perpendicular lines. Your signature."

I looked at him with a measure of both awe and defeat. Though the origin of my signature wasn't secret, I'd never encountered someone who knew the origins of the lines with which I sign all my paintings.

"Do you have a title for your exhibition, Mr. Hines?"

"Yes, *Red Snow*."

"How lovely. What does it mean?"

"Red snow is often seen close to gory dew, which is damp, blood-like algae appearing on walls."

"Fascinating."

Indeed. I'll have to ask the good Father about spilling.

AS I PREDICTED, I haven't slept. The rain has turned to wet snow. There are a surprising number of lights appearing up and down the street at this early hour. I can hear a baby crying in one house, and I imagine a man cursing under his breath in another, perhaps stubbing his toe on the corner of a chair in an unlit kitchen.

There are no sounds in my house aside from the gentle vibrations of the air blowing from the heat ducts beside my feet. Janet is always up at five-thirty and gone by seven, when I stumble out of bed. Usually, she's already had two cups of coffee before leaving, the scent of her morning Gitanes cigarette hanging in the air. She doesn't have another cigarette until the evening. I should be accustomed to greeting an empty house in the morning. And I suppose I am. But inhabiting this vacuous abode through the night without Janet is a new and unfamiliar experience. It's like looking at the discarded skin of a snake and wondering how something so intact can possibly be so empty.

It's ironic. When we were growing up, both of you looked to me to lead. If we wanted to stay up an extra half-hour past our bedtime, I made the case to Mom. And if we didn't want to eat the salted herring at dinner, I was the first to push away the plate. Shut in on a stormy Saturday afternoon, I chose the board games we'd play until supper. 'Course, it was always at Adrian's coaxing, but usually I took up the challenge. Now I can't even choose a pair of socks without consulting Janet. I depend upon her completely. She never rolls her eyes or displays any sign of annoyance. Because I'm never indecisive, I just ask for an opinion, which she graciously supplies.

Yet, there've been consequences, I realize. Last week I was sitting in my car outside the Gallery, listening to the end of a news item on the radio. Across the street, a man ran along the sidewalk to catch a bus. I watched as he stepped off the curb, then stumbled and fell flat out on his stomach. A woman approached and bent over him, said something, assisted him to his feet. I didn't do anything other than turn up the radio and look away. But I was thinking, could I have done anything, perhaps rushed over and aided the man? I was in conflict.

If Janet isn't with me, I'm anemic when someone drops his groceries, asks for directions, needs help crossing the street, or spills coffee on his pants. Invariably, I'm at the other end of the aisle, the bottom of the stairs, or across the room when these misadventures happen.

I'M STILL BAREFOOT and can't get Tally out of my mind. I've decided his eyes aren't icy, they're cold. Before he left, he warned me not to be overly optimistic about Janet's recovery, suggesting it might take awhile for her to get on her feet again. I'm no fool, I knew what he was implying, but Tally never leaves anything he says open to assumption, reminding me Janet is almost sixty.

I looked at him for a long moment.

I wanted to point out that when he climbed the eight steps to our front door, he reached the top huffing and puffing. Janet takes the stairs two at a time, she's always at least two steps ahead of me, I can't keep up with her on the street. And when she wakes up in the morning, she's awake. Fully awake.

Tally, tiring of my silence, shrugged his shoulders, pouring himself a second cup of coffee.

In all the years Janet and I've been together, I've only really

considered our age difference once. And it was during a conversation with Mom, on my last trip home before she died. Dad
had been complaining about his arthritis for a couple of days.

"He wants *liniment*," she said to me, smiling. "They don't sell
liniment at Zellers. I've told him that a million times. Ask for
Bengay, I tell him, or the young girls will think you're an old goat."

"Dad's ten years older than you are, isn't he?"

"I'm reminded of that every day," she said, still smiling over
the business with the liniment.

"What do you mean?"

"Is this about you and Janet?" she asked.

"No." At least it wasn't until that moment.

"I won't pry, Rory. But let me tell you something about your
father and me. As he gets older, I get older. But I only ever think
about *my* getting older. As for your father, I'm sure he still
thinks he's as young as the day we met."

"I'm not really following you, Mom."

"You're going to start looking at Janet and hoping that you'll
look the way she does when you reach her age, or have her energy.
She won't be sixty or seventy in your eyes. But you'll be very aware
of being forty or fifty. You'll never catch up with her, so don't try."

And I haven't.

I'VE GOT THE JOURNAL beside me as I let the car warm up. I was
just thinking about Father Sears, questioning his artistic sensibilities. My initial reaction to his suggestion of an exhibition coincid-
ing with the colours of church decoration was positive. But really,
when I consider it now, I must admit his behaviour is no different
from a certain class of art collector. Those who arrive at the Gallery

with a chequebook in one hand and a swatch of wallpaper in the other. The material is held up against several paintings to guarantee harmony with the interior design in their living room.

Father Sears had a shopping list. He wanted something red. Which is why Rory Hines is the first non–Western Canadian artist to be exhibited at St. Agnes.

I'M BEGINNING TO FADE, but I tell myself I can take a nap in Janet's room during the afternoon. I was right about the early *Red on Red* series. It was at the back of the container, and I might've unintentionally wrenched my back dragging the crates through the basement to someplace with better light. Normally I display them upstairs, but it was too early to transport them up two flights of stairs after a sleepless night.

Besides, Kolerus is familiar with my work. He quickly settled on two small pieces and these we effortlessly moved upstairs to more comfortable viewing quarters. Kolerus is a tall, heavy-set man and hunched over in the basement he looked cramped, even though there was room for him to stand erect.

I'll have to make a note to myself to re-crate what we left against the walls in the basement. I'd forgotten once before, only to discover four panels floating in three inches of water after a spring rain.

Kolerus was clearly in a buying mood. I temporarily left him to ponder the small canvases while I dashed across the street for some takeout coffee and donuts. When I returned, he'd tucked a cheque into the frame of one of the paintings he had chosen. This was vintage Kolerus. No negotiation. He always wrote a cheque without a quoted price and it was always about twenty percent above the asking prices I keep in my head.

WHEN I ARRIVED at the hospital this afternoon, Janet was sitting up in bed. She gathered her short black hair, just long enough to bob at the back, into her hands. I was afraid she'd knock the IV loose from her arm.

"Ivan dropped by after his rounds," she said.

Her colour had returned and the assertive hand was now extended, palm up, waiting for a gentle squeeze. She brushed the stubble on my cheek and chided me for getting no sleep, telling me in no uncertain terms I'd completely undone Dr. Aktky's good work under my eyes.

She already knew Tally had up and left the night before. He had called her from the airport. God, it must've been late. Probably had awoken her.

Then the telephone rang. It was the clinic. Something urgent about appointments being rescheduled, Janet whispered, as she listened to her secretary. I was furious. The idiot should know better than to disturb my wife's convalescence. All the while, Janet appeared to be more interested in the crossword puzzle on her lap, filling in a word here and there with a pencil while agreeing to whatever the secretary was saying on the other end of the line. When she reached over to hang up the phone, the paper slipped to the floor and I gallantly scooped it up. Only it wasn't a crossword puzzle. She was making alterations to her will.

I was shocked and mumbled something about it not being the time or place for such things. I was still holding it in my hands.

"Give it here, darling, I'll get back to it later," she said.

I crossed to the bed table and placed it on the bottom shelf, grumbling that this business with the will was morbid.

"There is nothing morbid about it." There was a slight rise in her voice as she fell back against the pillow in what I thought was mild defeat. "What I find morbid, Rory, is having you place it on that shelf," she snapped. "You know damn well I am not supposed to bend over."

"I—"

"How dare you take advantage of my situation. If I was on crutches, would you kick them out from under my legs so I couldn't cross the room?"

"Janet, please."

"Besides, this *is* the time and place to be looking at my will. Why shouldn't I give my attention to the things that concern me? Things I never get around to otherwise."

"Janet, I'm sorry. I'll put it here, beside your juice. It's not something you should leave sitting out. You don't want the nurses snooping—"

"Rory, for the love of God, don't take me for an idiot."

"I don't."

"Then let's move on. We've dealt with it now. But darling, it is quite natural. I can't begin to tell you how many times I am asked for advice on my rounds. And never about anything to do with post-op. It is usually about wills, and always from people on the mend." She sipped from her juice and continued. "I make revisions all the time."

"You do?"

"I look through my papers at least once a year."

"All these years. You've been making revisions to your will all these years?"

"Don't you?"

"No. Never. Why should I? Why should you?"

"Do your parents still stand as beneficiaries in your will?"

"I suppose they do."

"So, you've willed something to people who are dead. I would call that morbid."

"Well, the lawyers would figure it all out."

"Yes, but why should they? You're always saying that if the staff at the gallery would only think things through, they'd save everyone a lot of time and effort. I really think you should take a look at your own will. It may surprise you."

It did. I've got it beside me now. I couldn't think of anything else after I left Janet. And she was right. My will has surprised me.

I was young when I signed the damn thing. From the date under my signature I determined Janet and I had only been married a few years. My youth is clearly reflected in the document. For instance, I was surprised to discover our parents don't appear as beneficiaries. I clearly state, should I die, the bulk of my estate goes to Janet. In the case of her death, my share will be divided among my brothers. Not a word about our parents anywhere. It's probably because I felt they were squared away and anything I left to them at the time wouldn't amount to more than pocket change. 'Course I was thinking from the perspective of a twenty-five-year-old and calculating my current assets at the time of writing, not what might accumulate down the road. Pocket change, whatever it might've been at the time, would still feel heavy in the pockets of my dear brothers. That was my reasoning.

Now I can discern an element of spite in my youthful reasoning. I was upset with Mom and Dad in those years. It was the culmination of many things. They hadn't attended my college graduation, but more importantly they hadn't come to my wedding. I received a note from Mom. The wedding conflicted with their annual Florida vacation, it was planned six months in advance and I'd only given them two months' notice about the wedding. Nonetheless, they were looking forward to meeting this "Janet woman" when we visited Cape Breton during the summer. In the meantime, they were enclosing twenty-five dollars.

I wanted to convince myself their refusal was tantamount to their disapproval of my marrying a woman who was fifteen years my senior. But this wasn't the case. When we did arrive that summer, Janet was received with open arms. Janet was impressed with our mother and father. She'd never met parents who so completely accepted their children as individuals.

I wasn't so convinced. I thought Mom was condescending toward Janet, motioning for her to sit in the wing chair, telling her she'd enjoy the footstool, as if she was afraid Janet's feet wouldn't reach the floor. As for Dad, his eyes narrowed in that look he got when he wasn't comfortable, nodding absently to Janet when she spoke. His cheeks were ruddy, from his double whiskey, something else he did to get over his shyness around new people or if he was drawn into a discussion he didn't enjoy or felt unequipped to join. Two quick belts of whiskey to make him less visible.

"Not once did your mother or father treat me like an in-law," Janet said at the time. "There was nothing patronizing about their behaviour. It wasn't anything like what I endured in meeting Ivan's mother.

"When we were engaged, I was on pins and needles the first time I met that old witch. Imagine, Rory, we met over tea. She was judging me on the way I poured.

"But with your mother I felt that we were simply expanding each other's social circle. Circumstances had brought us together. It was refreshing. If my own parents were alive, they'd like your mother and father. They might have become friends."

Janet and our parents seemed perfectly content with their relationship. Mom and Janet kept some kind of correspondence going through the years, though there were no further face-to-face meetings after that one trip back east. Not to say invitations weren't extended in both directions. We encouraged Mom and Dad to visit Toronto and they always asked me to make sure to bring Janet with me on the next trip home. The Maritime air would do her good. "But make sure she packs a sweater," Mom advised. "For the love of God, she should wear something around that tiny throat." Maybe she thought any woman over forty came down with pneumonia if she didn't wear a sweater.

And then there's the matter of Tally and my will. I named him executor. Simply because he was our big brother. I'll have to change that. My estate is much too complicated for Tally. There are several progressive art funds I'd like to endow when I die. Tally would undoubtedly scoff at some of my choices. I don't want someone with an "I know what I like" attitude toward art guiding the disbursement of my money.

For much the same reason I'd never name you executor, Cameron. Though I credit you with astounding aesthetic sensibilities and an impressive ear for music, your cynicism takes the cake. As to where I have my studio at the cottage, judge for yourself. Since your schedule appears flexible, why not take a month or two and stay there? It'd do us good to know it's occupied. It'll keep the thieves away.

But let's get back to Tally. He was the first person who knew about my relationship with Janet, before we made a discreet and official announcement among friends. He just happened to arrive in Toronto the day after Janet and I decided to wed. When I told him I'd met her at a party and she was a doctor, not a fellow art student, he was puzzled.

What he didn't understand was how a student and a surgeon could end up at the same party. I should've known better. Tally still complains when lettuce is served on the same plate as his meat. Lettuce belongs in a salad bowl, separate from the main course. It's how our brother's mind works.

Puzzlement turned to condescension when I explained I'd been tending bar at her engagement party. This was followed by an accusation on his part, suggesting I'd come between Janet and her fiancé.

Yes, I was serving bar at their engagement party, but I didn't see her again until six months later, when, by sheer coincidence, she showed up at an exhibition of my graduating class at school. By this time the engagement had been called off. So there can never be any question of my coming between them.

Janet liked my work and wanted to buy a couple of canvases.

"You certainly like painting in red," she concluded, studying one of the paintings.

"It's a portrait. Myself, Cameron, and Adrian."

"The one in the middle, it's blurred."

"That's Cameron. He could never sit still for a picture. Adrian is on the right. All teeth."

"Laughing?"

"Yes."

"The other two are looking straight ahead. But your eyes gaze out to the side of the picture, away from your brothers."

"I'm the sentry."

"Keeping watch for danger?"

"Yes. That's also my work there." I pointed to a large canvas between the two smaller panels she had been admiring.

"That's amazing."

"It is?"

"It's so vivid. All those colours, it's like looking through a kaleidoscope. I really like this picture, Rory."

"You do?"

"Why are you surprised?"

"I find it noisy. I almost didn't put it into the exhibition."

"It's full of passion and rage. It gives me goosebumps. It's almost blinding."

"It's my brother."

"Adrian or Cameron?"

"Tally."

"Can I buy it?"

"It's already sold."

"Pity."

I didn't mention the picture to Tally when I told him about meeting Janet at the exhibition, only that after I delivered the self-portrait to her house, we started dating.

Tally wanted to know if we were planning on settling out east. A move wasn't possible, I explained, because Janet was going to open a practice in Toronto. He accused me of fickleness, reminding me I'd always claimed I'd return to Nova Scotia after graduation.

Tally did the math in his head and realized if Janet was starting a practice we obviously weren't the same age. When I told him she was thirty-seven he decided she was pregnant. As

I've said before, Tally never makes assumptions. This was the only reasonable explanation he could find for a thirty-seven-year-old woman marrying a twenty-two-year-old.

Still, he wanted to meet this *woman*. Cameron, the next time you run into Tally, ask him. Ask him if he remembers the night he met Janet. I'm sure the question will produce a blush. I'm convinced he thought he was on his way to meet a harlot. Poor Tally. Why do I antagonize him so?

I WAS TWENTY-TWO years old when I decided to get married. Other people, marrying young, might look back over a long marriage, sigh, and be inclined to say, "I was *only* twenty-two." But I don't share that sentiment.

The night I met Janet there were about fifty or sixty people at the engagement party. It was his house, Ivan Kolerus', shadowy and oppressive with all its Prussian furnishings and dark mahogany. The chairs and sofas upholstered in leather, the carpets Persian and brown with age. There was money there, old money.

Everyone was drinking imported ale in large steins. Everyone but Janet, who detests beer. She was slender, and the men in the room admired her figure. They towered around her in a semicircle and addressed each other above her line of vision, but she didn't act submissive, she didn't crane her neck, lifting her chin in an awkward pose to meet their gaze. Instead, she listened with her eyes focused in the centre of the room, escaping the confines of the pompous gaggle of middle-aged podgy men. Once or twice I'd move into her line of vision behind the bar, wondering if she was looking at me through the crowd, to escape all these strangers who surrounded but ignored her.

Periodically she approached the bar to have her white wine refreshed. All eyes followed her as she purposefully crossed the room, a reminder this was also her party and she was one of its protagonists, ignored or not. That's when we struck up a conversation for the first time. People came and went as the evening wore on. I lost track of Kolerus.

When I saw Janet pacing in front of the house, waiting in the rain for a taxi after the party, holding her shawl over her head to protect her hair, I offered to drive her home. She was smoking a Gitanes cigarette, and it took her a few seconds to recognize me as the bartender who had topped up her wine glass over the course of the evening.

"You're the smiler," she said. I didn't know what she was talking about. She stepped toward me and reached out and touched my cheek with her finger.

I felt the blood rush to my cheeks, and quickly camouflaged my awkwardness with a grin.

"Exactly," she said, "the smiler."

I knew she wasn't drunk. She had nursed the same glass of wine all evening.

Boldly, I made my offer.

"Drive me home? You don't even know where I live," she said.

"Does it matter?"

A look of astonishment fell over her face, and her features relaxed. A few times during the evening, I'd tried to guess how old she was. She was certainly younger than her fiancé, who reminded me of an instructor at school who made a point of telling us he was nearing sixty whenever we exhibited our obtuseness in an art history seminar, as if our somnolent response to his lectures was hastening his old age.

"I live in the Beaches," she said, stubbing her cigarette, the slit in her dress falling away to reveal a long thigh.

"It's only a drizzle," she said, climbing into the van beside me. "You would think there'd still be taxis available. Seriously, you're not driving me out of your way, are you?"

"I like driving at night. It feels as if everything is in slow motion. What's your name?"

"Janet."

"I'm Rory."

"Is that short for Roderick?"

"No. Rory."

"It suits you."

"How so?"

"It's a strong name. Comforting. Scottish?"

"Irish. It means red."

"You're not a redhead and I don't see any fire in those dark eyes of yours."

When had she noticed my eyes?

"I've a brother, Cameron. Cameron means crooked nose. He broke his when he was a teenager. An oar hit him over the bridge. I've another brother, Adrian. He was holding the oar. Adrian's the real smiler in the family. Adrian's a Latin name, meaning of the Adriatic."

"Does he live in Italy?"

"Montreal."

"Any other brothers?"

"Tally. . . Talbot. The woodcutter."

"He's a carpenter?"

"A teacher. But he does have a woodstove, and I know he chops wood for it."

"Any sisters?"

"No."

"Are you the oldest?"

"Tally's the oldest. He's thirty-two. Then me. I'm twenty-two."

"That's a long stretch. Cameron and Adrian are younger?"

"Not exactly."

"What do you mean?"

"Cameron is twenty-two and Adrian is twenty-two. We're all twenty-two, except for Talbot."

"Were the three of you adopted?"

"No."

She was silent for a moment and I thought she'd lost interest in the conversation.

"You're triplets!" she said suddenly.

"One-third, at your service."

"Identical?"

"Yes. What about yourself? Do you have brothers and sisters?"

"No, I'm an only child."

"Lucky you."

"No, lucky you."

We pulled up in front of her house.

"It's stopped raining," she said. "There's heat lightning over the lake."

I got out and came around to her side, opening the car door for her, offering her my hand. She took it and stepped out, still holding my hand while I closed the door.

"Can I offer you a nightcap, Rory? For the road?" She slipped her arm in mine and we walked toward her veranda.

Inside, she held up two bottles for my inspection. "Would you prefer champagne or the rosé?"

"Either one."

"Then I'll choose," she said. "You're a champagne man."

Soon, I was uncorking a second bottle.

"So why *are* you going to marry him?" I asked, our conversation circling the impending marriage between Janet and Ivan Kolerus.

"I'm not going to marry him," she said. "I know that now."

"What made you change your mind?"

"I think it was you."

Until that instant, the thought of bedding Janet hadn't been a meditation on my part. I'd fallen into the luxury of her company over the past few hours, coddling a conceit that had arisen within me, that I was only interested in her intelligent mind. But now I was twenty-two again, with an erection at three-thirty in the morning.

"Ivan is a romantic," Janet said. "He likes to hold hands in public, but drops my arm as soon as the door is closed. Romantics are great actors with all their props, flowers, chocolates, jewellery, and silk stockings. It is a performance that repeats itself night after night. There is never any variation. Are you hungry?"

I was already adapting to her habit of examining an emotional situation by offering a diagnosis. She approached all matters with objectivity, a clinical approach, composed. But it wasn't distant. Janet was always intensely passionate in her conversations.

I was to learn she was a popular doctor in emergency, instilling a sense of calm in her patients, diffusing their fears by looking them straight in the eye, patiently waiting while they cried or winced in pain, but eventually completing the task at hand because it had to be done.

We moved to the kitchen and she prepared an omelette and a salad. She told me when she was a resident she often worked odd hours, sometimes arriving home in the middle of the night, famished.

"I taught myself to cook in those years," she explained. "I would finish sixteen hours in emergency and need another four to wind down when I came home. Some mornings, I'd stop at the St. Lawrence Market after a shift, haggling over two fillets of sole with chefs from the best restaurants in the city. The sun wouldn't even be up. I'd get home and prepare a three-course meal for myself that was ready by eight a.m. Then I'd die for three hours and be back in emergency by noon, planning a candlelight dinner for one the next morning."

The champagne was replaced with freshly squeezed orange juice and the first of several cups of coffee. Janet loved caffeine, and often drank ten or twelve cups during the day.

I told her about college, and my uncertainty about whether to return to Nova Scotia or go abroad for a few years after graduation, noticing several religious icons on the wall above the kitchen table while I talked. The icons were hand-painted on wood, acquired, she explained, during a year she spent in Prague.

"I was there in 1967," she said. "A year before the invasion."

"It must've been exciting."

"It was a time of great agitation," she said. "I also visited Poland and Yugoslavia. I saw Tito give a speech in Belgrade."

"Would you like to go back?"

"Not really. I was actually in Europe once before, just after high school. My parents were born in Austria and they took me to visit Wösendorf, their hometown, the summer after my high school graduation. I was bored, seventeen years old, travelling with my parents, who were almost sixty at the time."

"Sixty?"

Janet smiled. "I was a love child. I came very late in their marriage. When I was growing up, most of the people I knew were old.

"In Wösendorf we stayed with my uncle who was a widower in his seventies. He was still using rations from the war years. Everything in his home looked like it was borrowed from a museum. I did not meet another young person the month we stayed there. I couldn't wait to return to Canada. So Europe does not hold much appeal for me. Except for the wine. My uncle had his own vineyard and he made a delicious Auslese vintage."

Janet poured herself a fresh cup of coffee.

"I'm thirty-seven years old, Rory. Between us, we've spread out almost sixty years of life and experience at this table. It makes for a rather handsome tablecloth, don't you think?"

We'd arrived at a curious juncture, the measure of our lives accommodating something new and valuable between us, the first of many emotional assets we were to acquire.

"Are your parents still alive?" I asked.

"No, they've both passed on. Would you like to see their picture?" I followed her to the living room and she picked up a framed wedding photo from the piano. Neither the bride nor the groom was tall, the husband gangly, standing stiffly beside his new wife, her back straight against the cane chair, both looking away from the photographer.

"Is this your grandmother?" I asked, spying another photo behind the wedding portrait.

"That's my mother," she said, smiling, "and I'm the little girl sitting beside her." She kissed the tips of two fingers and lightly pressed them against her mother's face.

"I think the shock of my mother's pregnancy was so great, my father didn't dare touch her again after I was born. They grew sad and quiet in each other's presence. Marking time. They grew old far too quickly.

"Which is why I can't marry Ivan," she said, settling on the sofa, lighting a cigarette, the first since leaving the engagement party the night before.

"For Ivan, the good life is always waiting for him. It's about tomorrow, next year, or a decade from now. There's no pleasure to be derived from living in the moment. I won't live that life again."

"I had no choice," I said, accepting her offer of a cigarette. "I was always living in the moment growing up. Threefold. If I tried something new, Cameron and Adrian could just wait it out, see how it ended, and then decide if it was something worth repeating or to be avoided. One of us was always trying our parents' patience. Or our older brother's. But only one of us ever had to get punished. Or caught."

"That was quite a gift," Janet said.

"I suppose. I had to do everything myself when I moved to Toronto and I was always wondering what they'd do in the same circumstance. It's really tiring when you're second- and third-guessing yourself all the time.

"But here's the funny thing. It never occurred to me to call them, because I never relied on either of them for guidance growing up. We observed each other, and I think it is vigilance that still unites us, even though we're not together anymore."

"And what is your vigilance telling you now?" she asked.

"It's telling me I want to wake up tomorrow, or this afternoon, and do this all over again. I want to spend the rest of my life with you."

"Are you testing my patience, Rory? Like you and your brothers used to do with your parents?"

"No. I want to marry you."

"Of course you do," she said. There was a hint of harshness in her voice as she butted her cigarette in the ashtray. "I've already told you that I don't want to spend my life with a romantic. I've learned two very important lessons in my life, Rory. The first is that if you allow a woman to mother you with kindness she's going to own you. And if you marry a romantic he's going to smother you. Neither of them want you to evolve, and their punishments are brutal."

"I'm not a romantic, Janet. For the first time in my life I've met someone whom I don't have to look out for or protect. I'm in love."

She reached for another cigarette and lit it, a wide grin spreading across her face.

"What are you grinning at?"

"Don't be angry. I'm not making fun of you, Rory. I'm correcting an assumption. Earlier, in the car, I told you there was no fire in your eyes. I was wrong."

Cameron

JUNE, GEORGIAN BAY

MARY ANNE'S SITTING out on the wharf and listening to the sounds around the bay, and once again I'm trying to decide whether she looks more like her mother or me. She's not as tall as Susan, but her hair is long and straight. Susan used to wear it like that when she was a teenager, only Mary Anne's hair is black, like ours. She has a round face, cherub-like, and has always had two laugh lines around her mouth. When she's not laughing she relaxes her face, but it looks like she's pouting. She refuses to wear sunglasses and her long eyelashes, a definite Hines trait, curl upward from her downcast eyes, which are almost always three-quarters closed. When she lifts her face to listen, you can see the whites of her eyeballs below her large eyelids.

She has small hands, so she didn't inherit them from us. But when she puts those hands on her hips she can look assertive. She's been striking that pose since she was an infant. Defiant, just like you, Adrian.

She's been sitting here on the wharf for at least an hour, feet dangling in the water, and occasionally cocking her head to the left or to the right. A second later I hear the call of a loon or the splash of a fish close by.

She isn't aware that she reacts before I even hear these sounds.

"It's a question of training," she laughs. "Like with fish, if they're moving upward through the water, getting ready to jump, the water makes a noise below the surface. And the loons usually ruffle their feathers before calling out."

"But the loons could be a mile away," I protest. "How can you hear them ruffle their feathers at that distance? Especially a city girl like you?"

"I don't know, Daddy, but in Vancouver, whenever I approach stray dogs, I know that one dog is going to bark and another will wag its tail."

"How?"

"Beats me. It's not like I can hear the dog or anything, but I don't really sense it either."

"So it's a mystery?"

"Yeah, it's a mystery. If I'm out walking with Mom, and I sense a mean dog, I warn her by pressing my hand into her palm. Usually the dog barks. You know, Daddy, there is much more to listen for in the country than in the city. There is less noise, but many more sounds. Sometimes it makes me dizzy."

And, as is always the case when Mary Anne explains the world to me, I clam up.

She was disappointed that we didn't get a chance to get together with you and Janet before heading to your cottage here on the Georgian Bay, Rory, but you had already departed for your vacation in Bermuda. Next time. So we drove up here the same afternoon and spent the rest of the evening getting her used to your cottage. It's always Mary Anne who makes the decisions about which pieces of furniture should be moved to the side or turned in another direction. She can adapt quickly to unfamiliar floor plans, but strange bedrooms always provide moments of uncertainty and it takes a few nights for her to settle in.

Blind people have an amazing sense of direction. She knew the layout of the cottage within a day and she also decided on which areas to avoid, asking me to keep certain doors closed so they wouldn't distract her. The only things she doesn't like, Rory, are all those small steps leading into the various rooms of the cottage. They annoy her.

Earlier today we were out canoeing for a couple of hours. This is a new experience for Mary Anne and Tenderfoot, her guide dog. I'm not really into animals, but Tenderfoot is a pretty amazing dog. He gets my nod, that's for sure. We were both a little cautious with him in the beginning, afraid he might get distracted by the sudden appearance of a rabbit or something. But Tenderfoot never allows himself to get sidetracked. He's Loyal with a big L. Which is what is so special about our canoe trips. It's the only time the tables are turned. It's like Tenderfoot knows he can't really lead out on the bay, but he insists on sitting at the front of the boat anyway. When we return to the wharf his tail starts to wag. It's the only time I've ever seen him exhibit real doggie enthusiasm.

The other day Mary Anne insisted I let Tenderfoot lead me around the yard. She tied her scarf around my eyes because she didn't trust me when I said I wouldn't peek. At first I kept stopping before Tenderfoot did, but after a while I got the hang of it. Mary Anne says that it's important to establish a rhythm with your dog.

"If you come to a stop, it should be because you have a reason," she instructs. "Otherwise, keep moving, let Tenderfoot make the decision instead of having to second-guess you all the time."

Apparently dogs don't like hesitation, which is why not all blind people can adjust to them. Some people are simply too jittery and nervous by nature. And a dog, well, a dog is a dog, training and unyielding discipline or not. Blind people have to be brave, for the sake of the dog. The dog, on the other hand, will always be courageous. That's when trust is really established. Another insight from Mary Anne. Tenderfoot and I didn't say a word.

I'VE NOTICED SOME CHANGES about Mary Anne this summer. For starters, she's wearing perfume. Or at least she wore perfume for the first few days. The black flies ate her alive, so she stopped. She's also wearing bangles on her arms.

"They're from Uncle Talbot."

"Talbot?"

"He sent them to me for my birthday."

"Beth probably bought them."

"Who's Beth?"

"His girlfriend."

"I didn't know Uncle Talbot had a girlfriend."

"Of course you did, I've told you about Beth."

"Not that I can remember. Mom's never mentioned her either. Do you like them?"

"They're pretty. But you might snag them on a bush."

"I'll wear them inside. I really like them, he always sends me something nice."

"He sends you other stuff?"

"Just birthday gifts."

"You're sure they're from Talbot?"

"What's the big deal?"

"Talbot's never sent me anything for my birthday."

"Poor Daddy."

Mary Anne also takes considerable care in choosing her wardrobe. I always assumed Susan dressed Mary Anne from head to foot, buying clothes based on what the other kids were wearing or relying on her own impeccable sense of fashion. When Susan picked me up at the airport in Vancouver, it only took me about three seconds to find her in the crowd, standing there, straight as a reed in her short black sweater, buttons open to reveal a white T-shirt falling perfectly against her flat stomach. She didn't look like one of those snooty models with a poker stuck up her arse, striking one of those snobbish poses. She was relaxed as she waited. She's always relaxed. I watched her for a few seconds as she checked the monitor for the arrivals, her shoulder-length hair expertly cut across the back of her neck, in an arc, like a gentle smile. She was wearing a thin gold chain, white gold, I gave it to her years ago, and earrings, the kind that hang, but not big ones, nothing that would tear those lovely earlobes.

Anyway, I was wrong about Susan choosing Mary Anne's clothes. She's been buying her own duds for at least four or five years. Clothes have different associations for her, they assist her moods. She takes the fabric between her fingers and rubs or pulls it, placing it against her cheek or arm.

When she arrived, I made the mistake of emptying her suitcase, tossing the T-shirts into drawers and the sweaters and jeans into the closet. She made me put everything out on the bed and then spent the next hour separating everything into different piles. She can be a little theatrical, because when I asked about one certain combination, she blushed. She said it was her just-leave-me-alone outfit, the one she wore when she and Susan weren't seeing eye to eye on something, like a curfew or an allowance. "Eye to eye" was Mary Anne's expression. What a twisted daughter I've got. God love her.

I asked her if she had a piss-off set reserved for her old man. She thought about this for a minute or so before answering. Then she said no, she never felt pissed off around me. And rather than be flattered, I completely surprised myself. I took sides with Susan and said it was unfair. Mary Anne bloomed, the folds of those lovely laugh lines deepening, telling me that Susan often said something similar when they were talking about me.

She's starting at Simon Fraser University in the autumn, continuing her music studies. She's even getting her own room at the dorm. Major step. It'll be weird for Susan, not having Mary Anne living under the same roof for the first time in twenty-one years.

MIDSUMMER'S EVE.

Mary Anne has always been fiercely independent, a trait she acquired from me, I like to think, with those hands of hers planted firmly on her hips when she wants to get her own way. It's even worse now that she's a young woman. It's a pain in the ass.

So it was a real surprise when she asked me to read to her before she fell asleep tonight. She told me she could remember when I used to read to her as a little girl. I said she would've been too young to remember. But maybe she's right. Maybe blind children remember better than sighted children. Mary Anne probably wouldn't like this assumption. She says people are always making assumptions about blindness.

"Give me an example," I asked her once.

I can't remember exactly what she said, but it went something like this.

"People think that if you put a blindfold on someone who can see, they'll experience what it's like to be blind. The only thing they'll experience is fear. They're only going to end up afraid of bumping into something or falling on their faces. I'm not scared of the dark," she said. "I don't know what darkness is, other than something familiar, so why would I be afraid of it?"

I think I made her uncomfortable with my sudden silence as I pondered this again tonight, so she was quick to add that she had forgotten to pack her audio books for the trip. That was the real reason she wanted me to read to her, she claimed.

She asked me to choose something from the books she got for her birthday. She likes books. Not everything is in Braille or recorded. Susan reads to Mary Anne a lot, although she often passes over questionable passages. Mary Anne can always sense something is about to be censored, because her mother's rhythm slows down and the words suddenly have clumsy little pauses between them as Susan glances ahead and bleeps out all the swear words and references to sex.

The book I choose isn't one of those long, literary *tomes*. It's raunchy in parts, but nothing she wouldn't hear on television.

She lasted through two stories before falling asleep. I sat there for another half-hour, singing to her, trying to count the sprinkle of freckles across the bridge of her nose.

She's been asleep for a couple of hours now and I've stuck my head in her room a dozen times to make sure she's still breathing. Typical dad. But the truth is, this trip is different from all the previous ones. It's only the second time I've had Mary Anne all to myself for more than a weekend. I was worried we'd tire of each other after a couple of days. Okay, I was worried she'd get tired of me. Then again, our vacation last year was pretty cool. I flew out to Vancouver to fetch her and we returned to Halifax the next day. I had a wicked case of jet lag, but those ten days together just flew by. The big test was her trip home to Vancouver, and Mary Anne insisted on flying alone. She didn't want me making a third trip across the skies on her behalf.

I started missing her as soon as she went through the gate in Halifax, but I was relieved when she finally called and told me she was home again. In fact, the relief was a natural high that I've never experienced before. I decided that I never wanted her to travel again. I figured that as long as she stays in one place, she's safe. Or at least I'm safe. Do you think all parents feel this way? What a stupid question. How could either of you answer that?

I've never gotten over the feeling that Mary Anne is only temporary. Sometimes I feel like she's going to be snatched right out of my fingers. Again.

When she was two and a half years old, the social workers wanted to take her away for good. Susan and I had been together again for over a year, thanks to the Big B's one-way plane ticket for Susan to Winnipeg, and I had been unemployed for the last three of those months. Susan was working the lunch counter at Woolworth's and I was home in our crappy apartment with the baby.

On this particular occasion I had just cashed my pogey cheque and scored a little hash to get me through the next week or so. The baby had kept both of us up the night before and I fell asleep in front of the TV set. Somehow, and I mean somehow, Mary Anne got out of the apartment and into the corridor. Our neighbour, a real bitch I might add, found her sitting and sobbing in front of the elevator. It came out in the report later that the neighbour in question had peeked into our apartment and saw me passed out in front of the TV with a six-pack on the coffee table. Which wasn't the case. I had only guzzled one beer. What the good neighbour neglected to say was that she had actually waltzed into the apartment and taken half my score of hash. But we'll let that pass. It wasn't the kind of thing I could say in family court to break down the credibility of the good neighbour.

Susan was livid when she got home and discovered that Mary Anne had been placed with Social Services. She started mouthing off, which didn't help our case, because the thieving neighbour taped the entire shouting match through the flimsy walls connecting the two apartments. More ammunition to use against us.

Mary Anne was kept from us for a month while they did a parental evaluation. Susan pleaded with me to straighten out and watch my temper when we arrived at court. In those days, any kind of pleading was an invitation for me to make more trouble. I've grown up since then. But on that day, the day of the court hearing, I was pretty wired, although I thought I appeared relaxed and in check, thanks to some Librium.

Obviously my mood had the opposite reaction on the *Powers That Be,* because Mary Anne wasn't coming home with us.

When the verdict went down, I pounded my fist on the table. Only once.

But once was too many. If the judge had any hesitations about her verdict, they vanished at that moment. Susan didn't say a word, but she was as white as a ghost and we walked to the elevator in silence. When we reached the lobby, she blocked me as I started to get out, and then she pushed the button to the basement and practically shoved me through the door.

The halls were deserted down there. That's when she started to beat me. She lit into me like there was no tomorrow. She started pounding my chest with both fists. Telling me I had to get her baby back. Demanding that I get her baby back. I was stunned. She kept pounding me and looked me square in the eye. "Get her back," she screamed, "get her back." Then she slapped me across the face.

"Do you hear what I'm saying, Cameron? Get her back."

Wham!

She cuffed me across the cheek. I shook my jowls like one of those bulldogs in a Looney Tunes cartoon after an anvil falls on its head. Then she cuffed me across the other cheek. All the while she was pleading. "Get her back. Get her back."

I got hold of her wrist after the tenth or eleventh slap. Her hand was going to split open any second. I was so numb I didn't feel a thing. I don't think it was because of the downers I had taken. It had just dawned on me that our baby was gone. Her pearly eyes wouldn't be there anymore to light up our days.

You see, Mary Anne was the name of the nurse who taught Susan how to wipe away the mucus from the baby's eyeballs. The eyeballs with no pupils. The nurse called her the baby with the pearly eyes. She made Susan smile and forget the loneliness surrounding her in those early days.

There in that cold basement, Susan was trying to get me to see, for her and for Mary Anne. Later she told me she would've kept on punching me, to make me see. Even if she had to kill me to do it.

The next day I entered a six-month drug program on an outpatient basis. After that, Mary Anne was home again with Susan and me. Those six months were hell for Susan. She was only allowed to see Mary Anne under supervised visits at the foster care home during those months and she was furious because the foster family had cut off Mary Anne's long hair.

When she was finally returned to us, she started to ask for a bedtime story. I always sang Mary Anne to sleep. Sometimes Susan would fall asleep as well, charmed by my magical pipes. The foster parents had read to her. The first night I had to make up a story because there wasn't one children's book in the apartment. The next day I bought out everything they had at Woolworth's. She was barely three years old and she already had her favourite stories.

I wonder if it's really me she remembers, reading her those stories as a child? Or was it the soothing voice of someone from that foster family? A soothing voice who almost became a permanent comfort for her.

JESUS H. CHRIST. Everything was going well this summer until the dog had to go and die. Mary Anne and I are barely on speaking terms, although she said she didn't mean the things she said yesterday. Whether she meant them or not, every word was true. You can't change history. Not mine, anyway.

My whole life is about history. It seems that I'm always on this side of what happened. Past tense. For once I'd like to stay in the present, where it's a lot safer.

It was the same when we were kids, wasn't it? I was always defying the conventional wisdom that triplets acted as one. Whatever you were doing, Rory, or you, Adrian, I was doing the opposite. I couldn't even find a place to stand that was safe. Dad took us fishing in Margaree once, and he told the three of us not to get behind him when he cast the line. You both had the good sense to move to the side. Me? I backed up about twenty feet, directly behind him. He cracked his fishing rod like a whip and the next thing I knew, he had hooked my earlobe.

The funny thing is, nothing ever seemed to feel like it was about to go wrong. I wasn't equipped with any of those premonitions that warn other people. I didn't have any antennas.

Eventually I realized that if I could just concentrate more on the *here and now* I'd make out a lot better. Stay where I was and let things happen to the world around me.

Like one of those mammoths stuck in the Siberian ice. They seem to have managed okay. Millions of years have passed and the world has changed a trillion times. But they say if you thaw out one of those suckers the fur is silky and the food in their stomachs is fresh. Being frozen in time has its advantages. Okay, those mammoths are dead, but that's beside the point. I'm not good at making analogies, but I'm sure you both get my point. Now is good. For too many years, yesterday, last week, or last month was shit. The last few years have been good. I haven't done any drugs other than weed. My meds keep my mood swings in check. I've got a good carpentry business happening and I sing in a wicked choir.

Then the dog died.

Tenderfoot was in his place of honour at the front of the canoe. The mist was rising from the bay and the sun was burning it off. It was going to be a scorcher, and we wanted to be out on the bay and back on shore before it got too hot. The canoe was gliding through the water and occasionally I took a swig of coffee from the Thermos. I'm no morning person, as you both know. So I dozed off. It was no big deal, it wasn't the first time. And when I say dozed, it was never for more than a minute. But maybe yesterday it was longer, I don't know.

I woke with a start because the canoe was rocking and Mary Anne was shouting after Tenderfoot. At first I couldn't see a thing because we were passing through a thick patch of fog. I could hardly see Mary Anne and when I did locate her, she was hanging over the side, dangerously close to falling in. I pulled her down into the boat. Immediately she tried to get back to the side, but I restrained her. She was screaming now. Telling me that Tenderfoot wasn't in the boat. I could barely see the prow, but it was true. The dog had gone over.

By this point I was yelling too. I told Mary Anne to shut up. Twice. I'd never told her to shut up before. But I was feeling panicky, okay? I didn't want her going over the side. I didn't want the canoe to capsize, didn't want to have to locate her in the fog. *Shut up.* The echo came back to me, but Mary Anne was calmer now. She crouched on the bottom of the canoe, her hands holding onto the sides, the dozen bangles on her arms making a soft jingling sound. She was sobbing. I tried to wipe away a tear, but she jerked her face away from me. There was no time to tell her I was sorry for yelling at her. She was almost hysterical. I would've explained this to her. But like I said, there was no time for that. I had to find the dog. So I kept very quiet and strained my hearing, best I could, trying to pick up the sounds of the dog paddling through the water. But I couldn't hear a thing. It was so goddamn quiet, except for Mary Anne's big sobs.

I asked her to listen for Tenderfoot. I reminded her that she could hear a lot better than me and if she listened carefully she could guide me to Tenderfoot. All dogs could swim, I told her. All dogs. Hadn't Tenderfoot proven that? This wasn't the first time he had leaped into the water. For the past week he had jumped over the side of the boat and paddled around the canoe. Then I'd haul him back in. I just didn't realize that Tenderfoot was short on endurance. Once around the canoe was probably his limit.

Mary Anne wiped away the tears and sat up. Neither of us dared to break the silence. Then Mary Anne began to shake her head, small shakes of doubt. She was mouthing the name of her dog, probably afraid that if she said it out loud, she might miss placing his location. My heart was in my throat as I watched her. I tore my eyes away and panned the bay.

I whispered to her. I asked her to tell me when he had jumped overboard. She whispered back. Maybe ten minutes ago. I ventured a second question. How long was she calling to him before I woke up? Maybe three or four minutes, she said. Too long, Daddy. You wouldn't wake up. It took you too long. The words sounded like the sharp hiss that comes from the pressure tube on a tire when you squeeze it. Too long.

We both started calling his name. Together. Then we took turns. Tenderfoot wasn't answering. Mary Anne made me keep paddling in circles, bigger circles each time. She made me stay out on the bay until all the fog had cleared. Only when she could feel the sun on her face from every direction did she let me take us back to shore.

It's in neither of our natures to hope, so we weren't expecting he'd be there ahead of us, sunning himself on the wharf. And he wasn't. Tenderfoot was gone. He had jumped out of the canoe and probably got disoriented. He swam through a fog bank in the wrong direction, farther and farther away from us. If he had struggled, we didn't hear it because Mary Anne was shouting. Or maybe he just fell below the waves with his lungs filled with water, pulling him down to the floor of the bay.

Mary Anne was shaky when we got out of the canoe. I was shaky. But it's dangerous for a blind person to be shaky and upset. She walked a few steps along the wharf, uncertainly, and sat down, holding her knees. Now she allowed herself to cry, for herself and for Tenderfoot.

When Mary Anne loses something, it's always just within reach. She's explained this to me a million times. When she drops a bookmark or one of her bangles, it's there, close. That's how she perceives the world, everything is just within reach. The world is neither round nor flat. Nothing falls off the edge. She's the centre of her own universe and all the edges bend toward the middle. Which makes losing a living thing harder to accept for Mary Anne. She half believes it will reveal itself as alive and well sooner or later if she just waits and keeps reaching. Sooner or later it will roll inward, a law of nature. Or someone else will bring it back to her.

Lost things and lost people, dead people and dead dogs, are only temporarily so. And when she finally accepts the death, long after the rest of us, the dead person or animal is never far away, never truly lost or forgotten. There's always the chance that gravity will roll it in.

Mary Anne sat on the wharf and hoped that Tenderfoot was close, if not visible. He might even be dead, but he was within reach. But Mary Anne was also bitter. What happened to Tenderfoot was my responsibility, she said. I should have kept an eye on him. Both eyes, she stressed.

Instead. Susan used to always say this, just before she shattered my present and hurled me into the past, creating more history for me.

Instead. "You were high, Daddy. How could you do that to us?" To us meant to her, to Tenderfoot, to Susan, not to me.

"I'm not high," I said. This was the truth.

"But you take all those medications," she answered.

"There's a difference," I pleaded.

Nothing more was said. I asked your neighbour to take me out in his outboard, Rory, to look for Tenderfoot, after we settled Mary Anne in the cottage. His wife insisted on staying with her, holding her small hand, while her husband and I went out to search. I was grateful. Mary Anne easily accepted the wife's generosity and comfort. That's another thing with the blind. There are no strangers. All people are close. Some closer than others.

AFTER THE ACCIDENT with Tenderfoot, Mary Anne didn't want to remain at the cottage. There was still a week left of her vacation. She would've been able to manage getting around. But it wasn't possible to manage with Tenderfoot filling all our thoughts. He was there, somewhere, close.

On the long drive to the airport she reminded me that she was sorry for calling me a junkie. I left it at that.

Many people are under the mistaken impression that joes like me choose to become drug-dependent. They never consider that some people are *made* drug-dependent.

We all know I was a hyperactive kid. It's no secret. Hyperactivity isn't something you can disguise or hide, it's all out in the open, and it's in the nature of the *syndrome* to involve anyone who comes into contact with the afflicted kid.

Fortunately, neither of you allowed yourselves to be sucked in by my whirlpool. We were all too busy asserting ourselves. From the outside, we looked like one atom. But inside, our molecules were bouncing in all directions, as if somebody had struck a match underneath us. And to anybody looking on, the folks, the Big B, we seemed to be bouncing in all those directions at the same time, leaving just enough space inside that atom that we didn't collide with each other. But on the outside, our atom kept knocking into everybody else's. Let's face it, we certainly weren't the poster boys for the "children should be seen and not heard" school of thought. But I was on overdrive. My molecule wasn't over a flame, it was on fire.

So I don't blame the folks for trying to cool off that fire. It was impossible for them to ignore it when I pounded a piece of pipe against a radiator two feet from the ears of their bridge partners in the living room. Especially when I wouldn't stop until they were forced to scream at me, two feet from the ears of those same guests. Or for realizing that they were buying toys for all the kids in the neighbourhood because I kept breaking them. Of course, you broke a few of those toys, boys, but we never broke our cardinal rule, no snitching on each other. It wasn't because I was evil or jealous, there were bits and pieces of my own toys strewn everywhere. I just didn't know my own strength. I was rough.

So what do you do? You listen to your doctor. The same one who takes his Willy Shears to every newborn male child without asking permission.

Snip snip.

"There, Mrs. Hines. That's better. You didn't want your baby hanging to his knees, now, did you?"

"You'd think there'd be some reason for all that extra skin," mom ponders, mindful of her tone in the presence of *Unquestionable Authority*.

"Sure there is! It gives me something to hang onto. It helps me pull the little bugger out," *Unquestionable Authority* says. Guff. Guff.

"Oh, Doctor."

Giggle. Giggle.

We'll fast-forward several years, boys. The folks are at their wits' end. My teachers insist that I have a learning disability, I can't keep still at my desk, maybe I should be moved to Special Ed. And the neighbourhood parents don't like me playing with their children. I'm too bossy and rough.

Maybe the Big B related all of this to you at some point. But what you probably don't know, is years later, *Unquestionable Authority* prescribed thioridazine for the boy he beheaded as a newborn.

Unquestionable Authority tells the folks thioridazine is used to combat excitability, competitiveness, short attention spans, and rapid mood swings.

"Yep," they chime in unison, "that's our Cameron."

They started me on the drug when I was nine, and the dosage was increased, steadily, until I was fourteen.

I had problems with my liver by that point. If you recall, I came down with hepatitis and was forced to stay inside for two months. My entire summer vacation. You weren't allowed to come into my bedroom without wearing a mask. Remember?

During my illness I wasn't given any medication. *Unquestionable Authority* had advised the folks to discontinue it while I was sick. My hepatitis cleared up and by September I was pretty wound up. I mean, really, wouldn't any normal fourteen-year-old buck be chomping at the bit after being confined to a bed for two months?

Our good parents didn't see it that way. I was put on a new drug. Peridol. Or haloperidol, as it's known in the trade.

At fifteen I started to break out in rashes every other week. I also started to piss my bed. Since we weren't sharing bedrooms, I kept that one a secret from both of you. I don't even think the folks told the Big B. So they bought me a rubber sheet. My hands also had a slight tremor, it was hard to hold a pencil.

Unquestionable Authority sent me to Halifax for tests just before our seventeenth birthday. They did cell counts, liver function tests, eye examinations, and electrocardiograms.

They told the folks I had Parkinson's disease.

Parkinson's disease!

I was seventeen years old!

Were they out of their minds?

More tests. Another trip to Halifax. I was put in the adult ward and shared a room with three men. One of them had a beat-up copy of the *Home Guide to Prescription Drugs*.

He let me borrow it and when I read what was in it, I pissed my bed that night.

I asked the nurse if I could see my bed chart. Under medication it read, *None.* Which was true. They weren't administering any medication at the hospital. But nobody had asked me if I'd been taking anything. In my best hand I made an entry on my chart. Under medication I wrote, *Daily dosage, 500 mg of haloperidol.*

The next day a bunch of interns accompanied the doctor on his rounds. This doctor was an arrogant son of a bitch. When he looked at you, he lowered his glasses and glanced down his long nose. He handed my chart to one of the interns without opening it.

"The patient is a seventeen-year-old Caucasian male. He suffers from a slight trembling of the hands. Diagnosis?"

The young intern consulted my journal for a few moments.

The doctor snapped his fingers. "Well?"

"At first glance, it appears the patient is suffering from the onset of Parkinson's disease."

"At first glance? What in the hell—"

"The patient is exhibiting a slight tremor in the hands. But the other two principal symptoms of Parkinson's disease, rigidity and abnormally slow movements, aren't evident. Nor is there any indication of physical imbalance, slurring of speech, or facial immobility. Based on the medical history before me, the patient is suffering from a toxic reaction."

"Give me that chart."

Snatch. The good doctor actually read rather than skimmed the bed chart.

"Who admitted this boy?"

No more haloperidol.

It also came out in the report that my hepatitis had been caused by a toxic reaction to long-term use of thioridazine. Only in the report the doctors sent to the folks, it was worded a little differently. The patient's long-term *abuse* of thioridazine, it read. It was my fault, my abuse, they claimed.

Pass the buck.

Which our good parents, like the doctors, did. They sent me to a psychiatrist. Maybe I was suffering from a mental condition? After all, I had graduated from rough kid to rowdy teenager.

Unfortunately, my use of haloperidol was stopped abruptly. Major withdrawal. Needed something to take the edge off. And there was still that problem of being hyperactive. Could the two be related? Withdrawal and hyper? But I'm getting ahead of myself. It's always easy to make conclusions after the fact.

Enter lithium. With the blessing of the good psychiatrist. No more hyper. Just active. Seemed everyone could live with that. I certainly could. Provided there was a ready and regular supply of lithium close by.

Susan didn't know anything about the thioridazine or peridol when I met her. Old news. But she knew about the lithium. She said I was hooked on downers. A junkie.

LET ME THINK about this for a moment. I need to get this story in the right chronological order. It was about a year after getting Mary Anne back from Social Services. The neighbour next door was gone. It was a calm period in our lives, what's called a lull. We were still in Winnipeg. Susan was still working the lunch counter at Woolworth's and I got myself a job assisting a Malaysian carpenter whenever he needed an extra hand.

I got the job through a guy I owed some money to for dope. His cousin, Kalim, had a small home renovation firm and the guy set me up with him to pay off my debt. I used to think

Kalim was watching my every move on the job. He has an arch to his eyebrows, it makes his forehead look higher than it is and lends intensity to his expression, which I misread as scrutiny in the beginning. My first three paycheques went to my dealer, but I stayed on with Kalim. He wasn't into dealing himself and told me never to carry any dope on the job.

Work wasn't steady because there wasn't much call for Malaysian carpenters in Winnipeg. You used to hear a story all the time in those days about the guy down the hall in your building whose living room ceiling leaked. Upstairs they found a Paki family watering a small garden in the middle of the living room floor. They just flung some earth there and threw in some seeds and watered it every day. Cross my heart, he says, it's a true story. Hey, I told this story once or twice myself to make conversation.

Kalim is dark, but not too dark. There are shadows under his eyes, which are brown. But I think it's his hair that makes him look dark, it's jet black and for as long as I've known him, he's kept it cut just above his shoulders. It tends to curl in the back, several tight little ringlets, and he keeps it greased, did so even before that style was fashionable in the Asian community. Man, if it's a sunny day the sheen on his hair can blind you when he takes off his baseball cap.

From looking at his hands, you'd never know he is a carpenter. The skin is smooth on his palms and long fingers. I think he gets his nails manicured, they're never chipped, there's never any black dirt under the tips.

Kalim speaks English, fluent English, with a really cool British accent. He worked on referral, and established WASP and mick carpenters farmed out jobs to him. But a lot of folks needing repairs had heard the urban myth about the garden in the living room and found reasons for wanting other carpenters. Not that Kalim was a Pakistani. He was Malaysian. But it didn't make any difference to those folks. They hated all light chocolate.

We turned the tables on them. Kalim had a business card made up with my name on it. From then on it was me who took the phone calls and met prospective clients, with Kalim in tow. On cue I'd send him out to the truck to fetch something and reassure the client it was me who was the foreman. Kalim didn't pass wind without consulting me first, I'd tell them with a big grin. Worked like a charm.

Kalim was content to stand back, his hands in his pockets, and watch me do the talking. He isn't pushy. But if you cross him or get lippy, he draws himself up straight, instantly growing three inches in height. The madder he gets, the taller he looks, just like you, Adrian, but he never raises his voice. You just know he's pissed off. But as I said, most of the time he was pretty quiet, hands in his pockets, even when he talked.

Business picked up. We started making a name for ourselves. But Kalim wanted to move out east. His parents and three sisters lived in Halifax. His father was also a carpenter. Seems Kalim had been apprenticing under his father since he was thirteen, mostly on weekends and during summer vacations, then after high school, putting college off for several years. Winnipeg had been his way of getting out from under his dad's control and trying to make some decent money on his own. Now dad wanted him back. As a partner. It was an offer he couldn't refuse.

Shit. Piss. Damn. Just when things were starting to pick up for me in Winnipeg. Those last few months were the first in almost two years when Susan and I didn't have to stop eating the last week before rent was due.

Kalim wanted me to come with him. Was I interested? Susan, Mary Anne, and I could stay rent-free in a rooming house his father owned until business picked up.

I talked it over with Susan, one night after her shift at Woolworth's. She had lightened her hair when she moved to Winnipeg, and chopped off a good foot of her ponytail. She put some curl in it, not much, just enough to take the flatness out of it and she looked like Lady Di. She was wearing contacts now, the big glasses from high school were donated to the Salvation Army, and she started wearing eyeshadow, the only makeup I'd ever seen her put on her face. She was still learning the art of application, though, and tended to apply it a little too heavy. It'd cake in the folds of her eyelids.

Anyway, I came home that day and told Susan about Kalim's offer. She thought it was a good plan, but said that I should go on ahead, alone. If it worked out then she and Mary Anne would join me in a couple of months. Otherwise I could come back to *Winterpeg*.

KALIM AND I DROVE to Halifax, and he expanded my knowledge of world geography during the trip. His grandparents came from a city called Kota Kinabalu, the capital of Sabah, a region on the island of Borneo that joined Malaysia in the 1960s. At the time, none of the names meant anything to me, so Kalim found a bookstore in Thunder Bay and bought an atlas.

"It's ten hours from Singapore or two hours from Hong Kong," he said. "Unless you're coming from Manila, then it's only about an hour. Look at the map, see for yourself."

Our first job in Halifax was to renovate the boarding house.

Kalim's father kicked out all the drifters and I moved in. I had the place to myself because Kalim was living with his family.

I was supposed to stay at the boarding house only until it was renovated. Well, that house stayed in a state of renovation for years. When we arrived in Halifax there was work all over the city. The boarding house could wait. So I started to do repairs on my own, between jobs.

Six months later, at the beginning of the New Year, Kalim's dad offered me a full-time job. Partly because he was short-handed. Kalim's grandfather had died and Kalim returned to Borneo for the funeral, to represent the family, and stayed there for three months. But also because I was a good carpenter.

With the promise of full-time work, I flew to Winnipeg. I didn't bother calling Susan before I arrived. I wanted to surprise her. As I walked through the lobby of the apartment building, I couldn't believe I had actually lived in this hole. Armed with a full-time job and a house for us to live in back east, I had suddenly become selective about my surroundings.

Susan wasn't home when I arrived, but by the time she came through the door with Mary Anne, I had all our things packed. Just clothes really, mostly Mary Anne's stuff, and all her books. I took Mary Anne in my arms and squeezed her really close. She was excited to see me. I thought she looked a little thin, but she was also an inch taller.

Susan looked around the room. I told her I'd lived up to my end of the deal and that we were going home to Nova Scotia. We'd fly out tomorrow.

She said she had to give notice at work.

I noticed the garish blue eye shadow was gone. She'd replaced it with a lighter shade, I don't know what colour you'd call it, but it was pretty, and she was wearing lipstick and some nice cologne.

"Screw Woolworth's," I said. "We're leaving tonight. We're staying at a hotel."

"But I have to pack," she said.

"Are you coming with us or not?" I said. "Because we're leaving now. We're not coming back." I was still holding Mary Anne in my arms. I'd managed to get all the suitcases to the door with my foot. That left Susan's couple of bags in the middle of the living room.

"Are you coming with us?" I asked, opening the door.

Susan had her eye on the suitcases. She just stood there for a minute, looking around. She was seeing the life she'd been living, the one I was about to leave, with our daughter. Across the room, Mary Anne and me were waiting by the door. We were on the way out. We were Susan's ticket. She had never expected that she'd look across the room and see her future, holding our daughter in its arms.

"Yeah, I'm ready, Cameron," she said. She picked up her bags and came toward me.

"You sure you don't want to take some time and look around?" I offered. "Maybe I missed something."

"I don't think so."

"Are you sure?" I asked.

She looked me straight in the eye. "Yes, I'm sure."

"That's good to hear."

"Then let's go," she said.

"Right," I said. "This was easier than I thought."

"Nothing's that easy, Cameron."

Those words from the embers of our old life would come back to haunt me. Sure as shit.

I always thought Susan was indifferent about Kalim. I asked her once if she liked him. She just shrugged and said he was my friend, not hers. I think the concept was too big for Susan, that I could ever have a friend. Until Kalim came along, the only acquaintances I had were other potheads and pushers.

Growing up, people were so busy staying clear of me that I never nurtured any friendships. The folks used to tell me to keep away from this or that kid. I'd only cause trouble, they said, after yet another parent had called to complain.

Susan was no better. She knew my reputation as a hothead and kept everyone at a distance. Whenever we went to a tavern for a beer, she'd seek out some little table for two in the corner where there was no risk of interaction with other bar patrons. If there was a band playing, she'd have me up for every dance. She never wanted any guy to saunter over to the table to ask her for a jig and get me all riled up. Figured it was safer to be dancing than sitting.

So Kalim was a puzzle for Susan. From her point of view, we didn't have anything in common because he didn't do drugs. She couldn't make the mental leap, to accept that he was a positive influence in my life. Because of Kalim, we could pay the rent. We were living in a three-storey Victorian house in downtown Halifax rent-free, a good deal. But Susan, she never once invited Kalim over to dinner. Maybe she found him too low-key. Kalim isn't much for chit-chat, so maybe Susan had a hard time figuring out what he thought of *her*. Kalim and I could spend hours together without saying a word. Well, he didn't say a word. He'd just work, putting all his concentration into the job. He seemed to save all his talking for dinner. I ate a lot of meals with Kalim and his family over the years, everyone talking at once, except me, because I couldn't get a word in edgewise, Kalim rolling his eyes at me from across the dinner table, pitying my attempts to keep the threads of half a dozen conversations untangled. I wish Susan had seen him around his family.

I spent time with Kalim and his family during those months I was alone, after Kalim and I drove out to Halifax. Kalim's dad had a habit of coming up behind you and squeezing the back of your neck when he wanted your undivided attention. Sometimes Kalim and I would both be leaning over a blueprint and his dad would stand between us, squeezing our necks and explaining something about rerouting a vent or expanding a porch. When he finished talking, he always slapped the back of our heads. It was his way of saying, "Okay, I've explained what to do, go do it."

I wasn't used to people touching me, especially men. As you boys know, there wasn't much hugging around the house when we were growing up. It wasn't in our folks' natures to smother us with hugs and kisses. With Kalim's family, all the affection came from his father. Kalim always kissed his mother on the cheeks before he left. Then he'd cross the room and kiss his dad the same way.

I didn't bother telling Susan any of this. It was like the advantages had escaped her. She missed her job at Woolworth's, she said. The new job, the one that paid double the old one, was as a receptionist at the Nova Scotia College of Art and Design. So yes, Rory, I have heard of it. She said the other secretaries were snotty. None of them watched *Another World*, the soap opera. She said she missed her pottery classes in Winnipeg, even though she could take any pottery class she wanted free of charge at the college.

This was our new life in Halifax. A paid apprenticeship in

carpentry and free college education for the taking. We even had a pet for a while. I found an abandoned kitten that had wandered into the basement through a broken window. The pussy hung around for a couple of months and then took off.

I wonder if Mary Anne remembers the kitten. Does she link it with what happened to Tenderfoot? That I was present when both of them disappeared?

I FOUND TENDERFOOT. The day after Mary Anne returned to Vancouver. I wanted to sleep under the stars. I took the canoe and wove my way through the string of small islands out on the bay until I found one I liked. I gathered some wood along the beach and lit a small bonfire. After I had it up and roaring I decided to stockpile some extra branches. I spied a log farther down that looked promising and went after it. I was no more than three feet away when I discovered that it was an animal. I experienced the same sudden flutter in my chest as the time I was walking along the shoreline in Mira and unexpectedly stumbled across a seal carcass. It was Tenderfoot. And he wasn't dead, but dying.

He was lying on his side, too far up the beach to have been washed in by the tide. There didn't appear to be any wound that I could see. He was facing the trees. I think he was heading for shelter when he collapsed. I didn't know that he was alive at first. He didn't move when I approached, not so much as a roll of the head in my direction. But I could see his stomach rise and fall, and that produced another flutter in my chest, plus a sudden squirt of bile in the back of my throat. He made no sound, so I can only imagine that he was beyond pain and suffering. Maybe he'd had a stroke.

My head filled with a thousand different thoughts. Should I lift him into the canoe? Go for help? Would he bite me if I tried to move him? Endless options, but no obvious solution. My knees turned to jelly. I fell to my haunches and began to sob, couldn't take my eyes off him and couldn't stop the flow of tears. I don't know how long I sat there. An hour, maybe two. But his chest stopped moving long before I stopped crying.

I didn't want to leave Tenderfoot there on the beach to rot and get pecked apart by crows. But I didn't have the energy or stomach to dig a hole and cover him with dirt. I dragged him to the shore and hoisted him into the canoe. I filled four or five plastic bags with sand and headed out on the bay.

It was dark and I had only the occasional sparkle of a light from one of the cottages in the distance to guide me if I got lost. I made sure I was far enough away from those small islands that the water would be good and deep when I pushed him over the side. I didn't want to risk his floating back to shore. I tied a bag tightly around each of his paws and dropped them over the side. With only a little more exertion his body quickly followed. He was below the water in a second and I paddled away.

As I headed in the general direction of the cottage I thought I'd call Susan and tell her to give Mary Anne the message about Tenderfoot. But Mary Anne didn't need Susan censoring all her heartaches. That was my responsibility.

THERE WAS A TIME when Susan censored many things in our lives. She didn't lie, but sometimes she kept things to herself. Big things.

Business was good, and Susan started to take some courses at the college. She stopped dyeing her hair. The perm was gone, and she let her hair grow to her shoulders. I had missed its silkiness when I brushed the side of my face through the perm.

This day, Kalim and I were working on different jobs, and the place I was at, the guy didn't feel too good, so he asked me to come back the next day. I had nothing lined up for the rest of the day so I headed home around one in the afternoon. Susan wouldn't be back until five-thirty, so I figured I'd just do some work in the attic. I'd been tearing out old insulation and putting new rolls in and I was eager to finish it so I could put up drywall and make a nice den up there. So I got at it, and around two-thirty I went down to the kitchen to make myself some fresh coffee.

Susan was sitting at the table with a half-empty glass of oj in front of her. She was pale and slumped in her chair. My first thought was that something had happened to Mary Anne.

"Where's Mary Anne?"

"She's fine, Cameron, there's nothing wrong with Mary Anne. She's still at daycare."

I felt this clicking happen in my brain, like I was just about to step over to the other side of now, with no turning back. Something wasn't right. I felt my anger scraping against the back of my throat.

"Then what's going on? Why are you home?"

"Cameron..."

"Don't Cameron me," I said, because I knew this tone. I'd heard it a million times.

"Please," Susan said. "Let me catch my breath." She pushed herself away from the table and I noticed the red spot on her crotch. Her lovely hair looked wrong. It was matted and limp against her forehead.

"What in the hell is going on?" I barked. "You're bleeding."

There was dead silence in the kitchen.

"Answer me," I shouted, more frightened than angry, pounding the table with my fists. Susan was behind me now, trying to get hold of my fists.

"Stop it, Cameron, for the love of God, stop it," she screamed, but it just fired my frenzy. I was trying to elbow her away, and then I was there. On the other side of now. Again. My elbow caught her in the gut and she collapsed to the floor. I'd never seen anyone fall so fast.

She didn't wake up, and my head was throbbing. I remember calling Kalim, who hung up and called for an ambulance. I don't remember arriving in the emergency room. I just remember the important part, a couple of hours later, standing beside Susan's bed. She was hooked up to an IV and she didn't look as pale as she had earlier. And she didn't look angry when I came in to visit her. I didn't ask any questions, I just stood at the end of her bed.

"I had an abortion, Cameron. I'm sorry," she said.

The edges of her mouth tightened. It was a look of pity, that much I could tell. There was no apology in the expression. "I should have told you," she said. "It was a mistake."

"That's one of them. Let's hear about your other mistakes," I said.

"Like why?" she suggested.

"No, I think I know why. It's because of Mary Anne. You're afraid that what happened to her might happen again."

Susan turned the side of her face into the pillow. Tears were rolling down her face.

"Yes, and it has, Cameron."

"I don't understand."

"With this pregnancy, and the one before that."

"You've been pregnant before."

Susan chose to continue talking to the pillow. "We lost the first one in the second month, a miscarriage. Just after we returned from Winnipeg. There were complications."

"And this time?"

"This time I didn't wait to find out. I couldn't."

"So you made this decision for both of us."

"I made it for you, Cameron. I didn't do it for me."

"Screw the charity." I was trying to put my arm through my jacket, but it was all twisted in a ball. It ended up under my feet and I kicked it under her bed. Only my foot hit the bed and Susan moaned. She was pale again, just for a few seconds. This time I decided to let her catch her breath.

"I can't have any more children. I won't."

"What were the complications, Susan? You said you had complications with the second baby."

"No," she whispered. "It wasn't me. It was the fetus, it was deformed."

"How?"

"It wasn't developing. The heart was too small. It wouldn't have been able to pump enough blood."

I felt my stomach cramp.

"The doctors think there's something wrong with your sperm. They won't know for sure unless you take some tests."

"Why do they think it's me?"

Susan propped herself up on her elbow.

"Maybe because of the peridol or the thioridazine. Maybe both." Her tears became a steady stream down the side of her face.

"Cameron?"

But I was out of the door, out of the hospital.

I was out of my mind.

Kalim found me in the attic three or four hours later. He just followed the racket to the third floor. I was trying to finish the insulation, which was about the only thing I hadn't been able to finish in the last couple of hours. A mickey of whiskey, no problem. A handful of downers and some hash to mellow out.

I was babbling to Kalim as he stood there in the attic with me. Mary Anne was with his sister, he says. She was going to spend the night. Susan would probably be able to come home in the morning. A lot of this information he had to repeat because I was pounding staples into the insulation with an hydraulic gun.

I tried to reload my staple gun and Kalim tried to help me. I didn't want any help. I didn't want him so near to me. I was going to hit him. I wasn't mad at him. I was just feeling like a fight.

So I chose to pick one with myself.

"I screwed up some good today," I said.

"Why don't you call it a night, come downstairs. I'll make you a cup of coffee," Kalim offered, outside my striking range.

"I didn't mean to hit Susan. She might've bled to death."

The sound of the staple gun startled us both. I'd driven one into my thigh, and my leg buckled. I was down on one knee. Kalim took a step closer, but I pointed the gun at him and he backed away.

"She says the doctors think all her pregnancies had complications because of me." I drove another staple into my thigh and the pain seared through my leg and up the back of my neck. It got dark for a few seconds.

"You know what that means, Kalim? It means that Mary Anne doesn't have any eyes because of me. I stole them from her." I was trying to lift the gun to my head, but my hand was shaking. I got it raised as far as my neck. The impact of the staple sent my head across the room, with my body clumsily trying to keep up.

For the second time that day I had no memory of an ambulance. Ninety days later, when they let me out of the asylum, Susan and Mary Anne had already been settled in Winnipeg for a month.

But I still had my job. And I still had my house. I signed and mailed the divorce papers the same day I moved home. No contest from me.

I've never won a contest in my life.

Adrian

A GAY MAN was wandering through the enchanted forests of Ireland when a fairy appeared.

— I can grant you one wish before I vanish, the fairy said.

— That's easy, the man replied. I want peace in the Middle East. He pulled out a map. Make all these countries stop fighting.

The fairy shook his head. —Listen, pal, I'm not a queen. That's too much for a little fairy like me to manage. Anything else?

— I want to live in a relationship filled with bliss from morning until night. No disease. No conflict. Honesty.

The fairy sighed. — Let me see that map again.

WHO CAN WILFULLY control the course of a disease? I couldn't. Otherwise Claes would still be alive. And who really has control over the discord that befalls them and the conflict they create for other people? As to bliss, it evokes infinity, a life of pious waiting on earth until Heaven opens its gates. I suppose for some people, that's the good life. Not me. The thought of it conjures an eerily impotent existence.

— *And honesty, little brother? What do you have to say about that?*

— *Don't be such a prick, Rory. He's getting to it. Aren't you, Socrates?*

NO, I HAVE NOT been honest. Claes wasn't alone when I met him in Venice. He had a partner, Nino Pavanati, who was also his lover. It was Nino who explained to me that St. Mark the Apostle was the patron saint of Venice and his traditional symbol, a winged lion, became the logo of the Venetian Republic. He spoke with his head slightly elevated, his gaze cast downward, past an almost perfectly straight nose. He showed me the lion on the Torre dell'Orologio, the clock tower on the Piazza San Marco, and another on a column in the Piazzetta beside the Doge's Palace.

There were lions on gate posts and bridges, in paintings and sculptures, and scores of them feasting on the kill, battling serpents and cast in all colours of the rainbow, including the red marble lions of the Piazzetta dei Leoncini. Nino seemed to know the location of every lion in Venice and I saw them everywhere, even when he wasn't around to cajole my eyes, luring the cats out of their hiding places throughout the city.

I chanced quick sidelong glances at him while he talked. Some people's good looks dissolve into mediocrity when observed in profile. Not Nino. His profile was strong, nothing in his face was compromised when you looked at him from the side, there were no sharp angles to his cheeks, no receding chin, his nose didn't end in an unflattering point or bump at the tip. He kept his dark hair short, with high sideburns, and although it was straight, there were tight little tufts of hair below his neckline in the back, which he didn't shave.

— *Did you ever notice that we're pretty good at describing people?*

— *I never thought about it.*

— *Maybe it's in our genes. You know, triplets and all. Maybe we're hard-wired to notice all the little details in others since we look alike.*

— *Have you been toking, Cameron?*

— *No seriously. You could have made a bundle, Rory, if you had chosen to be one of those folks who draw sketches for the police instead of an artiste.*

— *Cameron.*

— *What?*

— *It's not your turn.*

Nino and Claes were, to bastardize a cliché, like salt and pepper. Nino, the Venetian Latino, with dark skin and hair. Claes, the Viking, blond with a complexion that had never seen a blemish, a prominent Adam's apple bobbing in his neck, and deeply set, intense eyes.

They were both laughing, both had white, white teeth, gulping on beers at one of the coffee stands set up in the middle of the exhibition hall, both taking me in at the same instant, sitting at the next table, alone, sipping a tepid cappuccino and watching them.

— *I've heard this part of the story before, Rory.*

— *Yes, but it's different this time. Be quiet.*

I was watching Nino, in particular. Noticing that he hadn't shaved, the short, dense stubble cast dark shadows across his face and throat. He sat forward on the bar stool, one hand cupped over his knee.

That evening he sidled up beside me at the outdoor bar across from the hotel where we were all staying. Although I recognized him from the expo earlier in the day, he didn't let on that he knew me.

As Nino chatted with me, he told me that Claes had gone to bed early, and nodded across the street to the hotel. He, on the other hand, was just coming into his second wind of the day. He asked me to join him at a club and we wove our way through darkened streets.

All streets in Venice feel like back alleys, but there is no menace in these sober streets. People walk them with a sense of security and familiarity, never raising their voices. We ended up at an establishment with no sign out front, only the thumping rhythms of the bass track betraying the club behind the tall oak doors.

We are both tall and Nino's right hip swivelled inward against my thigh as we danced, our shoulders touching. Occasionally he grazed the bottom of my chin with his own, the stubble sharp against my cheek.

His scent was a musky sweat, little beads formed along the inside of his left jugular vein and I tasted them. Sometimes he pressed his cheek against my own and his breath rolled along my face and bathed my ears in damp, intense heat. A pair of lips greeted his neck as someone waltzed by us. This happened often during the evening, but each time he grasped my hand harder.

At the bar, he kissed me while we waited for fresh drinks and I washed away the pecks he had received on his neck from the admirers on the dance floor with quick strokes of my tongue.

We were quite animated as he led me back through the streets to our hotel, stopping often to kiss me roughly, his chest flattening my back against the wet stone walls and, later, into the mattress of my bed, then sleeping briefly, before removing himself to his own room and the bed he shared with Claes.

IN ALL THE TIME I was to spend with Nino, he rarely spoke about his past or his family. There was a father in Copenhagen and a mother in Venice, Claes explained the next morning, over breakfast, after introducing himself and asking if he might join me at my empty table, our conversation quickly turning to our professions and food. They were toying with the idea of refurbishing their bistro in Copenhagen.

Nino joined us as the waiter was setting the tables for lunch. We decided to spend the day together, the three of us. Nino wanted to show me some lions.

We spent the following days sightseeing and I slept with Nino on two of those evenings. Only on the last night did Claes join us at the club where Nino and I had danced the first evening. I was cruised by a young Italian and invited him back to my room. Nino and Claes left for Denmark and I returned to Canada. A week later I accepted their invitation to visit them. I flew to Copenhagen and they drove me immediately to the bistro.

I was infatuated.

With the restaurant. The city. Claes.

And Nino.

AMNESIC.

That is how Nino described his relationship with Claes.

We'd known for a year that Claes was HIV-positive.

I thought Nino and I were finally about to have our first discussion about it. Instead, he wanted to talk about amnesia.

Nino travelled often between Copenhagen and Venice. It had been his pattern for years, when they ran the bistro and then at The Little Supper. His mother lived in Venice and it wasn't unusual for him to hop on a plane once or twice each season and fly south for three or four days and meet with our Italian suppliers. After his mother died, he stayed with his aunt who lived on Burano, one of the many islands within the Venetian lagoon. In the weeks following his returns, equipment and other provisions arrived.

Each time Nino returned to Claes, the two of them spent the first few days adjusting to each other, as if meeting for the first time. Often almost colliding, at the apartment or restaurant, stepping aside to let the other pass, Claes mistakenly grabbing Nino's towel from the rack after a shower, both spearing the same piece of asparagus on the platter with their fork, one of them climbing into the side of the bed usually occupied by the other.

There was never a hint of irritation between the two, never a cross word or raised brow. Instead, tentative smiles passed between them, a slight blush on one or the other's cheek, as if they were courting. During those first days of each reunion they only wanted to sleep. Sleep seemed to be the only way they could recover memories of each other.

It wasn't long, during my first year in Copenhagen, the year we lived and worked together, before this affable choreography between Nino and Claes began to irritate and sadden me.

But when sadness did settle in, Nino was nearing his leave of Claes, The Little Supper, and Copenhagen, probably in that order.

OF CLAES.

Nino grew up in Copenhagen, the son of an Italian diplomat who settled in Denmark after his wife left him to return to Venice. Nino was seven when he arrived and was fluent in Danish within a few years.

Claes and Nino attended the same high school, passing each other in the hallways, but it wasn't until they met line-cooking a few years later at a restaurant that they ended up in Claes' flat one night. Eventually they gave up their apartments and bought a flat together. Then the bistro. They both enjoyed sex, together or with others. Casual sex was less frequent as they became busier with the bistro. Less frequent for Claes, at least.

Nino didn't like the sight of blood and always left the kitchen if a chef cut a finger shucking oysters or dicing vegetables. The chef was sent home to mend, even if the gash was minor, and wasn't allowed to appear in the kitchen again until the offending wound had healed. The blood from meat and fish didn't upset Nino, but the sight of human blood drained the colour from his face.

Unfortunately, Claes suffered from profuse nosebleeds, sometimes requiring a trip to outpatients to have the vessels in his nasal passages cauterized. Only once was Nino present when Claes had to rush off to the hospital, and Nino had to look out the window of the taxi during the entire ride. The next day, Claes couldn't find his blood-splattered shirt and pants. Nino had thrown them away. One of Claes' sneakers had also been stained and it was gone too.

Claes brightened as he recalled the episode one afternoon at our apartment, a couple of years later, long after Nino had left, pinching his nostrils while I provided him with a cold compress.

— Nino had only thrown away the one sneaker, he said. The one with the blood. The other one is still in the closet.

This is everything I know about Claes and Nino the friends, the partners, the couple. Probably in that order.

OF THE LITTLE SUPPER.

Nino loved chocolate, and on the day that he sat me down to ask me if I was interested in buying out half of his share of the restaurant, he served us a bowl of chocolate with strawberries for dipping, using the berries as a spoon.

— Montezuma drank fifty cups of chocolate to help him perform for his harem of six hundred mates, he said. Then. I'm leaving Copenhagen.

The echo I heard was *The Little Supper*. Fainter still, *Claes*. But he didn't say either, only that he was leaving Denmark. There was only the one question on the table, whether or not I was interested in half of his share of the restaurant.

In my experience of Nino, I wasn't used to forming questions for him to answer. I thought about this as I sat there, his tongue probing the chocolate on the end of an unripe strawberry. Had I ever asked him anything? He had an innate ability for dispensing information on a need-to-know basis, making Claes or me aware when orders had to be placed, how many reservations were on the book for the evening, or when the doors closed for the night.

Most restaurants advertise the hour their kitchen closes, but not The Little Supper. It varies from night to night. Nino installed a red light outside the restaurant. When it is on, the kitchen is closed, just like the red light at The Royal Theatre, alerting theatregoers that the performance is sold out.

Sometimes I overheard the staff place friendly wagers in the evening, trying to guess when Nino would flick the switch. For a few weeks I watched him to see if there was a system at play. I'd see him politely excuse himself midway during a conversation with guests to signal the closest waiter with a bantam dip of his chin to turn on the red light. It didn't matter if the night was slow or if patrons were lined up outside.

He ordered all the food, supervised and rejected the deliveries, and created at least one entree each evening. He was always in conversation with the sous-chefs and waiters, correcting a sauce, sampling the vinaigrette, or ensuring that his wine selections were germane to the night's menu. The staff never won their bets, they could never know with certainty when Nino would decide to close for the night. Now Nino had decided to leave the restaurant rather than close it.

My one question to Nino about leaving Claes inspired his anecdote about their amnesic relationship.

— I don't understand, I said. Why are you leaving Claes? Nino smiled.

— It takes too long for us to remember who we are, maybe even why we stay together.

Another smile.

— I love him, he said. I love The Little Supper. I love Denmark. I love you, Adrian. And I *love* Venice.

He tapped the side of his temple with his finger.

— I remember Venice up here in my head, he said. I don't have to dream about it to remember.

He glanced around at the dining room.

— I'm starting to see food when I dream. Will I forget how to cook if I stay here? Will I forget how to find my way home if I stay in Denmark?

— Have you forgotten how to love Claes? I asked.

Nino took my hand into his, cupped it, and kissed my palm.

— I haven't forgotten how to love you, Adrian, he said. That is something I want to remember. It has nothing to do with this place.

OF COPENHAGEN.

Although our sous-chefs prepared most of the soups, Nino always contributed at least one for the evening's menu. In the hustle and bustle of his day, making soup was a ritual for him. He rarely spoke during the preparation, it was meditative and restorative. The almond soup was his last for The Little Supper. The next day Claes and I agreed, separately, to buy out Nino's share in the enterprise.

— Copenhagen is sick, Nino said.

— Sick? I asked.

— Yes. Sick. Even the young men, he said. The baby boys at the clubs. They're all sick.

— I am not sick, I said.

— But Copenhagen is sick, Nino said.

— It could get better, I offered.

— Perhaps, he said. But without me. I prefer Venice, with her rosy cheeks.

CLAES HAD PROBLEMS sleeping after Nino left us. By the second week he was only getting two or three hours a night. I would wake several times, listening for the creak of his mattress through the walls or low murmurs from the television in the living room. We didn't talk about it, but it was wearing us both down. Then, at the end of the third week, I awoke to the creaking of my own mattress.

— I can't sleep, he said. Crawling in beside me.

— I know, I whispered. And settled into the embrace that would lull us into sleep every night after that.

One morning, leisurely tracing my finger along the tattoo of his seahorse's mane, I casually, and without intention, told Claes something about my own relationship with Nino.

— Nino didn't have any tattoos on his body, I said. Realizing, too late, that I had just told Claes I had looked everywhere.

A FEW YEARS LATER, I decided to visit Nino in Venice. There was nothing clandestine about it. He had extended an invitation to us both, Claes and I. And, perhaps, other men in Copenhagen.

Go to Venice, Claes said. Spend time with Nino. And miss me.

I had missed Nino's vivacity, noticing now that in the years since I'd seen him, fine laugh lines had appeared at the corners of his eyes and remained there when he didn't smile, his face animated even when he was silent.

He took me to visit the *Arsenale* to gaze upon the *bissoni*, ceremonial boats, some rowed by as many as eighteen crewmen dressed in costumes of the Renaissance. I saw *bissoni* outfitted with pairs of wooden horses galloping at the helm or tiny gilded pavilions.

But the most striking were those protected by a statue of Neptune stationed on the stern, athletic and youthful renderings of a tight-buttocked god, his nakedness sheathed only with a golden or silver skin, a mane of hair sculpted by the winds hurling the boats through the green canals, brandishing a gilded trident above his head.

— Many of the boats are handcrafted, Nino explained. Do you build boats in Canada? he asked.

— Nova Scotia is famous for its schooners. My dad built his own rowboat for fly-casting, I said.

— *I remember Dad's rowboat, Cameron.*

— *We borrowed it once without his permission.*

— *It was Adrian's idea.*

— *Of course it was. The little shit said we'd get it back before dad noticed.*

— *And we believed him.*

— *We always believed Adrian. And I always took the blame. I dove from the side, almost capsizing the boat, and Adrian's oar caught me on the bridge of the nose when I surfaced.*

Dad had attached a metal ornament to the stern of the rowboat. We three looked at it, wondering what its function was, as we sat on the shores of the river that afternoon, taking turns pinching Cameron's nose to stop the bleeding after I broke it with the oar. We hauled the boat up on the shore and collapsed beside Cameron to catch our breath before driving to the hospital.

Dad and I went back to get the rowboat later that afternoon and, during the drive, I prayed that we had dragged it far enough ashore so the tide wouldn't get it. It was where we left it and I breathed a sigh of relief. Too quickly, as it turned out. Dad took one look at the rowboat and started to swear a blue streak. Someone had stolen the ornament.

— You're never to take anything of mine again, he said. I carried that souvenir home with me from the war. From Italy, he said. From Venice.

It is the same ornament that adorns all the gondolas in Venice, I realize now. Only dad had attached it to the stern rather than to the prow, where it sits on the gondolas.

— I'm not going to punish your brothers, Adrian, he said. This was entirely your fault. You put your brothers up it.

— Why are you singling me out?

— Don't talk back to me. Jesus. H. Christ. You can't hide between your brothers forever. In a couple of years you'll all be out on your own. Something happens, they won't be around to pick up the pieces or take the blame.

— I can take care of myself.

— Can you?

ONE EVENING DURING my brief visit to Venice, Nino led me deep into the city's labyrinth.

He hopped down onto a small floating wharf and passed me a joint. I lit the joint and smoked it, offering him the spliff with a wave of my hand. He took a few deep puffs and passed it to me, humming all the while.

— My brother Cameron sings that song, I said. What is it called?

— *Domine Deus*, he said. Vivaldi. From the *Gloria*.

— He sings in churches, I said. But he doesn't go to church.

I closed my eyes and listened to the lapping of the water against the wharf. The dope was strong. When I opened my eyes again my head began to spin.

Nino had to grab me before I stepped too far forward and off the wharf.

— What's wrong? he asked.

— I feel dizzy.

— Are you ill?

I started to climb up off the wharf and Nino reached out to help me keep my balance.

— I can manage myself, I said. Without petulance.

— Can you?

I sat on the edge of the wharf, transported for a moment to the back seat of dad's car after the ornament was stolen from the rowboat. *Can you?* he had asked. I had refused to answer him, seething at his suggestion that I couldn't take care of myself. My eyes wandered over the top of Nino's head, settling on a sparkle in the water.

— There's a moonbeam reflected in the water. The clouds are gone, I said.

I waited until he turned to look at the reflection.

— Claes is very sick, I said.

Nino kept gazing at the water.

— You think I don't know that, Adrian? he said, finally.

— You never ask.

— Why did I invite you to Venice, Adrian?

— You invited Claes, too.

— Why did I invite you, Adrian?

— I don't know, Nino.

— Because I knew you'd come.

— You were certain?

— I hoped, he said.

— Why?

— I wanted you to take a vacation.

— From Copenhagen?

— Yes.

— From The Little Supper?

— Yes, he said.

I had trouble with what I needed to say next.

— From Claes?

— *Si*.

I was silent.

— You need to cry, Adrian, he said. Really cry.

— I miss Claes, I said.

— I miss him too.

I didn't tell Nino that Claes had sent me away to miss him, discussing the prospect of the trip while in bed, after changing the choreography of our lovemaking when he started to weaken, running my fingers through his thick hair, brushing it up off his forehead, and noticing then, for the first time, that the familiar raccoon-like shadows around his eyes were now permanent.

— I don't miss the sickness, Nino, I said. I don't miss it when I am here.

He wiped away my tears, kissing my eyelashes.

— Stay healthy, Adrian, he whispered.

The moonbeam on the water had glided closer to us and reflected off the prows of two gondolas tied to the wharf. Each had an ornament identical to the one from dad's rowboat.

— It's called a *ferro*, Adrian. The metal teeth symbolize the *sestieri,* the six districts of Venice, beneath the Doge's cap.

The *ferro's* silver teeth shimmered in the water. They reminded me of hooded ghouls.

I began to tremble, looking upon these demons, an effigy perhaps of Claes, of me, anchored side by side, cloaks shrouding the plague beneath the folds. They were sneering at me with their scissor-like teeth, clattering, the reflections biting the heads off the waves.

I kicked the side of the gondola nearest me. The ghouls in the water shimmered violently, breaking up.

I want to dance now, Nino, I said.

— ARE YOU THINKING *what I'm thinking, Cameron?*

— *That would be a first.*

— *Get serious. I think they're in love.*

— *So?*

— *What about the other guy? Claes?*

— *What about him? Adrian had a thing for both of them.*

— *I couldn't do that.*

— *Adrian's been doing it all our lives, Rory.*

— *I don't understand.*

— *Surprise of surprises.*

— *For the love of god, Cameron.*

— *Hold your bird. It's like this. Adrian loved the folks, right?*

— *Yes.*

— *Both of them.*

— *Yes.*

— *And he loves us. Both of us.*

— *Yes.*

— So he loved these two guys.

— And?

— That's it.

— But what if Dad was right?

— About?

— Adrian is only really comfortable when he's in the middle.

— Bullshit.

— He won't be in the middle forever. Mom and Dad are dead.

— We survived.

— But Claes is dead.

— He's got this other dude.

IT WAS TIME to go home. Nino prepared a last dinner before I departed in the morning. The knife slipped in his hand. Neither of us noticed the gash at first. It was only when he stroked my face, leaving a streak of blood across my chin that his own face whitened.

— You might need stitches. It is deep, I said after his nausea passes and the colour slowly returned to his face. He was holding the wet towel that I made him put on his forehead with his good hand, the thumb on the other hand wrapped in a bandage.

— Be careful of the blood, he warned.

When I looked into his face, tears were running down his cheeks. I drew him close, resting his head against my shoulder, and he quietly weeps.

— I loved him, Adrian, he said.

— I know.

— I was scared. The blood, it terrified me, he whispered. Recalling Claes' frequent nosebleeds.

— It doesn't matter, I told him. You didn't leave just because of the blood. But it did drain away your passion, I said. Look at me, Nino.

He raised his face and I wiped away his tears.

— He loved you, I said. Deeply.

This time Nino hugged me close, signalling a change, inviting me to walk along a new path that had opened between us.

— Will you return to Venice? And stay? he asked.

— No.

He cradled my face.

— Your cheeks are full of passion for him, Adrian, he says. Enough for a lifetime.

— He doesn't have a lifetime, Nino.

I SAILED AWAY from Burano the next morning. Nino's aunt kept repeating a word to me before I leave.

— *Paese*, she said.

— It means your village or town, Nino explained. Home.

— *Paese*, she repeated. Wanting me to know that their home is my *paese*. I'd be welcome if I returned.

— *Paese*, I said.

— *Si*.

All of this conveyed in Nino's bathroom, the two of us in a foamy tub, him resting against my chest, holding the bandaged thumb above the water. His aunt waiting to hear stirrings from his apartment, the sounds of the water pipes alerting her to our early rise. She walked into the bathroom and upon our nakedness to hand me a small box filled with earth, dirt from a nearby field. A little piece of Burano to take with me to Copenhagen.

— *Paese*.

We took the waterbus into Venice. Nino draped his arm loosely around my shoulder as we ride the choppy waters. As we neared our mooring, we passed a hotel where a water taxi, a *vaporetto*, ferried luggage to a ship anchored offshore.

The *vaporetto* rode low under the weight of all the bags and one of the suitcases slid over the side and into the harbour. I watched as it sank below the water. I wanted Nino to know that I loved Claes deeply and that he should never allow the memory of Claes to sink below the waves like the suitcase. But I said nothing.

Instead, I remembered a trick Nino's aunt had taught me and squeezed Nino's hand, pumping the last of my affection into his chest, creating our own brief *paesono*.

Rory

APRIL, TORONTO

DO YOU REMEMBER Skylab, Adrian?

The day it fell to earth we spent the day on the Mira River. You, Cameron, Susan, and me. We had Dad's car and Cameron drove us crazy with his obsession about the spaceship during our drive to the beach.

"Skylab circles the earth fifty degrees north and south of the equator at an altitude of four hundred and thirty-five kilometres. It completes an orbit every ninety-three minutes."

"Enough," we groaned.

But he continued while we sunned ourselves on the beach blanket, swatting horseflies as they flew around us.

"Three crews visited the station," he said. "The first mission lasted twenty-eight days."

"Cameron!"

"The second mission lasted fifty-nine days."

"Deaf. Are you deaf?"

"The last mission was eighty-four days."

"I've got beer." Susan rescued us, rummaging through the hamper, passing us pints of cold Alpine. We watched as Cameron chugged half the bottle, hoping it'd make him forget his tormenting.

"You know," he said, "they took x-rays of the sun from Skylab."

"For the love of God, shut up." I jumped up, my foot upsetting a bowl of potato chips on the sand.

"It might fall here," he said, ignoring my ire.

You applied a generous splash of coconut oil to your legs, Adrian, our long legs. You were the only one of us wearing shorts on the hottest day of the summer. "Nothing is going to fall on Cape Breton," you said.

"It could."

"But it won't."

"Oh great, Adrian's in one of his moods," Cameron said. "How can you be sure it won't fall on Cape Breton?"

"Cameron—"

"I love this song." Saved again by Susan, reaching in through the car window and cranking up the dial, Sting's whiny voice filling the car.

Cameron joined in and you and I filled out the chorus, Adrian, "Roxanne" echoing across the river.

We popped open more beers.

"Jesus, it's hot," Cameron said, and was out of his clothes in a minute.

"Christ, Cameron, put on a bathing suit. Adrian, tell him."

With his ass wiggling in our faces, he headed for the shore, took two or three long strides through the water, and dove in.

"I hope he belly-flopped."

You were on your feet in a flash, Adrian, stripping off your shorts. "I am going in."

"Your underwear. Where's your underwear?"

"Who wears underwear in the summer?"

Susan rolled over on her back.

"What's that on your shin?" I asked her.

"A tattoo. Adrian and I hitchhiked over to North Sydney." A few strands of her long hair had caught in her bra clasp. She tugged at the strands, setting them free in the only gust of wind to blow along the river that afternoon.

"When did you and Adrian become such good friends?"

"We've always been close. We like to talk to each other."

"He talks to you?"

She was standing in her panties, the brush of her pubic hair pushing against the silk fabric, her skin bronzed from head to foot, a sprinkle of freckles across her nose and ample breasts.

"Doesn't he talk to you?" she asked.

"'Course he does."

"Do you listen?" She tossed her panties at my chest and headed for the water.

I opened another beer and watched from the shore as you splashed each other, Susan jumping off the bridges Cameron made with clasped hands.

You were floating on your back, Adrian, while Susan and Cameron necked, disappearing below the water for twenty, thirty seconds at a time, their mouths locked together.

"You're soaking everything," I complained, when you and Susan came out of the water and collapsed on the blanket beside me. Cameron was at the car.

"Listen," he said, his head inside the car window now, the cheeks of his ass trembling, despite the heat.

"It's over," he said, turning to face us, towelling off, while making a big show of drying his balls.

"Where did it land, Cameron?" Adrian asked.

"Australia."

"Was anybody hit?" Susan asked.

"Hundreds, maybe thousands," he said.

'Course, it didn't hit anyone. Cameron knew that, he just wanted to be melodramatic.

He put on his pants and stepped into his sneakers.

"Do we have any toilet paper?" he asked.

"In the trunk." I tossed him the keys.

I lay back on the blanket, dizzy from the beers. It took a few seconds for me to place the roar of the motor and when I finally looked over at the car, you were already driving down the lane, Adrian, and Cameron gave me the finger from the passenger window.

"Where're they going?"

"Relax, Rory. They're picking up some burgers. They'll be fine."

"That wasn't the plan."

"Plans change," she said, pulling a T-shirt down over her breasts.

"You sound just like Cameron. Are you two joined at the hip now?"

But she ignored me, staring at my neck.

"What are you looking at?" I asked.

"You've got Cameron's Adam's apple," she said.

"It's *my* Adam's apple, Cameron's got his own."

"The three of you aren't exactly alike, are you?" she asked.

"No," I answered, firmly.

"It's not just your personalities, either, or your haircuts," she said. "It's other stuff."

"Like what?"

"Sometimes you look taller than Adrian and Cameron."

"I do?"

"When you stand up, you always seem to stretch a little taller than your brothers. And Adrian walks slower than you and Cameron."

It was the first time I'd ever been alone with Susan, and I realize now this was to be our first and only conversation of any substance.

"Your voice is deeper than Cameron's and Adrian's. Show me your stomach."

"What?"

"Show me your stomach."

I lifted my T-shirt a few inches.

"You all have different belly buttons."

"Yeah, we do. There were several nurses assisting at our birth. I guess they each had their own style of tying the knot."

"And you're left-handed."

"Guilty."

"Give me your hands."

She reached out and took them into her own.

"They feel lighter than Cameron's," she said.

"You've weighed his hands?" I asked. "That's creepy."

Susan sighed, dropping them. "I'm just trying to make a point. You're different from each other. Just in case you were wondering."

"Anything else?"

"Just one. What's that scar on your leg?"

"I was stung by a jellyfish when we were kids. It got infected and left the scar."

No one had ever taken the time to articulate our differences to me and for some reason, maybe it was the beers, I decided to give her something else, something of me.

"Here's something you probably don't know," I said. "I don't see things. I hear them."

"Little voices in your head?" she asked, smiling.

"No. Not like that at all. When you look at the river, what do you see?"

"It's blue, the sun is sparkling off the water."

"I see that too, but I also hear it. I hear the blue."

"What does blue sound like?"

"Cymbals."

"Cymbals?"

"Small ones, like the ones you'd wear on your fingertips, tapping against each other. Over and over, like a chant. It's not noise. It's not scary."

"What about Cameron and Adrian?"

"What about them?"

"Do they hear colours?"

"I've never asked them."

"Then you've never told them," she said. "It's a secret."

"We don't have any secrets, Susan."

"Everybody has secrets, Rory. I'll keep this one."

I turned away from her.

"You're blushing," she said.

"I'm hot, Susan. It's the heat. That's all. Can you pass me another beer?"

"Why don't you wait until they get back with the food?"

"I'm not drunk."

"You'd have to walk a straight line to prove it," she said, smirking.

"I can do it."

"Show me," she challenged, pulling me to my feet and dragging me toward the beach.

"Now walk a straight line," she ordered.

"It's sand. I can't walk straight in the sand."

"You're right." She lunged at me, pushing me hard on the chest. I stumbled backward into the water and lost my balance, falling on my back.

"I'm soaked."

"Then take off your clothes, the water's great."

"Damn it, I can't find my wallet."

"Relax. Cameron swiped it before he took off. Throw me your clothes, I'll wring them out while you take a dip."

I peeled off the wet clothes and tossed them to her.

"Crap," I yelled. "My underwear is full of sand." I stripped them off and let them float away, too embarrassed to let her touch them. The water was refreshing, my beer buzz cleared, and I ventured a little farther out, treading the water.

"It's great," I shouted.

"I told you."

"Are you coming in?"

"Sure." She took off her T-shirt, there was no bra to unclasp this time, and she let the towel she was wearing as a skirt fall to the sand.

She ducked and resurfaced about a foot away from me. We were both up to our chests in the water.

"Are you relaxed now?" she asked.

"You're always saying that."

"Saying what?"

"Telling me to relax."

"Well, you should. Doesn't the water feel great?"

"I'm not comfortable."

"You look comfortable. What's wrong?"

"I don't like skinny-dipping."

"Why not?"

"What if someone comes along?"

"The world's hiding from Skylab today, Rory, or in mourning now. Nobody's looking at you."

We bobbed in the water for a few minutes, both on our tiptoes.

"I'm in a cold pocket," she said. "Let's go in."

"I can't."

"Why not?"

"I can't, all right?"

"Do you have a cramp?"

"No, just go in, I'll follow in a minute."

"What's the matter?" she asked, nearing me.

"Susan, don't—"

"Oh," she said, drifting against my groin. "You've got a hard-on."

"I know that. It's why I don't go skinny-dipping. It makes me hard."

"It'll go away."

"No, it won't go away. Not this kind."

"Do guys get different kinds of boners?"

"Something like that."

"Well, you better whack off, Rory, your lips are starting to turn blue."

"I can't do it with you around."

"I'll wait on the beach."

"That won't work. You'll still be around."

"For Christ's sake."

I felt her fingers grabbing me.

"What're you doing?"

"Relieving the tension. And keep your mouth shut or you'll swallow a horsefly."

But I couldn't close my mouth. As she stroked harder my mouth widened. She edged even closer.

"Relax," she said and kissed me.

A few more strokes and I was done.

"Holy fuck."

"I didn't fuck you, Rory, don't go getting any ideas. I did you a favour. In honour of all those people Skylab killed today."

JANET AND I DECIDED to sell the cottage last year. We had spent little time on the bay over the past few years. Janet found the drive exhausting, preferring to curl up on weekends with a good book at our house in Toronto. We arrived one weekend to decide what to keep and what to throw away. Janet attached a story to each of her heirlooms. Picking up a vase from the dresser in the bedroom, she sat on the bed. "I broke this when I was eleven," she said.

"It belonged to my aunt. She told my father that I had to buy her a new one. He was very angry and put the broken vase in a box in her basement. Every time we visited her, the pieces were sitting in a bowl on the china cabinet. Neither of them ever glanced at it while we ate dinner." She turned the vase over in her hands.

"He glued it together after she died. Why have I kept this?"

I realized all the heirlooms she had inherited from her parents were at the cottage. She had kept them in dusky trunks, but over the years I'd displayed them throughout the rooms and it was probably this museum-like setting that distressed her. "They're just old things, Rory," she said, whenever I examined them, carefully, like antiques.

She glanced up at me from the bed and sighed. I was standing in the doorway with her mother's china teapot in my hands.

"You can take the bloody tea set, Rory," she said. "Put it in the gallery. I don't think it's made for use." She waved me away with her hand.

Her dismissal annoyed me further, as there was another purpose to this weekend, much darker, but I wasn't ready to confront her with it just yet. Instead, I took the teapot to the kitchen. I rinsed it under warm water from the tap and carefully dried it. I filled the matching sugar bowl and put milk into the creamer, carrying a kettle of boiling water to the table, slowly pouring it into the teapot, almost to the brim. The scent of Darjeeling filled the kitchen, the boiling water releasing a calming aroma into the air, which was in contrast to the anger brewing within me. I cupped my hands around the sides of the pot, then, horrified, noticed a fine crack form at the base of the handle and continue down the side. It split in two, the water spilling over the edge of the kitchen table. As I admired the teapot in those few seconds before it fell apart, I decided it would look nice in the Gallery. A place for things with no use, Janet had said. I decided then, as the water dripped onto the floor from the cracked teapot, it wasn't only the cottage I'd close, but the Gallery as well.

IT WAS EASY to tell you the story about Susan and me at the beach, Adrian. Probably as easy as it was for Cameron to relay another tale veiling deceit, only a shorter one, just fifteen seconds on my answering machine.

"Rory, it's Cameron. You sure the good wife isn't still porking this Kolerus guy? According to the Big B, she's been giving him a big payoff all these years. Catch ya later."

I'm not a jealous husband, Adrian, so I quickly dismissed Cameron's allegations regarding infidelity. But what prevented me from deleting his message was his mention of Tally. What information had Cameron chosen to misrepresent from a conversation with him?

I called Tally to find out what he and Cameron had talked about. He lost no time in coming to the point. It was Janet who had bought all my paintings over the years, not Kolerus. Every time he picked out a painting at the Gallery, Janet bankrolled it.

Suddenly I was mired in quicksand, and put several questions to Tally, standing on the tips of my toes, hoping with each answer I'd grow taller and put more distance between me and the muddied truth below. It didn't matter how hard I reached with those questions. I continued to sink. So I stopped trying and hung up the phone.

Why would Janet tell Tally any of this?

"Darling, it was years ago and you were going through a rough patch. Talbot was very considerate," she said.

This was said a few hours after the teapot had cracked, the weekend I spoke of earlier, after my conversation with Tally, when I couldn't keep my rage in any longer.

"I shouldn't have told Talbot, but I was desperate," she said, referring to a long dry spell following one of my earliest exhibitions. I hadn't had an offer to exhibit any of my work for almost four years. Worse, I hadn't sold anything. Other than to that prick Kolerus.

"Talbot was visiting. Every time you left the room he asked me why you were so moody. I tried to shrug him off. I know how sensitive you are about your private affairs. But Talbot is very persistent. He kept asking me if we were having problems, which really wasn't any of his business, and to make matters worse, Ivan dropped by the house. You were shopping. I made them coffee. Talbot kept bringing up your moods, Ivan said it was because you were struggling. I was wishing they'd both just leave."

She sat on the edge of the ottoman in the living room to catch her breath.

"It was only supposed to be one painting, Rory. Ivan said he always wanted to own some of your work. But he still wasn't offering to buy anything. That's when Talbot suggested I buy it for him. And that should have been the end of it. Because, darling, you were very happy. And you started to sell other work after that. But Talbot said that if you were to believe Ivan's interest was genuine he'd have to acquire a new piece on a regular basis."

I remained standing, intentionally choosing to challenge Janet from across the room, putting distance between the accused and the bench, my hands at my sides, clenching the fabric of my pants.

"Every painting Ivan owns. You bought every painting Ivan owns?"

"Yes."

"On the books, he's bought fourteen canvases, ninety-eight thousand dollars. You're my biggest patron, Janet. You're my pimp."

The colour drained from her face.

"You apologize to me," she said.

"Why should I apologize?" Raising my voice to Janet for the first time in all our years of marriage shocked us both. "You bought me a career. Everything I've painted is worthless."

Janet covered her mouth with the back of her hand, tears welling in her eyes.

"Ninety-eight thousand dollars is a lot of money, even for my rich wife. You can't deduct any of it."

"I don't care about the money, Rory."

"You should, because your investment was wasted. I went to Ivan's house to collect the paintings. He didn't even raise an eyebrow, just motioned me with a puffy finger to follow him to the garage. They were all stacked in a storage room, most of them had never been unwrapped. I took them to the dump and threw them in with the rest of the fucking trash."

I crossed the room to the fireplace, ignoring the offer of Janet's outstretched hand, and looked at the canvas hanging over the mantelpiece. It was the self-portrait I had painted of us. Me on the left, Cameron in the centre, and you on the right, Adrian.

"Do you remember when you bought this painting, Janet?"

"Of course I do. You were still a student."

"Do you remember what you said?"

"No, darling, I'm afraid I don't." Regret surfaced above the mounting unease in her voice.

"You said my eyes were looking away from my brothers. I told you I was the sentry, keeping watch." I followed the direction of the gaze I had painted on my own face over the frame and along the wall.

"I'm not protecting Adrian and Cameron in this picture. I'm looking for a way out."

"But you love your brothers. You were just asserting your individuality. That's why you painted it."

"I don't need you to define my world."

"Rory."

"Did I ever tell you our mother put us into our own bedrooms before we were five? By fourth grade, our teachers put us in separate classes."

I stabbed at the canvas with my finger. "There's no way for me to get out of this picture. Look at Cameron. He's a goddamn eel. He used to take running fits through the house. I'd grab him by the shoulders and he'd vibrate in my arms, slipping out of my grasp. One of our parents would charge into the room and shout at both of us. He didn't give a sweet fuck. And Adrian. He'd push and push, until they exploded, and then he'd laugh. At our parents or Tally. Everything was a big joke.

"In every picture my father ever snapped of the three of us, we lined up in the same order. So he started taking pictures of us by ourselves. And Tally? He made sure we were out of that house as soon as we graduated from high school."

I jabbed at a spot on the wall about a foot from the painting. "My mother is standing here. And that's my father there. Tally's beside him." The blood had risen to my fingernail.

"Look at it."

"At what, Rory?"

"Look at the fucking painting."

"I can see it from here."

"Look at it."

Janet approached the mantel.

"Closer."

"Rory."

"Closer."

"In the name of God, what do you want me to see?"

"I painted the truth. That's what you're looking at." I gestured toward the blurred image of Cameron at the centre of the picture. "Cameron was always in motion. Adrian was always breezy. Those are my brothers. And me, I'm doing what I did for years, watching, wondering where the next attack would come from."

My knees were weak and I sat on the ottoman Janet had vacated.

"I was a good sentry. I protected my brothers because I'm the oldest of us three. That's what you're supposed to do when you're the oldest, Janet."

"I didn't betray you, Rory."

"Then what were you doing? Protecting me? From Kolerus? Tally?"

"Yes, I was protecting you."

She sat beside me, misjudging the rage in my eyes for defeat, reaching across my lap to cradle my hand. I seized her palm.

"You're frightening me, Rory."

Her fingers flinched in my grasp. "You're not Cameron, Janet. You can't slip away from what I'm telling you. I'm always going to have to be the watcher. It's my fate. I can't escape from that picture no matter how hard I try." She exhaled as I slowly loosened my clutch on her wrist. "But I can leave this room. I can leave you."

"Is that what you want to do? Leave me?"

"No. I'm not going to leave you."

"Then we'll never speak of this again?"

"If that's what you've decided."

I brought her hand to my face, kissing each small knuckle.

"Funny," I said.

"What's funny?"

"I never noticed these before," I said, looking at the back of her hand.

"What is it?"

"Liver spots."

"Goddamn you."

I STAYED ON at the cottage for the rest of the autumn. Alone. I was deeply alienated from any sense of my work and needed to spend time with myself. I brooded for the first few weeks, disengaged, occasionally eavesdropping on whatever passed through my mind, ignoring most of it. I kept the curtains closed, shutting my eyes and ears to the tones of the colours around me, recalling my conversation with Susan on the beach at the Mira River, explaining the strange phenomenon that accompanied my puberty, synesthesia, a stimulus in one sense organ causing an experience in another. With me, it was hearing colour, sight and sound unifying, the tones and hues luring vivid sounds in my mind.

As a young student at the art college, I always faced an unsettling palette of colours, trying to make sense of the noise it unleashed in my head. It was impossible to concentrate during those early classes, nauseated by the oils and acrylics, finally stripping away the storming sea of colours so only two or three remained on the palette, gently lapping the edges of my brush so at last I could paint. My art teachers implored me to experiment with colour, and their urging turned to disdain by the completion of my second year. The instructors ignored me in the end, choosing to concentrate on other students. I disregarded them, convinced they were trying to extort my creativity.

I stopped painting anything that satisfied me, blaming the instructors, and was on the brink of quitting school when my curriculum advisor told me I might benefit from a term away from the college, at another school or as an apprentice with a studio where I could receive credits to apply to my degree.

So I chose Venice. The museums, churches, and palaces were still recovering from the cataclysmic floods that swept over the city in the mid-sixties. I joined a restoration project housed at a massive warehouse close to the *Arsenale* you mentioned, Adrian.

I don't share your vivid recollection of Venice because I didn't explore much of the city while I was there. Though I can still hear the church bells, pealing out over the city, especially in the early evenings while I walked home to the dormitory.

In one corner of the warehouse an art restorer reclined on a low scaffold, obscuring the lower two-thirds of a tall painting, a mask on his face, studying flakes of pigment on the canvas with a magnifying glass.

Over the course of my term in Venice I was taught to consider the myriad of details in a painting, sculpture, or icon, sometimes obscured by the restorer's body as I gazed over his shoulder. The work was done quietly, and we watched in agonizing silence, standing for hours as an artist mottled a tiny section of canvas with undercoating, repeatedly daubing it with his sponge.

I emerged from the gloomy warehouse at dusk after my ten-hour shifts, the early evening skies often overcast, devoid of any threat of colour to deafen me in my fatigue.

On my first free Sunday I decided to visit the Basilica San Marco, choosing it because our class had studied its mosaics during an art history seminar the year before. The mosaics in the Basilica are fashioned from thousands of small glass and stone pieces, anchored with mortar.

It wasn't a busy day at the church, the throngs of summer tourists long departed. Yet as I viewed the mosaics, low mumbling followed me and intensified into a barbed racket.

Suddenly sunlight pierced the cupolas high above my head, washing across the tiles that were angled by the artists to reflect as much light as possible. The gilded hues overwhelmed me, not with a feeling of elation but with nausea. It was then I realized the clamour distracting me on my tour was coming from inside my head. It was as if the colours were speaking to me, but I couldn't understand what was being said. It wasn't words I heard, but sounds. I sat down and closed my eyes, concentrating on my breathing, and soon the sounds abated, replaced by the timbre of light footsteps fron the other visitors or the catch of a cough in someone's throat.

As shocking as it was, the experience was familiar and I realized there had been other occasions when the brilliance of colour had seized me, listening to the chatter of the blue river when Susan dipped below the water or the echo of Mom's cranberry nail polish when she scolded me with her finger. Sitting there in the church, with my eyes closed, I realized I was able to hear colour. When I opened my eyes and glanced up at the golden cupola, the clamour started again, reflecting off the tiles, quieting as the sun outside fell behind a cloud.

At the warehouse, my eyes only ever fell upon the piece before me, sectioned off, dulled from years of grime, nothing too dazzling to distract from the challenge at hand. By the end of my apprenticeship I discovered the colour that *sounded* best to me, red.

In the meantime, I became a valuable member of the restoration team that autumn, the restorers trusting my judgment. I heard sounds as I mixed pigments, and waited until the sounds harmonized before passing the palette to my delighted master.

But I don't want to leave you with the impression the work I undertook was important in any real way. I cleaned brushes, ground and mixed the equivalents of fifteenth-century paints, and counted strokes as I applied layer after layer of the same colour to a practice canvas, in a scene reminiscent of the studios of Titian or Bellini. Only those apprentices, after months, maybe years, at least had the opportunity, under the watchful eye of their masters, to apply their skill to some small section of a great work, always in the style of their master.

The master restorer who headed my team was a great admirer of Titian. He kept urging me to visit any of a number of museums and churches in the city to view his work. The memory of my disagreeable experience at the Basilica returned each time he pressed me to get out and see the art of the city.

But on the day I left Venice, I decided to venture forth one last time, only I chose a venue less noisy than the Basilica. Maybe you've been to the Church of Santa Maria Gloriosa dei Fraci, Adrian, and have gazed upon Titian's *The Assumption of the Virgin*.

Walking down the centre aisle toward the altar, you were probably shocked, as I was, by the size of the altarpiece, more than twenty feet in height.

Titian baptized each of his canvases with a landscape of reds, imbued with a fire he later tamed through layer after layer of glaze, revealing an infinite canvas of light, shadow and colour.

This was to be my experience of the *Assumption*, a covenant between the view and the viewer, bound by a sense of unity. The sounds in my head were never as harmonious as at that moment, as I gently swayed on my feet and looked upon the masterpiece.

To steady myself, I applied the four questions of art criticism to the *Assumption*: *What do I see? How is the work organized? What is happening? What is the artist trying to say?*

Without doubt, the *Assumption* is a work of passion. Titian's flesh tones are blood-warmed, the entire canvas bathed in a resonant harmony of light. I try to place myself in Titian's studio centuries before, pondering the virgin canvas, washed in red grounding, then layer after layer of glaze applied to it. Was Titian attempting to still the noise in his head as he painted? Did he also hear colour? From my vantage point, standing at the altar in the Friars' Church, I counted twenty-seven shades of red. Twenty-seven notes chimed in my head.

I've been working with reds ever since, discovering more sounds, more shades of colour than I ever imagined possible. For a long time I wanted to return to Venice, to gaze again upon *The Assumption of the Virgin* and start counting each degree of Titian's red spectrum, opening my ears to sounds I missed the first time, sounds beyond what I've discovered in my own *Red on Red* portfolios these past two decades.

But I no longer want to do that because I have decided to stop painting.

I APPLIED THE FOUR questions of art criticism to myself during my retreat at the cottage last autumn. Standing before a mirror one afternoon, I wondered who was staring back at me.

What do I see?

I settled for the first answer that came to mind. A man of early middle age.

How am I organized?

Leaning close to the mirror, I turned my face from side to side, examining my reflection from the corner of my eye. My sideburns are trimmed high to remove the grey tufts sprouting below my ears. My hair is longish but not long, brushing the collar of my T-shirt, ringing the back of a long neck. Dark eyes, deep brown. High cheekbones, the same cheekbones as the two of you, and as our father. A small Adam's apple visible only when I swallow, not a forceful throat. Our father's wide shoulders and narrow hips.

My stomach is flat, legs slightly bowed. Long eyelashes, like all of my brothers, like pictures of our father's father. A solid weight, but not stocky, comfortably filling out a height of six feet. Thin wrists, often hidden by long cuffs, but appropriate on Tally's slighter frame. Good teeth, white, capped, the incisors a little too sharp, but there's nothing angular about the face, the eyebrows thick and arched. It's a nice face. We're a family of attractive men, worth a second glance.

Signs of my craft can't be found on the skin of my hands. I don't have Cameron's calluses or the burn scars from your hot ovens, Adrian. But I do have crow's feet, from years of squinting at canvases and from a vanity of sorts. I refuse to wear glasses.

My eyes don't have your sparkle, Adrian, and they lack Cameron's confidence or Tally's *legerdemain*. The green specks ringing my pupils are iridescent, shiny at times, like glass, possibly denoting a lack of depth, deflecting the view away from me.

What is happening to me?

Disillusion and smouldering anger stare back at me. I sought satisfaction in painting, stilling the noise of the canvas, replacing it with a timbre more assuaging to the ear than to the eye. That's why I've failed in my work, wanting people to hear rather than see the composition of the canvas, symphonic rather than visual. In assessing my modest collection of reviews over the years I find from the beginning I misunderstood the critics when they repeatedly referred to my "prolific brush," failing to realize that sometimes to be abundant is also to be adequate, average, and banal.

What is the artist trying to say?

It was the only question of the four I hadn't answered.

Closing my studio at the cottage before I returned to Toronto was an undoing, an act of deconstruction. I managed to pack away my supplies. All that was left was one unfinished painting of Janet I'd started in the spring. My first portrait in years. I stripped away the layers of paint, one by one, seeking a less guarded voice beneath, asking myself over and over, what was I trying to say with this painting in the beginning, what was its original language of sounds? Like unravelling a sweater and being left with a ball of yarn on the floor, neither sheep nor sweater, just wool.

I was searching for the inspiration of my work, the impetus that propelled me again and again to revisit one colour. Red.

What was I trying to say?

I liked the sound of red, comforted by rolls of dyed canvas, a warm and innocuous cloak between me and the world. I used the lulling refrain of red to protect the equanimity in my life, careful not to upset its serenity or set it vibrating. It was time to discard that cloak, because if I wanted to engage with life I had to stop painting.

Cameron

THE BIG B's SELLING the family home, boys, so you might want to give him a call, in case there's anything kicking around the basement or attic you want to get your hands on before the place is sold. Me, I'd like to check out the cubbyhole in his old bedroom to see if his monster models are still there. On the other hand, it might bring back some bad memories, seeing that he probably still blames me for smashing them. Of course, the Big B has been blaming me for a lot of things lately, but I'll get back to that later. That's what an act of kindness gets you. When he went off to college I packed the models in boxes and stored them in the cubbyhole so they wouldn't get busted.

He had quite a collection, Dracula, Frankenstein, Wolfman, Phantom of the Opera, Creature from the Black Lagoon,

Hunchback of Notre Dame, Godzilla, and the Mummy. Each of those plastic models was hand-assembled. I knew they were his pride and joy because he displayed them on three shelves he built himself. But they ended up in the basement after he went to college, covered in a thin film of dust that made them look even spookier. The glue wore out on some of the models and the limbs fell off. As a result, Dracula was an amputee, and the Hunchback was headless. I re-glued every one of those monsters, dusted them off, and put them away in the cubbyhole for safekeeping.

The Big B didn't see it that way. He came home one weekend from college and dragged me to the cubbyhole, shoving my head through the tiny door, the collar of my shirt bunched in his fist, pointing a flashlight into the far corner.

Every one of the models was smashed. He cuffed the back of my head and practically threw me out of his bedroom. He wouldn't let me explain that dad had insulated the cubbyhole and probably tossed the boxes around without caring what was inside.

Anyway, I wanted to give you a heads-up, in case you're interested in anything else still at the house.

ON TO OTHER MATTERS. I had a good chortle reading about you and Susan, Rory. I knew all about that, had forgotten all about it, really. When she found out nobody had died when Skylab returned to earth, she blamed me for her act of charity on you.

Most times, when Susan was about to tell me something she thought might make me crazy, she'd get this tightness around her eyes and mouth, waiting for me to explode, which I did most times. But when she told me about you and her, I felt something different. If Susan still wanted me after fooling around with you, then I couldn't be all that shabby. You had your head screwed on straight, Rory, you knew what you wanted to do with your life, you turned heads, even if you never seemed to notice the babes gawking at you when you walked past. You had all those qualities, Rory, and I could see why Susan took advantage of the moment that afternoon on the river. It made me feel good to know that Susan approved of you that day, because I did too.

Since we're revealing secrets, dirty and otherwise, I have one I've kept to myself for years. A big one. It came up in a conversation with mom after my mental *slide*. It seems the Big B, the first-born son, was actually son number two. There, I've got your attention, don't I? And, something else, the Big B was a twin. But I'm getting ahead of my story.

After my episode with the staple gun I was sent to the Nova Scotia Hospital for ninety days of observation. Although I was allowed to have visitors, I didn't encourage any, other than Kalim. I knew the institution had informed the folks, because Kalim told the hospital they were my next of kin and they turned to the Big B for advice, deciding, in the end, that it was probably best if I was left to myself to *heal* during those ninety days. They also thought it was best that I tell both of you what had happened, but I guess you could say that slipped my mind. I know all of this because I called mom a few weeks before I was released from the asylum and she told me. I thought a week at home would put their minds to rest in case they were harbouring any misgivings about my sanity. I didn't say any of that on the phone, just that I wanted to visit, and mom thought it was a good idea, asking me if lemon meringue pie was still my favourite.

Two days later, the Big B showed up at the hospital for a

visit. He spent most of the hour sitting in a chair across from me in the visitor's lounge, his fingers tucked under his chin like a praying mantis.

He didn't waste any time telling me the folks thought I might be more comfortable staying at his farm rather than with them. Let me tell you, if there was any comfort to be had, it sure wasn't going to be camping out with the Big B, but I didn't tell him that.

I wanted to know how I was supposed to fill my time at his farm during the days, while he was at school. At least I could do some repairs around the house for the folks. The house, he said, didn't need any repairs. When I told him there were always things to be fixed in a house, he placed his palms on the armrest of the chair and leaned toward me, as if he was getting ready to pounce.

In the last five years, he had put a new roof on the house and replaced the furnace and windows. The only other work the house needed was new wiring. And unless I was an electrician I should just back off.

He was so engrossed in his rant that he didn't notice one of the more colourful patients on the ward enter the lounge and slide into a chair directly behind him, rocking back and forth while he chewed on the hem of his johnny shirt, mumbling to himself.

And when I indicated that mom had hinted to me several times about getting the hardwood floors sanded, and that I was a carpenter, the Big B was ready for that argument too. Why sand the floors? She'd only wear them down again with her constant pacing and fretting about me.

Ouch.

The patient behind the Big B made a loud hacking sound, as if he was about to hurl a goober at the back of our Big Brother's head. The Big B didn't flinch.

Why did he think I was such a threat to the folks? Anyway, I told him it was none of his business. It had nothing to do with him.

He was on his feet in an instant, his shouts escaping into the corridor outside the lounge. The gibbering patient was rocking back and forth, mimicking the Big B's departing epitaph. *Nothing to do with me? They're my parents.*

"They're *my* parents, too," I answered, careful not to raise my voice. I didn't want to attract the attention of the interns who patrolled the hallways.

That stopped the Big B momentarily. Judging by his expression you'd think he had never considered this. And do you know what? I don't think he had. I honestly believe the Big B didn't see *his* parents and *our* parents as the *same* parents.

He was out of the room in a heartbeat. Not so much as a goodbye. I'll always be able to recognize the Big B in a crowd. All I have to do is look for his backside.

Realizing that a week of lemon meringue pies at the folks' house would soon taste sour if the Big B hovered during my visit, I called mom to tell her that I would wait until the summer.

"Your father and I were just thinking about you," mom said, when she figured out who it was on the other end of the line. I let it pass, but if there was any truth in what she was saying it was that they were just talking about me. While we chinned, I answered all the questions in my head that I wanted her to ask me, but she didn't: Where are Susan and the baby? *Vancouver.* Are they coming home? *Susan's lawyer served me with divorce papers a couple of weeks ago.* What about the baby? *Mary Anne will do fine. Susan will make sure of it. I'll do my part and stay away.* Forever? *For a while.* Are you working? *Yes. Kalim and I are full partners now.* Who's Kalim? *He's my best friend. He's been my best friend for years.* Do you miss Mary Anne? *Very much.* Are you angry with Susan? *No.* Do you love her? *Very much.* I think she loves you. *Do you?* Did you know we have new hardwood floors upstairs? *No.* Cost us a fortune.

Then I found myself responding to her actual questions, not the ones floating around in my head.

"Did you know your father and I never planned more children after Talbot?"

"Never planned or never wanted?"

"Is there a difference?"

"Between not planning and not wanting? I think so."

Had I missed something? Were we in the middle of a conversation about the grief I'd put them through over the last few months?

"Are you listening to me, Cameron?"

"Sure, I just got distracted for a second. I didn't hear what you were saying. Back up."

"I said Talbot told me he doesn't have any intention of planning a family."

"Is Talbot getting married?"

"Are you all right, Cameron?"

"Yes, yes. I just missed that last bit."

"Why? Did he tell you he's getting married?"

"No, mom, Talbot never mentions Beth. What does this have to do with a family? I'm not following."

"Then you should listen, shouldn't you?"

Dead air.

"I hate repeating myself, you know that."

More dead air.

"We were talking about children, and Talbot said he doesn't plan to have any. I told him he'd change his mind when he gets married. After his birth, your father and I didn't—"

"—plan on having any more children. I got it now. Thank you."

Wait a minute.

"Why?"

"Why what, dear?"

"Why weren't you planning any more kids after Talbot?"

"He was a difficult birth."

"I can imagine."

"When his brother died I was devastated."

"His brother? Who are you talking about?"

"Talbot's twin."

"Talbot was a twin?"

"I've told you that."

"First time I've heard a word about it."

"I thought I had told all of you."

"It's something I'd remember, mom. Rory and Adrian have never said anything about it. Or Talbot."

"Well, I'm telling you now. Talbot was the second twin. His brother was stillborn. Imagine the state I was in, Christmas morning, the nurse handing me a dead infant. Then the contractions started again. I was having another baby. A second one!"

"You didn't know you were having twins?"

"No. After the shock of the stillborn and the agony of the second birth, I couldn't even look at your brother. I was spent. It was a terrible time, Cameron. Terrible."

"Does Talbot know about this?"

"Of course he does. But. . ."

"But?"

"Nothing."

"Christ, mom, don't leave me hanging."

"Watch your language, Cameron."

"What were you going to say?"

"When the baby was born dead, he was buried the same day. We didn't tell Talbot about his brother until he was a teen. I wouldn't bring it up, if you're talking to him."

"Why not?"

"We didn't even name the child, Cameron. Don't bring it up. Ever."

"I won't say a word. To him. I guess you changed your mind later."

"About what?"

"Having more kids."

"These things happen."

"You must've been shocked when you got pregnant again."

"I bought a bicycle."

My mind wandered again, remembering the time the three of us decided to fix up some old bikes and sell them around the neighbourhood to supplement our meagre allowances. We spent the summer hunting the junkyards, searching for the prize, an old discarded bicycle with a good frame. We must've hauled home a dozen of those old bikes from the creek, which was known locally as the wash brook by older residents in the area, including the folks. It was a pretty sad collection, with flat tires and rusty handlebars. But the wheel rims were still good. Dad wouldn't float us the cash to buy new tires because he was afraid some kid might kill himself on a bike we sold him. He should've told us that before we spent weeks hammering those twisted rims into shape.

By the end of the summer we didn't have a dime to show for our enterprise. We waited until it was pitch black one night and walked the bikes to the top of our steep street on Hardwood Hill. Adrian led the way. We lined up, each of us straddling a bike with its naked steel rims. On the count of ten we were off. Rory first, followed by me, then Adrian. For the first five or ten seconds you could only hear a chorus of steel on pavement, but as the bikes picked up speed the friction between the steel rims and the street ignited sparks. We whistled like cattle rustlers as spinning lassos of flame rolled down the hill. An explosion of orange, yellow, blue, and green fireworks. The rims lost their strength halfway to the bottom of the hill and the flames sputtered as the bikes wobbled. A few last spitting sparks and we were off them, racing up the hill with three more bikes. Some of the neighbours were on their verandas, egging us on. The next day we found dozens of skid marks, carbon streaks that slowly faded from the asphalt over the next couple of weeks. I thought dad was going to skin us alive.

"I didn't know you had a bike, mom."

"I rode it every day the first four months I was pregnant with you boys. Rode it over every pothole in the city."

"To keep in shape?"

Dead air.

"I have to go, dear. Your father's pointing at his watch. You know what that means."

"You've been talking too long."

"Goodbye."

"Good—"

Dead air.

YOU KNOW, I keep thinking about that fairy powder falling on me when we were infants, because I'm really popular with the poofs, Adrian. The few times you took me clubbing over the years, you always said I was more at ease in gay bars than you were. I even had to teach you how to dance!

Remember that drunken guy hitting on you in that bar in Montreal? What was it called? Oh yeah, Cox, like I'd forget a name like that. When the drunk figured out we were identical, it turned him on, he wanted to have a ménage à trois.

I still remember that week I spent with you, Adrian, getting away from Oshawa for a couple of days, before Manpower whisked me to Windsor and then to Winnipeg. We had a good time that weekend, lots of bellyaches. You kept trying to convince me to move to the city. Even if you meant it, which I think you did, I didn't think you needed me hanging around, crowding your space. I knew you were spreading your wings in those years, even if you wouldn't introduce me to your beau of the hour. I miss you, Adrian, I really do. We've got to get together soon. Have some laughs.

I'm very sorry Claes died of AIDS. As far as I know, I've never met anyone who was HIV-positive or sick with AIDS. Take care of yourself.

And for the record, Adrian, just as with the folks, you never ever sat me down to tell me you were gay. Instead, you took me to that bar in Montreal to let me figure it out for myself. Which I already had. Even before you told the Big B about what was going on with your boyfriend in high school, Susan had tipped off Rory and me. I'll always remember how frustrated Susan was because she didn't get any response from either of us.

"Aren't you going to say something?" she asked, looking from Rory to me.

Silence.

"Adrian is a . . ." Susan didn't know what to call you, Adrian. This was before the word *gay* was common. "He's a . . . *bachelor*," she blurted, finally.

"A bachelor?" we said, in unison.

"Like your uncle," Susan explained. "Adrian told me you have an uncle in Halifax. He's a *bachelor*." We both grinned, probably not the response she was expecting, but it seemed to please her because she started laughing too.

She was referring to Uncle Theo. He was actually dad's older cousin, but we grew up calling him Uncle Theo. He was short and stocky and always giggling. He had a *friend* who *boarded* with him, mom explained, on one of our rare visits to Halifax as kids. I don't remember the *friend*'s name, but he was also short and overweight.

Uncle Theo had three jokes he told whenever we saw him, and every time he told one of the jokes, his friend tittered as if hearing it for the first time. When we stayed there, the four adults played bridge while we sat in front of Uncle Theo's TV in the living room, switching channels all evening because he had cable and we didn't. Mom and dad slept in the spare bedroom and the three of us slept on an air mattress in front of the TV.

On one of our trips home to Sydney I asked mom where Uncle Theo's friend slept. Mom exchanged a quick glance with dad in the front seat.

"They share a bedroom," she said.

"Why?" I asked. As far as I knew, only married people shared bedrooms.

"Because they're . . . bachelors," she said. "Bachelors share bedrooms."

I'VE JUST WRAPPED UP a three-week tour with the choir in Western Canada. Most of the time we were billeted, which was a real pain in the arse because many of our hosts were *devout*. Yawn. The time would have passed quicker had I remembered to pack our journal. When I got home after the tour I found it on the bed where I had left it when I packed my suitcase. I'm not a bed and breakfast kind of guy, so I dipped deep into my per diem several times on the road and took a room at a hotel to escape the bible talk among our hosts. I shouldn't bitch too loudly, though. Met some nice people along the way and even managed a satisfying rendezvous one night in Saskatoon after the concert. A sweet little thing she was.

Most of the time was spent on the bus that took us from Winnipeg to Vancouver. I sat across from the driver, more to keep him awake than for the conversation. And I didn't screw up on the tour, didn't lose my voice or keep anybody waiting at the altar. That's a pun. The concerts were in churches, so you know, church, altar.

We were all getting weary by the end of the tour. Folks wanted to get home to their hubbies or wives, and a couple of the boys to boyfriends. But while the rest of the choir was singing on their last note, so to speak, I was excited because our final concert was in Vancouver. I had tickets for Mary Anne, Susan, and her hubby, Jimmy.

It was my first time meeting Jimmy, and I was surprised to discover that he wasn't as tall as I had expected. He's quite youthful in the face, but you might think he was much older than Susan if you saw him from a distance, because his hair is completely white. When we met he gave me one of the warmest handshakes I've had in years.

It was a night of firsts, the first time Susan and Mary Anne ever heard me sing in public and the first time I was meeting the man in Susan's life. Privately, I was also celebrating an anniversary, no meds, prescribed or otherwise. Since dope is organic, I consider it an herb, one of the food groups, so it doesn't count.

It was also the first time I sang a solo in the program. One of our soloists lost his pipes just before the concert and the conductor asked me to replace him. And no, Adrian, I didn't sing the sixth movement from Vivaldi's *Gloria*. The piece is written for a soprano, although I didn't know that before joining the choir. I don't remember ever singing that piece when you were around, so I was surprised you mentioned it to your friend Nino. Years ago, when I lived in Windsor, I boarded with an Italian widow who sang arias while she made supper. She must have heard me humming the Vivaldi piece in the shower, because she insisted on teaching me the words.

That night, with my family in the front pews of the church in Vancouver, I made my debut as a soloist. When I finished I got a happy nod from the conductor, the only time I'd ever seen him crack a smile in concert. I didn't dare look at Mary Anne or Susan. But it must have charmed them, because after the concert there were plenty of hugs, not only from Mary Anne and Susan, but Jimmy as well. He shook my hand like I was Andrea Bocelli.

Next thing I knew, they were whisking me off to Chinatown for a late-night supper, and the only one not gabbing was me.

Now there was a first. Three sets of lips flapping faster than a flag in a hurricane. I felt connected. I was their flagpole. Mary Anne was leaning into my left shoulder and Susan's leaning into my right. Jimmy's head was on a pivot, his eyes more on us in the back seat than on the road.

"To Cameron," they said. The three of them, holding up their glasses in a toast at the restaurant.

"Thank you," was all I could manage, as I sheepishly looked at my plate, but not before I caught a familiar flame in Susan's eyes, a flame that had grown through the years. Affection. And it was directed at me.

I didn't want to look up from my plate, afraid I'd meet silence and discover that the last half-hour was only something I had imagined, met by the clacking of three sets of chopsticks, knitting needles stitching an awkward silence.

But it wasn't like that at all.

"So how'd you end up in the choir, Cameron?"

I met Jimmy's question with my eyes, and I hesitated for the briefest of heartbeats, wary. But there was no one-two punch behind his question, nothing in his tone that was going to hurl me to the other side of now.

"I love to sing," I said.

"Daddy always sang me to sleep," Mary Anne said.

"Me too," Susan added.

"When did you start singing?" Jimmy asked.

"The truth?"

"I've told Jimmy to expect nothing less than the truth from you, Cameron," Susan said, squeezing his hand.

"Did you now?" I said, grinning.

"Daddy started singing in the asylum," Mary Anne said.

"Is this my story or yours?" I asked, the grin spreading to deep corners of my mouth that I didn't know I had.

"Sorry, Daddy. It's your story."

"I started to sing in the asylum."

I THINK MOST PEOPLE are under the impression that you enter a mental institution to get cured. In truth, you spend most of your time waiting. You wait for the next round of meds, the next smoke from the orderly, which isn't too enjoyable because he holds the lighter and sits with you while you puff out your lungs. It's waiting for breakfast, lunch, supper, and a night snack.

While I waited, I didn't spend much time in my room. I preferred the common areas, playing chess or perfecting my hand at *crazy* eights. There wasn't a hell of a lot of rehabilitation going on. At most, I met with a busty shrink three times during my ninety-day incarceration and she seemed satisfied with the answers I gave to her litany of who, what, where, when, and why, ticking off my responses on a chart.

Name?

Cameron Hines.

Occupation?

Carpenter.

Address?

Maynard Street, Halifax.

A bunch of other banalities before we came to the big question.

"Do you ever feel angry?"

"Yes."

"Do you get angry with other people?"

"Yes."

"Toward yourself?"

"Yes."

"Toward your twins?"

"My twins?"

She looked down at her notes for clarification.

"We're not twins," I said.

"Is that important to you? Identity?"

"I don't have twin brothers. We're triplets. We don't refer to each other as twins."

"Do you ever feel anger toward your brothers?"

"Sometimes. We're brothers."

"Did you ever hit your brothers?"

"No."

"Why not?"

"Should I have?"

"You tell me."

"People in glass houses shouldn't cast stones," I said.

She arched her eyebrows. "That's profound."

"Isn't it."

"What do you mean?"

"If I threw a rock at one of my brothers, I'd be hitting myself."

"So you never fought as children?"

"We fought all the time. We just never hit each other."

"Did you feel like you grew up in a glass house?"

"Sometimes. Sometimes it was like living in a house of mirrors."

"Mirrors?"

"The ones at the circus. The house of mirrors. It's the same face looking in all the mirrors, but the person who's looking back is all wrong. Sometimes Rory was tall and skinny and Adrian was short and fat. I could never figure that out."

"What about your parents? What did they look like in the mirrors?"

"They always waited outside."

I think the chesty doctor was looking for a pattern in my responses, my own moronic code.

nO. Yes. Yes. nO.

Patient cognizant of events leading to being institutionalized.

Yes. nO. nO. Yes.

Consistency in responses to queries.

nO. nO. Yes. Yes.

Recommend ninety-day conditional release.

Yes. Yes. nO. nO.

Patient fixated with my big bOObs.

There was a skinny kid on the ward, no more than nineteen or twenty, he was all angles, with long, stringy hair and some deep acne scarring on his forehead that he tried to keep covered with his bangs. He had a beat-up guitar and sat in the music room every day, strumming for hours. Well, it felt like hours. After one too many games of chess, I moseyed on into the room and picked up another guitar and started strumming along with the kid. At first he didn't pay any attention to me, but it wasn't long before he noticed I was following him on the chords. When he got to the chord where he'd been making the same mistake for the last hour he eased up with his fingers to hear me play it right. He flashed a big smirk and watched my fingering and the next thing I knew he was following my fingers and after another ten minutes he wasn't sounding too bad. I started singing while we played and he was humming along with me. His voice was a little high, so I lower my pitch and the kid adjusted his pitch to match.

"You should sing in a choir," he said, still strumming.

I stopped playing and looked at him as if he's . . . nuts.

"A choir?"

"Or a band," he said, quickly, looking down at his fingers again, striking the wrong chord.

I don't know what was wrong with the kid, if anything. He was still there when I left, but at least he was a better musician.

During my last session with the shrink, she asked me if I had any hobbies. Hobbies must be a good thing, I thought. So I lied.

"I sing," I answered.

"Are you in a choir?"

Dead air.

A couple of weeks later, after I was home again, I told Kalim about the shrink and the kid, how they'd both mentioned the choir.

"I told you to stay away from my dad's records," Kalim said, stringing his tennis racket, acting like he's not really listening to what I'm saying, but I can tell he's interested and pleased.

When I first took over the rooming house his dad owned, I found a box of Mario Lanza records in the attic.

"Mario Lanza was really popular in Malaysia," Kalim told me. "They used to play him on the radio all the time. My dad spent a lot of money on those records. I think it made him feel more British. Even though Lanza was an American."

The only operas I'd ever heard of growing up were the daytime soap operas. I gave a couple of the records a spin, and the next thing I knew I was singing along with the great maestro in the attic. Months after Kalim's dad collected his records,

I was still humming Puccini while I drywalled. It just stuck with me.

"Have you ever thought of joining a choir?" Kalim asked.

"When did everybody start listening to my voice?" I asked, sucking back an India Pale Ale.

"We've been listening for years, Cameron, you couldn't hear our praise over all that yelling going on in your head," he said.

I don't know why, but my body started to tingle.

"How do you audition for a choir?" I asked him.

"I guess you have to join a church," he said.

As it turned out, I didn't. I strolled over to Dalhousie University one afternoon and found a secretary in the music department, and she gave me a list of choirs around the city. She asked me what kind of choral music I like, rhyming off styles and Latin names.

I shrugged my shoulders, wondering if she was just having fun with me, humouring me.

"Are you a tenor? Bass?" she asked.

"I don't know."

She asked me to sing a few bars.

"Right here?" I asked.

"Sure, the phone's not ringing. And the copier's broken," she said.

"Do you like Christmas carols?" I asked.

"Knock yourself out."

I was only going to sing the first verse, but she sat there with her mouth hanging open, so I sang everything I had memorized from "The Coventry Carol."

"Can you wait a minute?" she asked, dialling the phone with the eraser tip on her pencil.

Five minutes later I had an audition scheduled with the Nova Scotia Choir. Secretary girl's boyfriend was the choirmaster.

"By the way," she said, as I was going out the door, "you're a counter-tenor."

Now you have to understand, boys, the whole concept of an audition was foreign to me. During the days leading up to the tryout, I cancelled at least ten times in my head.

So I was there on the day of the audition, wearing a new sweater and clean skivvies. I'd practised "The Coventry Carol" a million times, figuring that if it had worked the first time it should work again. About twenty of us were auditioning that day and the section director split us into groups.

He positioned us on a set of risers, pointed to the guy standing beside me, and asked him to hum a note. Then we all sang the note. Next, we sang a scale and built some chords. Of course, I didn't know that's what we were doing at the time.

Everybody's nervousness had turned into concentration. The section director split us into groups of three and we were herded over to a piano to sing warm-ups, instructed to ascend as high as we could go, and then down. He assigned each of us a different note to see if we could hold our own note in the triad.

Finally, we're called to the piano individually by the choirmaster. He played a chord cluster over and over to see if I could hear and then sing all of the notes he'd played. Which I could and did. All the while, I'm singing the words of "The Coventry Carol" in my head, waiting for my big moment. When it arrived, when he finally tells me that he wants to hear a song, it isn't the carol I've been rehearsing in my head. Instead, he asked me to sing "Happy Birthday to You."

Stunned, I looked around the room to discover that there

were only five of us left. During the afternoon his assistant had gone quietly around the room and dismissed the others. When the last of us finished singing the world's most popular song, I asked the choirmaster why he had made us sing that one.

"Because it's my birthday today," he said with a wink. "And you did it very well."

But not well enough to get an invitation to join the choir that day. Although he liked my voice, he wasn't impressed with the fact that I couldn't read music. Nonetheless, he made me an offer that afternoon, telling me that if I audited a course he taught on sight-reading at Dalhousie, he'd let me sit in with the choir at practice.

"What you're saying, then," I suggested, "is that we'll play it by ear?"

"Hopefully not for too long," he said, with another wink.

I NEVER MISSED a choir rehearsal, and I took two music courses that semester. It was easy to focus on the choir, school, and work because I had a void to fill. Susan and Mary Anne were gone. This void must have been deeper than the Bras d'Or Lake, because I enrolled in three more courses in the autumn and before I knew it, I was majoring in music. Between my happy trinity of activities, the early nineties flew by and graduation day quickly approached.

In the meantime, I'd stopped dating. I didn't even miss it, truth be told. The dating, that is, not the sex. I'd get home from a day's construction work, shower, and head off to class or the library. In between, I hung out with the choir three nights a week and on Saturday afternoons. Not that I was planning to replace sex with celibacy, a modern-day Gregorian monk, I just didn't have the energy or the patience to waste courting some babe over a couple of beers, hoping to score before last call, then dragging myself out of bed the next day to get to an early class or rehearsal.

Kalim was also busy during those years and made two trips to Borneo, returning with hundreds of photographs each time.

"That monkey has a hard-on," I said, after his first trip, referring to a monkey with a bulbous drooping nose, perched on a rock.

"They always have an erection," Kalim said, deadpan.

"Always?"

"Almost always."

It was the closest we had ever come to talking about sex. In all the years I'd known him, Kalim had never mentioned a girl-friend. I knew it was a sore spot between him and his parents. They had been pressuring him since high school.

He had several pictures of Mary Anne in a small bedroom he had converted into a meditation room after his first trip to Borneo.

"He's been very generous to her over the years," Susan told me during one of our late-night phone calls. Kalim had just sent Mary Anne a box of classical CDs. "And he's been a good friend for you, Cameron."

"I never thought you actually liked Kalim," I said.

"I liked Kalim a lot. I still do," Susan said.

"We never had him over for dinner."

"We never invited *anybody* over for dinner, Cameron. I hate cooking. Remember? We always ate out. Kalim joined us dozens of times."

"I'm glad you're telling me this."

"I'm sorry you didn't notice, Cameron. Besides, I didn't want to interfere too much."

"What do you mean?"

"Kalim was your *only* friend when we were together, Cameron. You needed him. *We* needed him."

Kalim called me from Borneo on the morning of convocation. We didn't chat for long. He was calling from a satellite phone in the jungle, every second costing a fortune. I had to repeat our two-minute conversation a dozen times for his father and mother, who were proudly sitting in their reserved seats waiting for me to receive my music degree.

Susan also graduated that summer, from UBC with a major in visual arts.

Susan never gave up on me. Okay, she divorced me, but she didn't shut me out of Mary Anne's life when they moved to Vancouver. We ended up having a good gab every couple of weeks and she often stayed with me for a couple of nights when she and Mary Anne came home to visit her mother in Sydney. And I made quite a few trips to Vancouver. They were good years and, how do I say this without sounding all Oprah, but Susan and I ended up as good friends.

SUFFICE IT TO SAY, Jimmy didn't get all the dirt at the restaurant that night. He got the crib notes. I studied music so I could join a choir. I sang with the Nova Scotia Choir for several years, and I've been with the Halifax Men's Choir since then.

After my story, we wrapped up dinner. It was late and Mary Anne had an early class in the morning. I noticed she looked a little tired, as if she'd missed a couple nights' sleep. I had a second concert the following afternoon and needed to get some shut-eye myself.

"Do you have any plans after the matinee?" Susan asked, slowing her pace as we headed for the car, keeping Mary Anne and Jimmy out of earshot.

"I've got a few hours to kill before the flight back to Halifax."

"Let's go for a drink," she suggested. "Just the two of us."

"Do we have some unfinished business?" I asked, poking her in the side with my hip.

"I've got some news. I want to bounce it off you before I decide whether or not it's good news," she said, poking me right back with her hip. "Tell you what, we'll go for a drink after the concert and I'll drive you to the airport."

"Deal," I said.

The following afternoon, we were sitting in a quiet bar, waiting for one of those seven-dollar strawberry daiquiris to come to our table.

"So what's on your mind?" I asked.

"Mary Anne wants to get married, Cameron," she said, with a chirp to her voice.

"It's still Jonathan, isn't it?" I asked. Mary Anne had met Jonathan in the first week of her music program at Simon Fraser University two years before. The first time I met him, I thought he was a basketball player, an Asian basketball player. Jonathan is Cantonese, all arms and legs, towering over me by four inches. Two inches is hair, which he wears high on his head, like Lyle Lovett. His eyes are set deep in his face, and when he looks at you, it feels like he's peering inside your skin. He's one of those people who never takes his eyes off you when you're talking to him.

"Of course it's Jonathan," Susan answered.

"So what's the problem?"

"They want to get married before the end of this year," she said.

"And you'd prefer they both wait until they finish their degrees?"

"Mary Anne's pregnant, Cameron."

"Oh," I said, grabbing for a handful of cashews.

"I'm not judging them," she said.

"But she'll have to take some time off from school," I said. "Are you afraid she won't go back to finish after she has the baby?"

"I want her to have amniocentesis, Cameron."

I looked at my hands, but not before I noticed her searching my face for a reaction.

"How do you feel about that?" she asked. I was aware that she was cupping my hands on the table. I was looking at her fingers and I started stroking her hands, kneading her palms with my thumbs. I was trying to find some response, but my mind was racing and I could feel my heart thumping in my chest.

She kissed the tips of my fingers, then folded my hands around her face, drawing me forward till my head found her shoulder. I lay there while she stroked my back.

"I love you, Cameron," she said. I leaned deeper into her neck, saying nothing.

It was a discussion we'd put off for years. As far as we both know, Mary Anne has never sought a link between the toxic residue floating around in my body when she was conceived, poisons I passed on to Susan in my sperm, and her blindness. Mary Anne was born blind and will be blind for her entire life. I left all the *how come* and *why me* discussions in my doctor's office years ago. Maybe Susan did a little digging of her own, but we've never talked about it. We can't change what is. All I have to do is look at the scars of thirty-seven stitches in my thigh and neck from the staple gun to remind me of the demons that masqueraded as grief and guilt in the attic.

"She should definitely have the test," I said. And we left it at that.

Mary Anne's expecting in March. That should give me just enough time to be able to look in the mirror and say the word *grandfather* without wanting to hurl.

IF EITHER OF YOU is planning on calling the Big B, you're in for a surprise. He's changed his telephone number. Not only that, it's unlisted. But then again, he probably gave both of you his new number, it's just me he's shutting out.

I don't blame him. I'd be pretty ticked myself if I found out that one of you had stolen my wallet. Do you remember the wallet, Adrian? The one the Big B lost the time we all went for lobsters in Main-à-Dieu? That would be, what, twenty-five years ago? So why, after all these years, does the Big B suddenly think that the wallet he lost on a beach was stolen, and by me?

Because you told him that I stole it, Rory. You were pissed off with me when I left the message on your answering machine. All I was trying to do was tip you off, and let you know that the Big B was talking about you and Janet behind your backs.

But you got mad at me instead of him. And you were still mad when you called him. The conversation probably went something like this.

You said, I hate it when Cameron gets high and leaves messages on my machine.

He said, How long has Cameron been doing drugs?

You said, For the love of God, Talbot, he's been a pothead for years.

He said, Coke? Heroin?

You said, Grass.

He said, It's all expensive.

You said, Cameron always finds the money. Stole your wallet once to pay for it. Remember? Anyway, why were you having a conversation about me, with Cameron, in the first place?

He said, You think your name never comes up? Back up for a second, are you sure he stole my wallet?

You said, He wasn't working that summer. Had a bag of grass the next day. You do the math. Now, back to the call. Cameron mentioned something about Janet and Kolerus.

On top of everything else the Big B thinks about me, I'm now a thief, and that doesn't sit well with him. I should have realized that something was brewing, because I hadn't heard from him in quite a while. Normally that wouldn't mean anything, because we don't always return each other's calls unless it's something urgent. It wasn't until I returned from the tour with the choir in June and opened my mail that I realized I hadn't spoken with Talbot since last summer! In fact, the last time I spoke with him was when he told me about the paintings, Rory. I have to admit, I felt a twinge of guilt.

But the eviction notice I was holding in my hands countered the guilt. And the eviction notice was from Talbot's lawyers.

I wish I could see the expression on both your faces right about now. When did Talbot buy Cameron's house? you might ask. Or, why would Cameron ever sell his house to Talbot?

The truth is, it was never mine to sell.

As you both know, I've been living in this house since I arrived in Halifax. Kalim's dad was always looking out for me, right from the start. For the first year, I didn't pay a dime in rent, and even after Susan insisted we pay something, it still didn't amount to much. Then Kalim's dad asked me if I wanted to buy the house. He wasn't asking much, but Susan and I didn't have any savings. I called the folks and asked them if they would lend me the money for the down payment. They needed a day to think it over. Two days later I got a call from Talbot. I knew he was going to tell me that the folks weren't lending me the money. Which he did. But then I must have let out a deafening and dramatic sigh of disappointment, because he had to repeat his own offer. He wanted to lend me the money. I accepted without thanking him, was going to but then I went crazy because this all happened just before I found out about Susan's abortion.

After I got out of the asylum, Talbot changed the terms of our agreement. If they had to put me away again before I repaid the debt, he might never see a dime from the money he loaned me.

The down payment was off the table.

But he was willing to offer me a private mortgage. If something should happen and I couldn't make the payments, he'd still have the house.

It wasn't as if Talbot was my landlord. He was the bank, he explained. He was offering me good terms over the life of the twenty-five-year mortgage. As long as I made my payments and kept the house insured, he didn't care what I did with it.

I wasn't so naive as to believe that it was an absolute act of charity on his part, despite his doe-eyed expression. The Big B was going to make a tidy profit from the house over the life of the mortgage, asking twenty-five percent more than Kalim's father.

I still thought it was a good deal. I couldn't very well accuse him of extortion when I was practically stealing the house from Kalim's dad. When the documents were drawn up, Talbot insisted that I come to Sydney and sign them in his lawyer's office. And it was during the drive to Sydney that I finally realized why the Big B was so eager to become my private banker. In his mind, it was only a matter of time before I lost my mind again. For good. I'd be in a straightjacket and he would get the house after all.

I would never give him that pleasure. When I arrived at the lawyer's office, I didn't want to spend any more time with Talbot than was absolutely necessary. I told him I had to be back in Halifax that evening because of a big job I had to start in the morning. I signed the documents and was gone again before the lawyer had a chance to put the cap back on his pen.

That was a big mistake.

In my haste to avoid a confrontation with the Big B, I declined his lawyer's offer to review the contract. I never did read the fine print. Until the eviction notice this summer.

Talbot had exercised his right to sell the house at any time during the life of the mortgage. My lawyer suspects the clause was inserted as an insurance policy so that the Big B could raise some ready cash by selling the house if he ever ran into financial problems. And although the clause stipulated that every penny I had paid into the mortgage, less interest, would be repaid to me, the Big B stood to make a lot of money from the sale.

I can't plead fraud or deception, because I kept on signing the papers every three years when the mortgage came up for renewal without reading them.

So why did he do it? Why is the Big B stealing the house out from under me after all these years? Because you told him that I stole his wallet twenty-five years ago, Rory. Steal a wallet. Steal a house. His eye for mine.

After he sells the house, the money he has to repay me, less interest, won't amount to enough to buy a house in Halifax in today's market. Of course, there's always the family home in Sydney, now on the market. If you do have the Big B's new number, Rory, tell him I'd like to put a bid in on it. Just don't remind him about all the smashed monster models in the cubbyhole upstairs.

Adrian

OCTOBER, COPENHAGEN

A YOUNG BUCK meets an old man at a bar, crying over his beer.

— What's the matter? the young man asks.

— I have a twenty-five-year-old lover at home. He cooks all my meals, cleans the house, and makes love to me every day.

— Then why are you crying?

— I can't remember where I live.

Aside from Nyhavn's schooners, brightly painted Dutch-styled build-ings, brawls, and vermin, the canals of Copenhagen are also renowned for tattoo parlours where sailors from around the world, on a night of revelry, haunt the canals, ending their evenings slouched on the tattoo artist's bench, the pricking of needles dulled by whiskey and beer while

their nervous hands frantically grasp hidden pockets sewn into their
shirts for reassurance the pickpockets who skulked along the cobbled
streets haven't lifted their worn money belts weighted down with the
tarnished coins from their meagre seafaring earnings.

IT IS A RATHER laboured description, written in Old Danish, from a faded guidebook among the stack of magazines in the waiting area of the tattoo parlour. Despite my comprehension of Danish, I have to read the passage several times to understand it.

This is my third session at Tattoo Anker. The hundred-year-old splintered bench is upholstered now, its legs groan when I shift my weight after half an hour. I have been lying on the bench for almost two hours, and the tattooist, Ole, grandson of the original Tattoo Anker, decides we should share a beer before he slips his hands into a fresh pair of rubber gloves to finish the last area of the motif he started on my back three weeks ago. It should take another couple of hours, another beer, and my only piss of the night.

Ole says I am tense this evening. I do not tell him I was angry when I arrived, angry with Talbot, angry for both of you. I'd suggest you do the same thing. Be angry with him, not each other. Otherwise, Talbot throws a switch, and you're two locomotives headed for a collision.

I haven't heard from him since mom and dad died. He doesn't write to me. I don't miss him. The only time I ever think about Talbot is when I am reading the journal, or writing in it. Even though we decided not to include him, it feels as if he is on every page.

Ole reaches behind to the base of his back, his long fingers manipulating his vertebrae. The result is a sudden cracking sound that I can feel through the floorboards. He's a long-limbed man, with big feet. Pale, but not sickly pale, he just looks like he doesn't get much sun. He wears slacks and an open-collared shirt, the pleats in the sleeves have been ironed, and there's a sprig of white hair at his throat. His brown leather shoes are old, but the leather is rich, there are no scuff marks, his fingernails are clean and manicured.

He looks like other Danish men of his generation, the pharmacist, the loan officer at a bank, or the clerk at the hardware store, always dressed casually but well. He's an attractive man, not handsome, his ears are big with droopy earlobes and his hair is wispy, cut straight across the back of his neck, unevenly, as if he does it himself, scissors in one hand and a mirror in the other, but his looks are dignified, if plain. And he has warm eyes. They remind me of Claes.

There is a lot of activity on the street outside. People laughing at jokes shouted across the canal. Choruses of voices raised in drunken song. Every once in a while somebody knocks at the door, but Ole has it locked, the Venetian blinds drawn. Still, we hear a hand pulling the latch, despite the sign he's hung in the window.

Ole doesn't want to be interrupted, not even for a moment. My back is a large commission for him, so losing a dozen tourists wanting coaster-sized butterflies on their arses is no great loss tonight.

The younger crowd prefer the tattoo parlours in the trendier parts of the city, especially those specializing in Celtic designs and offering piercing. They spend hours leafing through the thick photo albums, the flash books, scanning the tattoos.

Ole likes to work with colour, and this tattoo is important to him. He's designed it himself.

— Most people have no imagination, he says. They might look at a dozen flash books, but in the end it's always the same. Roses. Skull and bones. Pierced hearts.

— Anchors? I ask.

— No, he says, smiling. I haven't done any anchors. Foreigners think the name of the parlour, Tattoo Anker, is the Danish spelling of *anchor*. But it isn't, he explains. Anker is a man's name in Denmark.

Claes took me on a tour of the tattoo parlours in Nyhavn. We visited Ole's parlour last.

— Take a good look at the flash books, Claes said.

— Why? I asked. The albums are the same in all the shops.

— Not these, he said. Every one of these tattoos was created by Ole, his father, or his father before him.

Tattoo Anker's portfolios are unique. From a distance, tattoos of red hearts are blue. But if you look closely, there are red veins running through the hearts.

— They're worth the view, Ole had said. You just have to decide who it is you want that close to your skin. Who's worth getting the best view.

He said this to me when Claes and I decided to get our tattoos. Waves, tucked into the crooks of our groins, the ocean spray salting our hips.

Last month I walked into Ole's tattoo parlour for the first time since Claes died. Ole looked older, his hair completely white. He still had his trademark cigars, the sweet stale aroma something I remember from my first visit. He erupted in a short muffled cough every ten or fifteen minutes. I told him I wanted a tattoo on my back.

— Where on your back? he asked.

— All of it, I replied.

He took a few puffs on his cigar and asked me to remove my shirt.

— Turn around, he said.

He slid his wheeled chair toward me, running the palm of his hand along my skin, tapping the vertebrae.

— Take a deep breath, he said.

Fingers poked the skin.

— Twist your torso. Now to the other side and bend over.

He rolled the chair a few feet away from me and puffed deeply on his cigar.

— You have a long back, he said. A lot of canvas to fill. What kind of tattoo do you want?

— Nothing from the flash books, I said.

— An original?

— Yes.

— Colour?

— Yes.

— It will involve water, he said. Does that suit you?

— Yes.

He took a few more puffs on the cigar.

— I'll work on your back for three or four hours each time. If you want, we can do it over several days or once a week.

— Once a week, I said.

He placed the closed sign in the window, locked the door, and drew the blinds facing the street.

— I did another tattoo for you, he said.

— Yes.

— Show it to me.

I pulled down my pants to expose my hip.

— When did I do this one? he asked.

— Several years ago.

— I'm going to take some photos. Take off your pants, he said. Take everything off. I won't shoot your face.

He admires my nakedness, allowing his eyes to wander along my torso, cock and legs. His smooth hands cup my hips and he rotates me so that my back is facing him. With his finger he traces patterns, the muscles shift beneath his touch. He blows warm gusts of air over the skin, to see if goosebumps appear that could mar the lines he will paint with his needle.

He asks me to raise my hands above my head and with his fingernail caresses the skin under my armpits down to my hips. I am not ticklish. There will be no sudden convulsions as he tattoos my skin, jerking the needle from its path.

He takes several photographs of my back and I face him so that he can take a few more of the waves on my groin. Only now the waves are capped with foam. He hands me a paper towel to dry myself.

— I will touch you many times over the coming weeks, he says. You must understand that. And be comfortable with the lashing of the sea waves between your legs.

TONIGHT OLE AND I are discussing King Frederik, the current queen's father, who was famous for the tattoos that covered his body. Ole doesn't like it when I become quiet. And he doesn't like it when I tense up, like tonight, every time Talbot intrudes. So he tells me stories so I'll relax.

— There's a joke among tattoo artists, he says. A customer comes into the shop and is nervous about getting a tattoo that is permanent. What if I change my mind? the customer asks. How long will it last? Six months, the artist answers. That's not too bad, the client says. Yes, the artist says, it'll stay there six months after you're dead.

I laugh.

— Don't move, Ole says.

I remember Claes showing me the outline of the starfish tattoo he had on his shoulder. One of the arms was crooked.

— It's because I laughed, he said. You don't laugh when you get a tattoo.

Ole did all of Claes' tattoos and they were all connected with the sea. Ole and I share a cigarette. He holds up a mirror, angling it so I can look at the work he is finishing tonight.

— I remember Claes, he says.

— What do you remember? I ask.

— He didn't talk much.

I smile.

— Yes. I did enough talking for the two of us.

— You do like to talk, Ole says.

— Too much? I ask.

— No. You're one of those people who can talk. I'm more like your boyfriend Claes.

— A man of few words? I ask.

— Yes, he says.

I think about this for a few seconds. I have never considered myself talkative. Susan used to tell me that I ended all of my sentences with a smile. Most people use periods, she said.

— What would you prefer? I asked.

— Smiles, Adrian. Your smiles.

— You like it?

Ole has caught my reflection in his mirror. I have been smiling with the memory.

— Yes, I say.

I tell him what I have just been thinking. About smiles.

— Eskimo women had tattoos on their chins, Ole says. Sometimes they were used in choosing wives. If an unmarried girl smiled too much when she was tattooed, the lines were uneven. Men looked for girls with thin, tight lines on their chins. They were considered serious and hard-working.

Ole doesn't offer any further comment on Claes.

He puts on a fresh pair of gloves. The snap at the wrist is sharp.

I don't like the sound of rubber gloves. Once, Claes came down with a bout of food poisoning and it resulted in violent vomiting. He was too weak to clean the sides of the toilet. He insisted I wear latex gloves before I cleaned it. In case, he said.

— Wipe your tears, Ole says.

He passes me a Kleenex. I check my reflection in the mirror on the wall. He uses it to keep an eye on his clients when they're on his table, facing away from him. There are tears in my eyes.

— Do you want me to stop for tonight? he asks.

— No, I say.

— It's not too painful?

— The needle?

— Yes, the needle.

— No. Continue.

— Half an hour, Ole says. It'll be finished in half an hour.

ON A LOW TABLE, at eye level, Ole has placed a lava lamp, the kind that seesaws on a pivot, sending a gentle wave of blue glutinous liquid from side to side within the tank, reminding me of ocean breakers rolling toward the shoreline at high tide on a calm afternoon in Cape Breton.

Watching tides has always nauseated me and I don't like to be in anything bigger than a rowboat. But I love to swim. We three often raced each other into the waters at Ingonish Beach or Kennington Cove, diving into the waves, waiting for the next big breaker to carry us toward the shore, using our stomachs as surfboards.

Claes and I used to go swimming at the indoor saltwater pools in Copenhagen. The buoyancy of the water always surprised me. After four or five laps I discovered I wasn't a strong swimmer and had no real stamina.

On the beaches around Cape Breton during the summers, swimming was restricted to short ocean sprints, treading water, or floating on those rubber inner tubes in the rivers and lakes. In and out of the water a dozen times during an afternoon. I don't remember the time you got stung by the jellyfish at Mira, Rory. But when Claes and I went to the crowded beaches north of Copenhagen, it was to sunbathe and watch the crowds, a quick dip in the water to cool down. For Claes, swimming was a sport, for me it was recreation.

I wouldn't be surprised if a pair of flippers or a plastic snorkel is still tucked under the rafters in the basement of mom and dad's house. Do they belong to me? Or to you, Cameron? Or to you, Rory?

Will Talbot find them if he goes searching? Or will he find something else hidden on the beams? Like a wallet?

A wallet I hid under the rafters all those years ago, the wallet with his driver's license and all his other identification and a fat wad of bills. The wallet I had hidden to punish him. Because he had humiliated me once too often.

It was after being stalked by Joseph's father that I dropped the note in Talbot's mailbox, alerting him to what was going on that early summer. He knew Joseph's mother, that's the only reason I chose to tell him. If he talked to her, he might be able to settle things. Keep it from mom and dad. As I have told you, Talbot wrote a note back to me, insistent that I should return to Montreal. When I saw him a few days later, his eyes didn't hold any judgment when he looked at me. If anything, his eyes looked beyond me, as if he had decided that I had already left for Montreal. I was invisible.

It was lobster season and we three decided to have our only feed of the summer before I returned to Montreal the next morning. Talbot always bought his lobsters from a guy called Bobby, a former classmate at teacher's college who helped his father fish off Main-à-Dieu in the summers. I don't remember who told Talbot about our excursion, but he offered to drive us to Main-à-Dieu. Talbot liked to get fresh lobsters and cook them on the beach.

The four of us arrived at the wharf just as the boats returned to the harbour. The sky was full of gulls and there were three or four other cars waiting along the wharf. There was a haze over the water and thousands of tiny sparkles erupting from the waves. Visiting Main-à-Dieu always made me feel lazy. It is a quiet village, and the only real noise is the squawking of the birds when the boats return to harbour.

Talbot's friend Bobby beckoned us onboard to inspect his

catch. His fat cheeks were splotchy and the hair under his base-ball cap looked like it hadn't been washed in days. He wore a pair of old rubber boots and dirty, faded jeans.

Usually we bought a couple dozen lobsters and drove the car to one of the coves that dotted the coastline to cook them. The sudden lurch of Bobby's boat startled me, and it took me a few seconds to realize we were heading out into the harbour.

You both looked as surprised as I did, knowing I had no sea legs. I immediately collapsed on the bench at the back of the boat and stared at my feet while we crossed the harbour.

Any appetite I had had for lobsters was gone. There were plenty of coves, but Talbot kept urging Bobby to the next one, and the one after that. When my feet finally hit the sand on a beach an hour later, my legs were wobbly and I had to sit down to steady the spinning in my head. This is the worst part of sea-sickness, the vertigo I experience when I am onshore again, washing over me in waves for the next several hours.

While I stared at the sand, Talbot and Bobby kept both of you occupied with building the fire to boil the water. I was use-less. The only thing worse than the nausea and the dizziness was that I knew we had to cross the harbour again on the return trip.

Talbot ignored me the entire time we were on the beach.

You brought me a plate of lobster, Rory.

— I can't eat it, I said.

— In case you get your appetite back, you said. Reaching down to put the plate on the sand.

By the end of the afternoon I could finally close my eyes without feeling like I was going to pass out.

Bobby took one look at me as we boarded for the return trip and started to chuckle.

— Seasick? he asked.

I nodded.

— Sit up front in the wheelhouse, he said.

He shoved a plastic bucket at me.

— And don't you dare puke on the deck, he said.

I sat on a small hutch behind the wheel. Bobby gunned the engine and I buried my head in the bucket.

— We've got a rule onboard, he said. You clean your own puke. That bucket starts filling up, you rinse it over the side of the boat. It'll cure you.

Talbot wandered into the cabin, wanting to know if I was giving Bobby any trouble. I was looking at their backsides. Bobby shook his head.

— Is this the one from Montreal? he asked.

Talbot nodded.

— City kids, Bobby said, snarling. Sissies. He glanced over his shoulder at me.

— Likes the little boys, does he? he asked. Then they both laughed.

I felt another wave of nausea and knew I was going to vomit. I staggered to my feet and headed out onto the deck. You were both at the back of the boat, watching a flock of gulls following the wake. I spotted Talbot's wallet on the deck and somehow scooped down to pick it up without falling flat on my face. I slipped it into my pocket and headed to the rail of the boat, emptying my guts into the water as the gulls dove after the warm lunch.

Neither of you would sit up front with Talbot on the drive home. You joined me in the back seat. As much as it irritated him when we all spoke at once, it was our silence that Talbot really detested. But he had never encountered this before, us three shutting him out as one. His fingers fiddled with the dials of the radio, seeking out a station to fill the permanent vacuum inside the car.

At home, I headed straight for bed and didn't even bother to get out of my clothes, collapsing on the blankets I had left rumpled from the morning. It wasn't until well after midnight that I woke up, to a quiet house, everyone asleep.

There was a note on the fridge to me from mom. Talbot had lost his wallet. Did I remember seeing it earlier today?

My appetite had returned, but when I opened the fridge and saw half a dozen lobsters on a tray, I remembered my humiliation from the afternoon and felt Talbot's thick wallet in my pants pocket.

I stole dad's car that night. Put it in neutral and rolled it out the back driveway and along the street before starting the engine. I had intended to wake you both, but decided that this was something I would do entirely on my own. A first.

Bobby's boat wasn't hard to find when I got to Main-à-Dieu. I filled the gas tank with sugar.

Back home, I headed for the basement and stashed Talbot's wallet under the rafters. There was almost eight hundred dollars in it. I wiped the dust from my fingers.

Bad men. I remembered. Talbot and Bobby were the first I had ever met. I would never let any of them victimize me again.

A couple of hours later, you drove me to the airport, Rory, to catch the first flight of the day. It was foggy and you waited with me, in case the flight was grounded, which was common.

— Talbot lost his wallet, you said.

— I heard, I said.

— There was a lot of money in it.

— Why would he carry around all that money? I asked.

— After he dropped us off yesterday, he was going to his landlord with a dozen lobsters, and a down payment on the farm. Now he doesn't have enough money to buy the place.

— Maybe he dropped it somewhere on the beach yesterday, I said.

— He's going out there later today. Tide probably got it.

— Yes, I said. Tide probably got it.

— It's too bad.

— Yeah, *bad*.

— YOU'LL CATCH FLIES, Ole says.

I am yawning. The buzz of the tattoo machine has an anaesthetizing effect upon me, much like the sleepiness that overcomes me in a dentist's chair during a cleaning.

On my first evening of tattooing, Ole drew a broad outline of his design on my back.

— *Det vil modnes mens jeg arbejder.* It'll ripen as I work, he said.

He wanted to create something that involved the ocean and asked me if I had any ideas. I told him when I thought about water I thought about Neptune's trident. Like those that adorned the *bissoni* boats in Venice.

A skilled tattooist knows how much pressure to apply to the machine to get a proper depth and clean, unbroken lines. Too shallow and the lines are scratchy after the tattoo has healed, if he goes too deep it will be more painful and produce more blood.

When Ole finished the outline the first night, he washed my back with antiseptic soap and water. He lit a fresh cigar and studied his handiwork before he continued, making the lines thicker and adding shading, pausing every ten minutes or so to continue disinfecting my skin.

— I'm retiring, he said. This will probably be my last canvas.

It wasn't until my second session that he started to fill in the design with colour, overlapping each line to guarantee solid and even hues. Splashes of water as Neptune rose from the sea.

— A lot of people come to me with holidays, Ole said.

— Holidays?

— Botched tattoos, he explained. Some tattooists are sloppy, the colour lifts out with the scab while it heals, or they miss a section. That's why they're called holidays. The artist took a vacation.

— Are you going to take a vacation when you retire? I asked.

— I'm not big on vacations.

— What will you do?

Ole laughs. —I'm not going to die, son. I have a lot of life in me yet. I'm getting older, not old.

I look at the rolls of paper towels on Ole's counter. He's gone through four tonight, pressing the paper on my skin to collect the blood and plasma excreted during the tattooing. Claes used to go through a lot of paper towels too, to wipe up grease and spills at the restaurant, or to soak up his many nosebleeds.

In the months before his death, Claes was admitted to the hospital four times. There were two things that interested him each time he came home from the hospital, brushing our dog every day and wanting to get another tattoo. Whenever the dog saw Claes holding the brush, he sat on the floor in the centre of the room, pawing the air with his leg and waving his tail in excitement.

Just before Claes went into the hospital for what would be the last time, I overheard him leave a message on Ole's answering machine.

When Ole called back the next day, Claes was already in the hospital and I took the call. Ole told me he wouldn't tattoo Claes. Claes had been a difficult client because of the hemophilia and the risk of bleeding each time Ole tattooed him. With full-blown AIDS, his immune system was almost completely shut down.

— I won't hasten his death, Ole said.

— Does it matter? I asked.

— Yes. It matters to me, he said.

Three months later, at Claes' funeral, a man approached me on the steps of the church, after the service. He looked familiar, but I couldn't place him.

— I'm Ole, he said.

— Ole?

— Tattoo Anker.

— Of course, I said.

— I saw the notice in the paper, he said. I spoke to Claes on the phone. He wanted a tattoo.

— It was me. You spoke to me, I said.

Ole shifted his weight from foot to foot.

— I'm sorry, he said. It was a while ago. I did his tattoos. All of them.

I was making him uneasy by detaining him on the steps, realizing he'd come to pay his respects, nothing more, eager to move on now that he had shook my hand. I smiled and it immediately put him at ease.

— It's a shame, he said, clearing his throat. He wasn't very old.

— No.

— We were cousins, did you know that?

— No, I didn't.

— Distant cousins. We both have the same last name.

It hadn't occurred to me that Ole had a last name. He was Tattoo Anker.

— Morgenstierne, I said. Ole Morgenstierne?

— Yes. I think Claes and I are third cousins.

— Did you know each other? Growing up?

Ole smiled and shook his head.

— No. I don't have any immediate family. We got to talk, that's all. At my parlour. It's not a common name.

Morgenstierne. The morning star.

Several staff members from the restaurant approached. Ole gave a quick nod of the head and moved on, making room for the fresh group of mourners behind us.

— WIPE YOUR TEARS, Ole says.

He's not embarrassed about my reminiscences. He hugs me, careful not to touch the area where he's been working on my back.

A ringing phone breaks the embrace. Ole takes the call, telling the person on the other end of the line he'll be home soon. His tone is one of ease and comfort, affection even. A young lover, perhaps.

About a week before I first visited Ole, I came home after a late shift and pressed the play button on our antiquated answering machine. Half listening, I leafed through the mail and headed upstairs to change. In the kitchen, I filled the dog's water bowl and opened a bottle of wine. Finally, I collapsed on the sofa, feet up on the coffee table, and sipped the wine.

— *Hello? Adrian?*

The dog and I both looked around the room to find out who was there.

— *Adrian? It's Claes.*

I closed my eyes and listened.

— *I still want to get the tattoo, Adrian. If Ole won't do it, we'll find someone else. Maybe get them to come to the hospital. Could you ask around? I love you. Bye.*

I closed my eyes. The worn-out tape on the answering machine had continued to replay all the old messages I hadn't erased. When I opened my eyes, his dog was sitting on the floor in the centre of the room. Pawing the air with his leg, the old brush between his teeth.

— ALL DONE, Ole says.

He positions his mirror so I can observe the tattoo from different angles and he takes several photos. Then he applies some gauze to the section he has finished tonight.

He sits on the bench.

— You must be tired, I say.

— I'll dream well tonight, he says. His eyes are heavy but relaxed.

Claes used to tell me he always dreamed about me just before he woke up. As I took my leave of him the afternoon he died, it comforted me to imagine that his eternity might include me.

— Can I ask you a question? Ole asks.

— Sure.

— Why Neptune?

— His trident. One tine for me and one for each of my brothers.

— I thought you had three brothers, Ole remarks.

— My back isn't big enough for three, I say.

— You could put on some weight, Ole jokes.

—The tines are also for each of my parents. I am in the middle. And there's also one for Claes.

— You and Claes are only two tines. Who's the third for?

— I don't know.

Ole brightens. Five years erode from his face.

— Listen, he says.

— To what?

— Outside. What do you hear?

— People.

— Happy?

— I suppose.

— I might see a dozen people here during the day, but there isn't much talking. It isn't natural to be surrounded by people all day and still feel alone. So when I close up, I walk right down the middle of that noisy crowd. By the time I get home I've shaken off all that loneliness.

Ole slaps my knee.

— Are you hungry, son?

— Always.

— Good. I'd like you to meet my man. Now he's *old,* but a hell of a cook.

Rory

MARCH, TORONTO

FOR THE SECOND TIME in these pages I'm writing to thank you for expressing your condolences. Though I'm not quite ready to return your kind telephone calls, I do want you both to know you've been in my thoughts.

It was difficult for me to read your pages, Adrian. It astonishes me to realize five years have passed since you lost your companion. And it overwhelmed me to read several of your moving epitaphs, wondering if Janet will be as present to me in the years to come. Isn't time supposed to erode the conviction I carry around that she's just in the next room? In bed, I can still feel her breath on my neck with such vehemence I tear away the covers to shake her from her hiding place.

It's been two months since Janet died.

She's so close. So far. Already I harbour guilt, fearful amnesia will overcome me as memories of her slowly ebb. But I'm also absorbed by a contrary sentiment, reinforced by your intimations of Claes. An unsettling desire to be released from the enigmatic and constant attendance of Janet, because it's unbearable to imagine her within me, but not beside me, in the years to come.

Janet was approaching two cancer-free years when the blood disease struck. It claimed her within eight weeks of the diagnosis. She said her goodbyes to friends and colleagues in the hospital seven days before she died. Those days and visits were difficult. She died at 4:45 p.m. on New Year's Day. Her body was cremated the next day during one of the worst snowstorms to hit Toronto in years. Janet hated winter. I've scheduled a memorial service on her birthday, June 21, when it'll be warm and green.

I made only two telephone calls when she died. The first was to her long-time partner at the clinic, Diana, who contacted all their colleagues and relayed my request for privacy in the coming months. But I still had to contact my own family, realizing too late I hadn't informed any of you about her illness. Between its discovery and her impending death, I brashly believed there'd be a remission and I'd be calling my family to say the worst had passed.

For my second call I chose Beth. I didn't want her to find out about Janet from Tally. I believe Janet was more connected to our family through Beth than through any of us, because Beth included her in the details of her life, independent of Tally.

She knew Beth's middle name, her preference for perennial flowers over annuals, her allergy to shellfish, which is why she always wears a MedicAlert bracelet, if you've ever wondered, and the details of the car accident that claimed her favourite aunt's life. Two or three times a year they called each other, and their Christmas cards always contained long handwritten letters.

When I was trying to decide whom to call first, I leafed through the unopened Christmas cards I'd thrown into a basket on the kitchen table and found the card from Beth. I hadn't even broken the seal. I picked it up, guessing there was a four- or five-page letter inside. For Janet. That's when I decided to call Beth, poised without dread for her immediate grief and the many minutes of sobbing while I recounted, in an unbroken monologue, the circumstances of Janet's final months. Then we spoke easily for an hour or more. As always, I was lulled by the slight girlish lilt to her voice. We spoke of ourselves, within the comely choreography of lifelong friends, picking up the thread of conversations set aside months or years before. I'd forgotten something, when Beth spoke to you, even when we were children and she was an adult in our eyes, it was easy to respond to her.

We didn't talk about Tally, other than a brief assurance from Beth that she'd call him after we hung up. Nor did we talk about their breakup. Beth wrote about it in her Christmas letter to Janet. From what I can gather, Tally and Beth haven't actually been together as a couple for a few years. As to reconciliation, it isn't going to happen. Beth has been dating the past year and is getting married this summer.

I'VE JUST RETURNED from Sydney. I wanted to spend a few hours at the house before it's listed on the market again, properly this time. Tally was probably shocked when Mom and

Dad's estate lawyers contacted him and told him he couldn't sell the house without our consent.

All of Tally's things were gone, the rooms were empty, even the cubbyholes and attic were cleaned out. So I was surprised when I went down into the basement and discovered it mostly untouched, a dozen old car tires stacked under the stairs, rusted bed frames behind the sump pump, and boxes of old shoes and boots, mouldy-smelling and covered in dust.

I found two pairs of flippers, not under the rafters, but in boxes with old shoes. There were stacks of *National Geographic,* and Tally's wallet was still hidden where you had left it, Adrian. Actually, where Cameron and I'd left it.

It was Cameron, while stashing a bag of grass, who found the wallet later in the summer and showed it to me. It'd never occurred to either of us you had nicked it, Adrian. Cameron and I thought Dad had hidden the wallet under the rafters, perhaps punishing Tally for his carelessness in losing it, then waiting a sufficient period of time before returning it to Tally with a lecture. But we both realized this was far-fetched, because we couldn't recall any occasion when Mom and Dad had ever disciplined or browbeaten Tally for negligence or a lack of common sense. Parental castigation was always reserved for me or for one of you.

We decided Tally was involved in some kind of scam. Maybe he faked the loss of the wallet to file an insurance claim so he could double the down payment on the farm in Bras d'Or. That made him less than perfect in our minds. Like us, flawed. Like us, brothers. It was probably the first time either of us had felt any sense of covenant with Tally, something akin to, but not quite, a fraternity.

Tally's money was still in the wallet. Eight hundred dollars in an assortment of green, reddish brown, blue, purple, and olive bills, their backsides an illustrated atlas of Canada, depicting places I've never been, Alberta's Moraine Lake, Vancouver Island, Baffin Island, and Sarnia, Ontario. I leafed through my own wallet, studied the images on the newer bills, the atlas replaced with a nest of loons, osprey, and a lonely snowy owl.

I shoved the eight hundred dollars into my pocket, for the United Way donation box I saw at the airport when I arrived.

Why didn't you take Tally's money to pay for your plane ticket to Montreal that summer, Adrian?

Or why didn't we split the money when you showed me the wallet, Cameron?

Because the money belonged to Tally, that's why we didn't take it. We didn't want anything from him. Not then. Not now.

I put the dusty empty wallet back up under the rafters, but not before my apology to you, Cameron, for suggesting to Tally, in a moment of spite, that you had stolen it. Hoping, if he found it now, in one last sweep of the basement, he'd read the message I wrote with my finger in the thick layer of dust. *Cameron didn't take the wallet. Yours truly, Rory.*

I WAS SUPPOSED to be in Sydney for two nights only, but a fierce storm delayed my return to Toronto by two days. I stayed with Beth, arriving on the last flight of the night via Halifax, my stomach unsettled by the constant turbulence in the small Dash-8. It was a slow drive from the airport to Beth's house.

I don't remember exiting the highway, navigating half a dozen side streets, or the sudden silence of the car when she turned off the engine. The falling snow outside and a creeping fatigue that had started several hours before disoriented me.

"We're here," she said.

We braced ourselves against a gust of wind. On the doorstep I held open the storm door, absentmindedly watching a plow seal the lip of her driveway with a foot of snow, as Beth put the key in the lock.

"Would you like a cup of tea?" she asked, settling me in the living room in front of the fire.

"I'd love one," I answered, with an assurance that ambushed me after these many weeks of emotional temperance. She also set out a pie.

"Is that lemon meringue?"

"Yes."

"We used to torture Tally when he babysat us, always begging him to let us stay up an extra hour after our bedtime. He'd counter with half an hour. Mom and Dad always left us a bedtime snack when they went out. Three slices of lemon meringue pie. Only this one time, two pieces were missing. Tally held the pie plate over our eight-year-old heads while we three accused each other of eating the missing pieces. I don't think I've eaten it since. I love lemon meringue."

Early the next morning, coming awake, I heard a scraping sound in the distance, placing it outside the room, outside the house. Beth was in the driveway, shovelling the snow that blocked access to the street.

Up and down the street her neighbours were doing the same thing. Two or three inches of snow covered her car.

She was bundled up, wearing a scarf over her mouth against the wind chill and a woollen toque pulled down over her ears.

She pushed a last few chunks of icy snow toward the tall banks lining the driveway, then disappeared around the side of the house, stomping the snow off her boots before coming inside, her cheeks ruddy, a warm smile across her face when she saw me.

"School's cancelled today," she said. "I'll make us a good breakfast before I drive you to your parents' house."

Arriving there, an hour later, Beth didn't want to chance getting stuck in the unplowed snow across the driveway.

"Do you want to come in?" I asked.

I didn't think she'd heard me. She was staring at the drifts in the driveway.

"Your parents waited three years before they invited me inside," she said.

I looked at her in disbelief.

"When Talbot and I started dating, he didn't own a car," she said. "I used to pick him up to go to the show."

It'd been years since I'd heard anyone refer to movies as *the show*.

"Talbot never invited me inside. Sometimes, in the summer, your mother and father were sitting on the patio out back and when they heard the car in the driveway they'd lean around the side of the house and wave to me. Less often, your mother came over to the car, stood at my window and chatted for two or three minutes until Talbot came outside."

"What did you talk about?"

"Nothing I can remember," she said.

"My parents didn't entertain much. They were always on the go, visiting friends or playing cards a couple nights a week. But I don't remember if my mother ever entertained her bridge club at home."

"I didn't know she played bridge."

"For years, as long as I can remember."

"She never mentioned it. Of course, I only saw them twice a year. They'd join Talbot and me for supper at his farm, once at Easter and then at Thanksgiving dinner. I haven't stepped foot in your parents' house since."

"Even at Christmas?"

"I never saw Talbot on Christmas. I spent the day with my family, and Talbot and I got together on Boxing Day. He's not big on holidays. And birthdays? Forget it. I can count the number of cards I ever got from him on one hand."

"When we were young teenagers, I don't ever remember him showing up for dinner at Christmas," I said. "He'd drop by early on Boxing Day, probably before he visited you. We always thought you spent the twenty-fifth together. In fact, he'd make a point of telling Mom and Dad you had wished them a Merry Christmas."

"Then you've learned something, Rory."

"And what would that be?"

"He didn't spend Christmas with your family and he didn't spend it with me."

"So where did he go?"

"Is this important to you?"

"I suppose it is."

"He went to the graveyard. You do know Talbot had a twin brother?"

I nodded.

"On Christmas Day he visited the graveyard and placed roses on his brother's headstone. An additional one for each year that passed."

"My mother told Cameron she hadn't named the baby. Why would there be a headstone?"

"Maybe she didn't know about it. Talbot put it there."

"Have you seen it?"

"Once. The year we were engaged. He showed me the grave on Christmas Day. It was bitterly cold and windy. He gave me a few flowers from the bouquet and when I bent down to put them on the gravestone the wind blew them away. That upset Talbot and he never invited me back."

Beth returned for me after my morning of rummaging at the house and took me to lunch.

"There aren't many people out today."

"It's been a long winter. One storm after another."

"We used to love snow days as kids. Our mother was exhausted after stuffing the three of us into snowsuits. We'd stay outdoors for a couple of hours, building forts or tobogganing on a hill at the ravine down the road. The house smelled of fresh buns when we finally came inside, and we smothered them with molasses."

"Kids don't spend much time outdoors these days," Beth said. "But you boys were always outside. Talbot wasn't that active, was he?"

"Not really. I don't think he planted a vegetable garden at the farmhouse all the years he's lived there."

"No. He didn't. He said he would never invest a penny in something he didn't own."

The waitress brought menus. We were the only customers in the dining room.

"Is that Celtic music they're playing?"

"Yes."

"If I ever moved back to Cape Breton, I think I'd pass on the fiddle music. Adrian and Cameron and I used to go to rock concerts at the old Sydney Forum. April Wine. Crowbar. Dr. Hook."

"Did you ever go to the Venetian Gardens?"

"In Toronto?"

"No, here. Across the street."

I glanced out the window. The wind was blowing a plastic garbage can lid across the road, toward the harbour side of the Esplanade.

"I vaguely remember it. It was built out over the water, on piles, wasn't it?"

"They had great dances there," Beth said. "It was pretty old by the time I was a teenager. They tore it down years ago."

"That reminds me, Cameron's choir is going to Venice in the autumn."

"I love Venice," Beth said.

"You've been there?"

"Twice. It's one of my two favourite cities in Europe."

"What's the other one?"

"Copenhagen."

"Adrian's still in Copenhagen."

"I was there the year before your parents died, but he was out of town. I had a great chat with his boyfriend."

"Claes?"

"Yes. I kept saying Klaus."

"He died."

"I didn't know that."

"A few months before our parents were killed in the train crash."

"I'm sorry to hear that. Adrian never mentioned it when your parents died. And Cameron?"

"He's good. We're good. Things got a little messy when we found out about Tally's shenanigans with Cameron's house in Halifax. Did you know about that?"

Beth nodded. "Yes. I feel bad for Cameron."

"It cost Cameron a lot of grief. But we've dealt with it, put it behind us."

"You should go see him."

"He's been staying with a friend since the eviction. I'm going to invite him to the memorial service in June. Maybe he'll stay for a couple of weeks."

"I meant Venice. You should go see him perform."

"I never thought of that."

"You and Adrian should both go to see him."

"I'll give it some thought."

The waitress came round with our drinks.

"Are you seriously thinking about moving back to Cape Breton?" Beth asked.

"It's funny you say it like that."

"Like what?"

"*Back* to Cape Breton. If I was talking to Tally, he'd say *home* to Cape Breton."

"But it isn't."

"Home?"

"Yes."

"No, it isn't home. Hasn't been for years."

I found the fiddle music loud. Beth motioned for an ashtray and I asked the waitress to turn down the music.

"There's no art on the walls," I said. "It looks so drab."

"They have one of your paintings out at the college."

"Really? I didn't know that. In storage?"

"It's part of their permanent collection. It's been hanging in the Great Hall for two years now. There's a lot of art on the walls."

"That's nice. Did Janet tell you I was teaching?"

We grew silent, the ping-pong bantering of our conversation fell to the floor. Invoking Janet's name brought a third chair to our table. Beth put down her fork, dropped her eyes to the plate. I watched a single tear roll down over her hand and wrist, patiently waited for her to meet my gaze again.

"I know how you feel, Beth." I inched my arm across the table. As I touched her, her flesh softened, submitting as I bundled her fingers within my hand.

"When I suddenly mention her name like that, I expect a confirming look from her, as if she's just out of view. And I can't understand why she won't move in closer, where I can see her."

The wind rattled the panes of glass.

"If we're snowed in today, I'll have to call Toronto. I'm supposed to teach tomorrow morning."

"When did you start teaching?"

"I started last July. Summer school. Then I taught two courses in the autumn. Until Janet took sick. What about yourself? How's school?"

"I'm retiring in June."

"No. No!"

"Thirty-five years."

"And Matthew?"

"He retired last year. We're moving to Vancouver after the wedding."

"Vancouver?"

"Most of my family is out there. Except for my mother. She has Alzheimer's. She hasn't recognized me for a couple of years so she won't even know that I've gone. Still, I'm a little torn about moving away before she dies."

"I'm sorry to hear about your mother."

"She had great affection for Talbot and liked to mother him. She always cooked a three-course meal when he visited and beamed when he asked for seconds. Her face always brightened when I mentioned his name on my visits to the hospital. Even after she no longer recognized me, she seemed to remember him and smile. Anyway, Matthew's family is from Seattle."

"Susan and Mary Anne live in Vancouver. Susan's teaching at UBC and Mary Anne's married and expecting. I'm going to be an uncle. Any day now."

The window started rattling again.

"That's the second time you've looked outside, Rory. What are you thinking about?"

"I just realized with you moving away, I won't know anybody in Cape Breton when I visit, other than Tally."

"Talbot isn't in Cape Breton, Rory."

I sat there with my jaw hanging open.

"He applied for a transfer before Christmas. When I called to tell him about Janet, his unlisted number was disconnected."

"Where did he go?"

"Antigonish."

"The lawyers didn't mention it."

"They might not be aware of it," Beth said. "It could all be handled through his own lawyers. And there's something else you should probably know."

"Yes?"

"Talbot is married."

"To whom?"

"A young teacher's aide. They have a daughter."

"Was he cheating on you?"

"I don't think so. This all happened after he stopping seeing me."

"Did he tell you he was getting married?"

"No, I knew the girl's mother. I met her at the supermarket and she told me. I taught her daughter, but I didn't mention that. I don't think she knew about Talbot and me."

"How old is the baby?"

"A year. Maybe less. The mother showed me a picture. She's very pretty."

"You must've been devastated."

"No. I don't think about Talbot all that often. But there is something else. He's stopped visiting his brother's grave. We were still together when I put my mother in the home. Then, two years ago, a bouquet of roses arrived for my mother, at the home, on Christmas. From Talbot. I drove out to the graveyard on Boxing Day these last two years. There were no flowers on the grave."

The wind was whipping snow into a tall drift across the Esplanade. I urged the squall to drive this news about Tally away from the table.

"Rory?"

"I've never vacationed in Cape Breton. Whenever I visited, it was to see my parents. Tally would drop by, or I'd have dinner at your place or his farm."

"They were always short trips."

"I never did take Janet around the Cabot Trail."

"Did she ever visit the island? I don't remember her mentioning it."

"Once. When we travelled, it was for a vacation. Coming to Sydney wasn't a vacation. It was an obligation. On my part. To be honest, I never pushed the idea of the two of us coming out here on an extended vacation."

"You both travelled a lot."

"We loved Bermuda. And the cottage on the bay. We enjoyed the long weekends over the years. I don't think I'll ever have reason to return to Cape Breton. In the back of my mind I always thought I would, someday. I'd buy a cottage in Boularderie, and spend the summers or autumns painting. But Janet was never in those romantic daydreams. I don't know where she was. Probably in Toronto, in our home. Safe from the jet lag of my armchair travels. Anyway, here I am today. In Cape Breton. And I know this will be the last trip. Yet everywhere I look since I've been here, I see Janet. It's confusing and frightening."

"What are you afraid of?"

"I don't want to leave these memories of her alone here when I leave."

I took a sip of coffee, tepid, the way we like our coffee, and I shook off the musings of the last few minutes.

"Travelling. When I'm not thinking about Janet, I'm thinking about travelling. I think I'm up for a journey."

"Is there anywhere in particular you'd like to go?"

"I enjoy teaching, Beth, and art history. A friend of mine, he offers art history tours in Europe. I'm thinking of looking into it. I'm interested in Italian art. I spent some time in Venice, years ago. I worked on a restoration project. Anyway, I'm going to look into it."

It was Beth's turn to watch the feud between the winds and snow outside.

"I love snow days," she said. "You just follow your feet on days like this."

"The first thing Janet used to do when she got home from the clinic was take off her watch and put it on the tray in the hall," I said. "It'd sit there until she left for work the next morning or all weekend. I do the same thing now."

I held up my bare wrists for Beth's inspection.

"For years, I wouldn't get voice mail," she said. "People think a teacher's day ends at three in the afternoon. But they don't have to put up with parents and students calling you at home, at all hours."

"What made you change your mind and get one?"

"Your brother."

"Tally?"

Beth sighed. "He stopped calling me. We were still seeing each other, it's just that *his* calls stopped. Then he stopped returning *my* calls. I guess I got it in my head that I was missing the calls when I wasn't home. That's when I got voice mail."

"I'm sorry, Beth."

"He did it to me. He did it to your parents. I don't think you or your brothers will ever hear from Talbot again."

"My parents? Tally doted on them."

"Talbot didn't like your parents, Rory."

"That's foolish."

"He never believed they liked him. For the first ten years of his life he felt ignored, as if your parents were grieving over the baby who died in childbirth, perhaps blaming him because he survived and the twin didn't. Then you were born. All the attention went to the three of you. Out of necessity."

"My mother used to use the same expression, *out of necessity*. But it can't be true, Beth. Not about Tally."

"It doesn't matter, Rory. It's what Talbot believed. Trust me. He had many theories and I've heard them all. Then he stopped."

"Stopped?"

"Stopped talking about you and your brothers. Stopped talking to other people. I used to watch him at functions. People would come up and talk to him. He'd smile. Wouldn't say a word. Like he was in a royal receiving line. Waiting until the poor fool moved on, knowing if he spoke, he might not get rid of them. Jackie Onassis used to do that. Jackie O and Talbot. He stopped talking to your parents. Stopped calling them once a week. Stopped visiting regularly. The last time Talbot saw your parents was about two months before they died."

"Why?"

"He didn't think they cared, one way or the other."

"That's not true."

"Of course it isn't. But he used to complain bitterly about always having to call them. According to Talbot, they never picked up the phone to call him."

"But that was their way. We all did that. We called, they answered. Big deal."

"But you never tested his theory, Rory. If you had stopped calling your parents and they didn't call you, what would you think?"

"Probably that they thought when I had something to tell them, I'd call."

"If weeks went by, months? And you didn't hear from them?"

"I'd think something was wrong with them."

"And when you finally called and found out everything was fine, how would you feel then?"

"That they had nothing to say to me."

"So why continue calling. Why bother?"

"Because they're my parents."

"But you never felt you were unwanted, like Talbot did. Every week that passed without a call from them just proved his point. That's why he stopped calling, why he stopped coming around. There's your answer, Rory."

"But why did he do it to you? You cared, you continued to call him. Why?"

"Because he was mean."

"Didn't that make you furious?"

"Of course it did. But my sister Clare got tired of all my hand-wringing about Talbot. She finally told me that if a naive person is betrayed, nobody cares. Stop whining."

Beth reached across the table and patted the back of my fist.

"He didn't even send me a card when Janet died," I said. "I thought he was using Janet to punish me. When I think of Tally, I think about her. And it's shameful she's in there with those thoughts about Tally, and the anger and the bitterness he makes me feel. It's unforgivable."

"Yes, it is unforgivable, Rory."

"So why do I suddenly feel better, knowing it's because he simply didn't care?"

Beth squeezed the anger out of my fist.

"Because it's a comfort to know it wasn't about Janet. Maybe it wasn't about any of us. Maybe it's all about Talbot. I think you're going to have to learn to stop thinking about him. That's what needs to be done."

Beth rose. "We should go home. Or think about ordering supper," she said.

"What time is it?"

"Four-thirty."

"No!"

"It's a snow day, Rory. Time stands still."

I ARRIVED HOME from Sydney five days ago, after a long day of flight delays. No sooner had I sat at the kitchen table than the doorbell interrupted me.

Ivan Kolerus barrelled into the hallway and embraced me in a bear hug. He looked as if he'd been crying, but I think he was just having a bad day with his runny eye ducts.

"Rory," he exclaimed, forcing any lingering air out of my lungs with a second hug.

He held me at arm's length, his eyes curiously scanning me, as if he were trying to decide whether all of my appendages were in the right places.

"Why don't you answer your phone?" he asked.

"Did you call?" Wondering if I'd missed hearing the phone ring since getting home.

Kolerus marched across the room and pressed the play button on my machine. There were several messages, most from him. After the fourth or fifth message I stepped in front of him and pressed the stop button.

"Was there anything you wanted?" I asked, exasperated with having to stand there and listen to multitudinous variations of the same curt message, *It's Ivan, call me*, or *Call me, it's Ivan.*

"It's not like you," he said, peering down his nose at me over the top of his glasses.

"I was out of town."

He waited for me to elaborate.

"Ivan, you're annoying me. What is it you want?"

He was stymied by my frankness and his lower lip quivered for a few seconds.

"I was worried about you, Rory."

He reached into his coat pocket and removed a bottle, passing it to me.

"Thank you. You'll join me for a glass?"

I poured us both a stiff drink. No water, no ice.

"I was in Cape Breton. Family business."

Kolerus ripened, the colour rising to his cheeks, readily accepting what I said as if it were a confession. He celebrated by downing his whiskey and holding out the glass for a refill.

"It's good to get away," he said, in an arbitrary act of closure, throwing back his head to swallow the second shot in one gulp. He slapped his knees with his hands and sighed. "I should be going," he said, in a spiritless attempt to rise from the sofa.

"Stay awhile." I poured him two fingers.

"Thank you."

"Ivan, I'm quite capable of taking care of myself."

"Yes."

I could feel the blush of the whiskey on my cheeks. "I'm no more likely to fall down the stairs now than when Janet was alive."

I said it lightly, trying to dispel a creeping suspicion about the motive behind his mercurial appearance at my door.

"I just wanted to be sure," he said. "*To be sure.*"

"Did you think I'd had an accident?"

"No, no." He blinked as he said this. It might've been a wink, or the fluttering of his lashes.

"I knew you wouldn't hurt yourself," he said, the lashes flittering madly. He looked as if he were about to take an epileptic seizure, embarrassed with the turn of the conversation, dodging the pretence for his visit. Knowing I knew why he was there, to check up on me, to make sure I hadn't killed myself to escape my grief.

"I wouldn't hurt myself. Really."

His eyes locked on to me, as if daring me to blink to prove it was a lie. But I wouldn't blink.

"I've made an ass of myself," he said, finally.

"No, you were concerned."

Kolerus chuckled. "Suicide is the most sincere form of self-criticism," he said, with complete levity, holding out his glass again.

I poured us another drink.

"Here's to famous suicides," he said. "*Famous suicides*."

"Van Gogh."

"Kleist."

"The expressionist?"

"Kleist. Kirchner. Lehmbruck," he said. "All fine artists."

"All Germans."

Kolerus' chuckling erupted into chortles.

"And Jesus." I continued.

"Debatable." He poured his own drink this time. "Suicide is a serious business. *Serious business*. It all has to do with the stars," waving a finger through the air. "What's your sign?"

"I'm a Libra."

"Ruled by an optimistic attitude."

"And you, Ivan?"

"Sagittarius. Repelled by any kind of violence. We view suicide as an act of aggression, even if it is toward ourselves."

Kolerus smiled, impishly, like a child. "One must be skeptical, always," he said. "There was an astrologer and prophet by the name of Girolamo Cardano. He predicted his own death would take place in a specific year. The year arrived and he fulfilled the prophesy by taking his own life." Kolerus reached across the table and embraced the back of my neck with his large, warm hand.

"I'm glad you're a Libra," he said.

"And I'm glad you're a Sagittarius, Ivan."

"Now, be a good friend, *a good friend*, and call me a cab."

I STEPPED INTO a blanket of fog this morning when I went out onto the porch to fetch the newspaper. The snowman on the lawn across the street was melting, its carrot nose and coal buttons fallen to the base. The boy who'd so proudly rolled those three mounds of snow the day I left for the airport cast a languid gaze at it now from his living room window. It's curious, but as I contemplated the snowman I was also dwelling on Beth's advice about letting Tally go.

Years before, I'd almost done just that, deciding to exorcise him from my life after he'd insulted Janet when he met her. I think Tally considered Janet my undeserved trophy, and wanted a closer look to see if it, she, was tarnished. As we wandered the aisles of Honest Ed's bargain store in Toronto, rooting through a bin of discounted socks, Tally decided to tell me Janet wasn't pretty.

Who in the fuck says such things?

He so completely blindsided me with his insult I was numb, and he chose to interpret my silence as licence to continue.

"Mannish. You're telling me Janet is mannish?"

He shrugged.

"Do you mean she looks like our mother?" I asked.

The skin on his face tightened, the lips pinched. I don't know what made me bring our mother into the conversation. But it was true, Mom kept her hair short, bristled. It was a look she acquired in her early forties, like so many other women in the area, all looking as if they'd met the onset of mid-life with a visit to the barber, acquiring an androgynous style, the hair sliced straight across the back of their necks. Walking through the shopping centre as teenagers, Adrian used to call them the menopausal battalion.

Janet had thick, short hair, but it didn't look like a helmet. She had a habit of bobbing it up the back of her head, lifting it off a slender neck to reveal the dangling pearl-drop earrings she so loved. Her complexion was dark, her eyebrows full, and long eyelashes edged deep brown eyes. The muscles on her arms and legs were long and smooth, like those of a dancer. She was fond of wearing sleeveless blouses in the summer. She detested covering her neck and she never wore turtlenecks. When she came home after work she liked to change from slacks to jeans, blouses replaced with loose cotton sweaters. She was only five-four, but all of my memories are of looking into her eyes, never casting my glance downward to meet a question. I think she was aware of this, learned early in life to position herself so she always appeared at eye level, adding inches to her height.

Later, when I told Janet what Tally had said, she frowned.

"Some men are threatened by dark women," she said, dismissing the comment as misplaced candour from a precocious child. "Although I'm surprised he didn't have the gallantry to at least refer to me as *handsome*. What else did your brother have to say?" she asked.

"Nothing." Though Tally had lectured me on how pretty our mother was in comparison to all the other mothers in the neighbourhood.

"He thought I was a whore," Janet said. "When he slipped out of the booth behind me at lunch, he patted my ass."

"What?"

"Rory, I don't know your brother, but my initial impression is that he's a bit of a prig. They all have double standards. Does he have a girlfriend?"

"Yes."

"Is she younger than him?"

"No."

"He probably won't marry her. Men like Talbot seek virtue in younger women. And they certainly don't think women of their own vintage can do the same."

"Fall in love with a younger man?"

Janet considered me for what felt like ages before she answered. "Yes, fall in love with a *delightful* younger man."

I'd misled Tally, telling him Janet and I hadn't started seeing each other until after the exhibition in my graduation year. In truth, we had spent almost every weekend together since her engagement party. Much of that time was spent in conversation or private thought. Janet hadn't set up her private practice yet and many weekends she was on call at the hospital, performing emergency reconstructive surgery. I enjoyed those nights, staying awake until three or four in the morning, listening to music or cooking, my heart skipping a beat when I heard her key in the door.

She liked long baths and I enjoyed drawing them, sometimes slipping into the tub before her so she could lean against my chest as I massaged her shoulders and sponged her neck. Janet liked to make love in the middle of the day, never at bedtime when we were exhausted or in the rush of mornings before work.

It wasn't our custom to show affection in public, but I always offered my hand when she got out of a taxi and gently grasped her elbow entering a restaurant or walking along the street.

We filled in the years between us with quiet growth, nurturing acquaintances, mine within the Toronto art scene and Janet's among other doctors, never intruding on the other's friendships. I enjoyed Janet's colleagues and she my artist friends. But for the most part we enjoyed our time together at the house, at the cottage, or strolling along the beaches of the Caribbean.

The last time we ever discussed the difference in age between us was during our conversation about Tally's callous assessment of the woman I loved. I was intensely angry and told her I was thinking of cutting him out of my life entirely.

Janet's advice was to let it go. It wasn't up to us to make an adjustment to suit Talbot, she claimed.

"Even if he found me pretty and young, it wouldn't change things," she told me. "From what you've told me, Rory, your brother doesn't seem to really like anyone. Let's work within that. Give it a chance."

She said it with a flicker of impatience in her eyes, and I was to learn this expression was reserved for discussions and situations where the outcomes couldn't be changed and therefore weren't worth debating. It was still early in our relationship, however, and something in my face told her I'd mistaken her impatience for a dismissive attitude.

"It doesn't really matter what Talbot thinks about me or about us," she said. "I'm thirty-seven and you're twenty-two. It won't matter when you turn thirty and I turn forty-five, or when you're fifty and I'm eligible for a senior's discount. What's important is that we're going to arrive at the same time, in the same year, on the same day and hour. Together."

It was the dampness of the porch, finally, that jarred me from my daydream. My eyes were still on the snowman across the street. A few weeks earlier I might've wondered what I would get for my efforts if I did meet Tally now, after everything that's happened. He'd probably toss a carrot and three pieces of coal at my feet and walk away. But I knew there would be no meetings.

Before leaving Sydney, I took a taxi out to the university and strolled through the halls. Classes were still cancelled because of the storm, and the campus was mostly empty. I stood before the painting the university had added to their permanent collection, the painting Janet had referred to as a kaleidoscope of passion and rage when her eye fell upon it during my graduation exhibition twenty-five ago. The vibrant colours appealed to her, the skin on her sleeveless arms erupted in goosebumps. It was my portrait of Tally, and its sensual impact upon Janet made me intensely jealous.

So I lied, telling her it was already sold. I crated and stored it away for years until I unloaded it for a pittance with a dealer in Toronto.

When I painted the portrait I was still in my first year at art school and angry withTally for convincing me to give up my plans to study in Halifax. When I mentioned it to him that first Christmas when I was home on break, he couldn't even remember his lecture about choosing schools far from home. I didn't choose Tally as a topic, it was an assignment, to create portraits of our family members. In painting it, with each stroke of the brush, I had become increasingly nauseous, not yet aware of the synesthesia that afflicted me. Assuming I was stricken with the flu, I persevered nonetheless, determined to finish my portrait of Tally and to recover from the virus and the bouts of vomiting that accompanied it at the same time. On the day I capped the last of my paint tubes I gazed upon the portrait for several long minutes, and the last of the bile erupted from my stomach. When I left the studio I was cured.

I kept a distance from the portrait as I viewed it, knowing if I stepped closer the hushed halls would erupt in furor. Walking away, I banished the painting from my mind and eternally exiled Tally within its frame.

As I closed my front door on these thoughts, the boy across the street let the window curtain fall between him and his view of the shrinking mound of snow on the lawn.

THERE WAS ONE other caller on the tape, besides Ivan. Father Sears had telephoned to express his condolences.

I thought about Father Sears again this morning, while scanning the headlines in the paper. I haven't spoken to him since the Vancouver exhibit. I picked up the phone, punching in the digits of his number slowly as I formulated in my head the question I needed to ask him. I could picture him on the other end, passing a hand over his five o'clock shadow as he listened, running his fingers through his wispy hair, the missing joint and the stout gold ring looking far too big for the remaining digit.

"What can you tell me about grace, Father?"

He lapsed into silence for a short time.

Something had changed in the three days since seeing Ivan and visiting with Beth in Sydney. I cleaned the house from top to bottom, packing away Janet's clothes for the Salvation Army, bundling her magazines for recycling. I acknowledged all of the sympathy cards, calling Diana at the clinic for addresses, accepting an invitation for dinner at her house later in the week. I looked through Janet's appointment book and even notified her dentist, to cancel an impending cleaning she had booked months before, to save the receptionist an embarrassing reminder call. I remembered Adrian's surprise call from Claes, left on his answering machine all those years, and replaced Janet's voice with my own in a new recorded message. As I moved through the house, I realized I was making more room for myself.

I'd found a broker to sell Janet's jewellery and decided to use the money as an endowment for a medical scholarship. I returned all her medications to the pharmacy and threw away her toiletries, pausing briefly to remove a few strands of hair from her brush, feeling the slightest sense of her at my side. Less so over the past few days. In its place, a sense of quiet has settled, replacing the storms of grief that have battered me, over and over, these past few months like the waves smashing against the shore I watched as a child. Now I feel as if I'm standing on the same beach, but the tide is low and the waves just ripples.

"What's on your mind, Rory?" Sears asked, after my question about grace.

"I've stopped mourning. I think I've given it away."

I told him about the force with which Beth had squeezed my hand as she wept in the restaurant. How Ivan was buoyed by our few short hours together, dissolving in my embrace before he stepped out of the house to his cab.

"The comfort of the comforted," Sears said.

"But you don't just stop grieving in a matter of weeks."

"Some do. Most will with time. Grace can be like water to a seed, entering you through the favours of friends, and in your search for more water you reach out like roots, favouring them with your grace.

"But grace can't be exercised where there is the slightest human merit to be recognized. If you do a good deed to be rewarded, it isn't an act of grace."

"I wasn't implying—"

"Let me ask you a question, Rory. Did you love your wife?"

"Yes."

"Did she love you?"

"Yes."

"Were you good and kind to each other?"

"Yes."

"And to others?"

"I think so."

"Did all of this fill you with joy?"

"Yes."

"Grief has ebbed in the face of something stronger, my man. It isn't a sin to allow joy to fill the rooms of your house again and to settle in your heart."

Grace was Janet's middle name. I used to call her *my saving Grace* whenever she found my car keys or spied an empty parking spot.

Cameron

DECEMBER, VANCOUVER

TALK ABOUT BEING out of the loop! I arrived in Vancouver at
the end of March as planned, five days before Mary Anne's due
date. She insists on meeting my plane at the airport and goes
into labour half an hour before it landed.

My plane was at the gate, everyone was agitated, wanting to
be the first off, when the steward made an announcement, asking
Mr. Cameron Hines to please identify himself, which I did. A
stewardess motioned me to the front of the plane. The only thing
I was thinking was maybe, and it was just a maybe, I'd exceeded
the limit on my Canadian Tire credit card, and the airline wasn't
going to let me leave the airport unless I reimbursed them.

An attendant met me outside the door and we walked
through the sleeve connecting the plane to the transit hall. She

was talking into her walkie-talkie, telling them Mr. Hines was with her now. At the transit hall I was passed over to another attendant sitting in one of those golf carts they use to transport the *infirm,* and she backed it up before I had both legs inside. The cart beeped as we backed up, and she turned on the flashing light. It was only then that she told me there was a taxi waiting at the exit to drive me to the hospital, courtesy of the airline.

"Your daughter went into labour an hour ago, Mr. Hines. Congratulations. Write down your address and we'll make sure your luggage is delivered. Two bags?"

"Four," I said.

A dark shadow fell over her face for a split second.

"They aren't heavy," I assured her, lying.

Meanwhile, Mary Anne, Susan, and *Surefoot,* Tenderfoot's successor, had been whisked away from the airport by ambulance to the nearest delivery room. I arrived at the hospital and walked straight past Susan in the waiting area. I mean, how dense could I be? I walked past the dog, a guide dog! You'd have thought I'd clue in! I was almost at the end of the corridor before the little hamster running on the treadmill inside my head woke up and started pedalling some sense back into my head. "Follow the dog," I told myself. "Follow the goddamn dog."

Susan grabbed my arm on my second pass by Mary Anne's room.

"Cameron," she said, "breathe."

I gave her a hug and a quick kiss on the cheek.

"Mary Anne?" I asked.

"She's fine," she said. "They're all fine."

"Good," I said. "Good." The hamster was running a marathon now. "All?"

"The babies."

"The babies?"

"Mary Anne just delivered three healthy girls."

"Triplets?" I whispered. "She had triplets?"

"Yes, Cameron."

"Our Mary Anne," I say, "our little Mary Anne?"

"Yes, Cameron."

"Why didn't I know?"

"You told Mary Anne you wanted the sex of the babies to be a surprise."

"I meant the sex of the *baby*. She didn't say anything about *triplets*."

"She didn't want you to worry. I was sworn to secrecy. Anyway, surprise! Cameron?"

But I was sliding halfway down the wall. The hamster must have had a stroke from all the exertion. And turned out the lights.

"HI DADDY."

I blinked madly, trying to place the voice.

"I'm right beside you," she said.

I looked over from the bed they had me on and saw Mary Anne sitting up in hers.

"Hi, pumpkin," I said.

"Welcome back, Mr. Hines."

A nurse took my pulse. Susan and Jimmy stood behind her. Across the room, at Mary Anne's bedside, Jonathan and his folks were beaming. Jonathan's long, slender face lit from ear to ear with a big smile, his chiselled cheekbones flush with pride. He rivals your smile, Adrian.

"Did I faint?" I asked.

"Yes," Susan said. "How are you feeling?"

"I'm okay." The nurse nodded an assurance to Susan and left the room. I swung my legs over the side of the bed.

"Easy, big fellow, drink this juice before you get out of bed." Jimmy passed me a glass and I finished it as three nurses walked into the room, each with a baby in her arms.

"The babies," I whispered, "are they all right?"

"They're perfect, Cameron, ten fingers and ten toes."

"And two eyes?"

Susan leaned forward and kissed my forehead.

"Yes. Two eyes. On each of them."

Jonathan took one of the babies and put it in Mary Anne's arms. She gently traced the outlines of the tiny face, placed a light kiss on the forehead. Susan brushed Mary Anne's long hair away from her face, tying it in a ponytail so it wouldn't fall on the faces of the babies. That's something I've seen Susan do a million times, a routine Mary Anne has always enjoyed, like when I count her freckles, running my finger across the bridge, always ending with a gentle poke on the end of her nose. She always smiles. Always.

The nurse took the first baby and Jonathan passed Mary Anne the second. No one said a word. All eyes were on Mary Anne as she touched her babies for the first time, breathing in their unique scents. Each of the babies made her own sounds and Mary Anne held each one to her ears, committing their tiny unformed voices to memory.

The nurses were as enthralled as the rest of us.

Mary Anne was amazed by the full head of hair on each of them, and combed each head with the side of her cheek.

The nurses returned the babies to the nursery and we all gravitated around Mary Anne's bed. Susan was the first to give her a hug, and then everyone headed down to the nursery for another peek.

Before I was even at the side of her bed, Mary Anne reached out her arms to me.

"How are you feeling, Daddy?" she asked.

"Wobbly."

"You're not going to faint again, are you?"

"No."

"I love you, Daddy." Her arms were around my neck and she was crying.

"Hey, it's okay," I said, rubbing her back, making little circles with the palm of my hand, like I used to do when she was a little girl.

"I'm so happy, Daddy. I think my heart is going to burst."

"Mine too," I said. I put her hand on my chest.

"I know how happy you are, I can feel it. It's so good."

"Yes, pumpkin, it's so good," I said, as I buried my face in her neck. "You've got to rest now, sweetheart."

"Okay," she said, her voice soft, on the edge of sleep.

"I'll just be down the hall."

"Okay."

"I love you."

And I did it, poked the end of her nose with my finger. And she smiled. Like always.

I JOINED THE REST of the family at the nursery. Jonathan's father shook my hand and proudly told me we were both grandfathers now, although there was a measure of disbelief in his eyes when they fell on me. I could understand his bewilderment. Jonathan was the youngest of several children, born when his father was fifty. I gazed at the face of this seventy-five-year-old man who had become my peer through marriage, and the birth of our children's children, and wonder if I was disrespectful in daring to consider myself, like him, a grandfather.

THOSE WERE HEADY WEEKS, boys. The next day my furniture arrived from Halifax and I spent the day moving everything into the house I bought, thanks to the boost to my savings from the sale of the folks' house. It needs work, but I started with the garden and landscaping. I want to take advantage of the ten-month growing season they have here on the West Coast. I left Halifax in a blanket of snow and arrived to the sweet smell of cherry blossoms.

Kalim packed up and moved to Borneo, leaving Halifax two days before I headed to Vancouver. I'm going to visit him next year. I started a vacation fund. I can't wait to see all the places he's described over the years. Sometimes we float in the sulphur hot springs he loves, where I finally put my divorce behind me. Other times, I close my eyes and walk alongside him through the busy streets of Kota Kinabalu, watching the faces of the people strolling along the sunlit roads, jostled as we walk along the crowded sidewalks. The last time we took a stroll, I dropped my anger at the Big B like a bag of oranges, and watched my resentment toward him roll away, out of reach. I grabbed a new orange from a cart, sweet and juicy, happy the bitter oranges landed in the gutter.

LIKE JONATHAN, the babies are going to have western names.

"Something my dad decided when he came to Canada," Jonathan said, when I asked him why he doesn't have a Chinese name. "He gave us all names from the Bible."

"Is *Jonathan* in the Bible?" I asked, my knowledge only extending to Peter, Paul, and Mary.

"I didn't like John," he said. "I started to call myself Jonathan when I was about six." As usual, he was taking up an entire sofa, the rest of us squeezed into the matching one. Unlike some tall people who try to squeeze themselves into nothing when they sit down, Jonathan had one arm flung lazily across the back of the sofa, his left leg stretched halfway across the carpet, his polished Doc Martens almost touching my foot. He has an easy comfort about him, and I like that.

He knew lots of blind people before meeting Mary Anne at university. Jonathan's brother is blind, and Jonathan worked part-time with an agency in Vancouver that matched guide dogs with blind people. He eventually matched Mary Anne with Surefoot, and they're both musicians, so there was a lot of common ground.

But when they first met I was curious. Did Mary Anne understand the concept of different races and skin colours?

"I know about cultural differences from reading," she told me.

"That's not what I mean. When I tell you someone is black or white, what does that mean to you?"

"Daddy, we've talked about this," she said. "About colour." Mary Anne wasn't being cheeky. Born blind, she doesn't see any colour, or even its absence, black. Her brain doesn't process any information from her eyes. A black man might as well be purple or green.

"I know that people are different through learning about their history. Colour is about politics," she said. "Is this about Jonathan?"

"No."

She wasn't quite ready to let it go. "He's very handsome," she said.

"Yes, he is."

She smiled at me. "Is he better looking than you are?"

"Much."

"You're lying," she said, giggling.

"Of course I am."

We were sitting in Stanley Park. Mary Anne had introduced me to Jonathan for the first time earlier that day. It was a scorcher. A gust of wind blew over the water and cooled us down. Mary Anne reached across the bench and took my hand in her own. The familiar jingle of her bangles soothed me.

"I remember you gave me a shoulder ride in this park," she said, "when I was a little girl. It was a windy day."

"I remember."

"I kept on asking you to get us out of the way."

"Of what?"

"The wind. It was really strong, and the dirt from the path was stinging my eyes and nose. I couldn't understand why you weren't walking around the wind, like you would if it was a tree."

"I'm remembering," I said, eyes closed, seeing us walk along the shore. "You thought I could see the wind."

"Why wouldn't I? Nobody told me it was invisible."

JONATHAN AND MARY ANNE have selected the names for their babies. *Eve, Ruth, and Faith.* I was sitting in their living room with Susan, Jimmy, and Jonathan's parents. Typically, Jonathan had one of the sofas to himself.

"We'll start with the oldest," Jonathan said, and everyone laughed.

Eve.

"Because she's lively," Jonathan said. We tasted the name in our mouths. "She's the oldest," he said.

Ruth.

"Lovely and dignified," Mary Anne said. "Ruth is the middle baby. It's a traditional name. She'll always have the benefit of knowing what came before and will use it to guide her in the future."

Faith.

"She's the baby," Jonathan said. "We did consider filling out the trinity with Hope and Charity, but we felt it had too much of a Puritan ring to it."

I was thinking of our mother, telling us if she could do it all over again, she'd have chosen three short names. "Chasing the three of you around the house all day, by the time I got all those syllables out of my mouth, the three of you would be into something else. I should have called you A, B, and C."

Eve. Ruth. Faith. Simple, lovely, and elegant.

Everyone likes the names, although Jonathan's mother is a little unsure about who is who.

"How do I know it's Ruth and not Eve?" she asks. "Or Faith?"

"I'll know. This is Ruth," Mary Anne said, stroking the folds of the baby's ears with her finger. "I'll always know."

Mary Anne sensed her mother-in-law wasn't quite satisfied.

"Besides, they're not identical. In a few weeks, you'll be able to tell them apart."

I remember your insistence about establishing our birth order, Rory. I reminded you about that when I called, waving the white flag, before Janet took sick.

"It's not true," you said.

"What's not true?" I asked.

"The birth order thing," you said. "Mom couldn't remember. She based it on our birth weights, figuring that I was the first because I was the heaviest. She said she read it somewhere, in an article about twins. The heavier twin was always born first. She said it probably applied to triplets too. I was the heaviest at six pounds, you were five pounds fourteen ounces, and Adrian was five pounds twelve ounces."

"So I could be the oldest," I said.

"Do you want to be the oldest?"

"God no, Rory, I want to be the youngest. Don't you?"

We both laughed. Major thaw.

"I should never have told you about the paintings, Rory."

"I shouldn't have told Tally you stole his wallet."

We grew silent for a moment, digesting each other's impromptu apology.

"Is all this business with Talbot behind us now?" I asked.

"I should be asking you that."

"Bygones?"

"Nothing would please me more, Cameron."

"Then it's done. Thanks for not hanging up on me."

"Cameron, when have I ever hung up on you?"

"Never. I know I get on your nerves, Rory. I think I do it to keep your attention."

"Does it mean that much to you?"

"Yes. By the way, I'm thinking of pulling up stakes and heading west."

"Vancouver?"

"How'd you guess?"

"Mary Anne. The new baby on the way. Family."

"I've got family in Toronto," I said.

"Is that a threat?"

More laughter.

"Seriously, Cameron. You're more than welcome to stay with us. For as long as you want. I mean that."

"I know you do. How's Janet?"

"She's good. Well, she's been a little tired the last few weeks. I'm trying to get her to go see her doctor. I think she's working too hard."

"You guys should get away."

"Janet doesn't like to travel in the winter."

"Then you and I should get away. Go to Copenhagen for a couple of weeks and see Adrian."

"I suppose we shouldn't wait for another funeral to see each other again. I mean, how long has it been since we've laid eyes on each other? Four, five years?"

"Yes."

Then Janet died. You finally called me in April. I knew you had to wait until you were ready. And I knew it was going to be very difficult for you to make the call. I just didn't realize how difficult if would be for me to listen on the other end of the line with a lump in my throat, not knowing what I should say.

"I don't think she was in any pain, Cameron," you said. "She just got tired. And then she slept. A lot. She slept for the last four days of her life. Cameron?"

"I'm here."

"I used to talk to her in the hospital. All the time. Right up until she died. Sometimes I wished you were there."

"You did?"

"Janet said you used to have good chats on the phone."

"She was easy to talk to, Rory."

"She really liked it when you called."

"YOUR MOTHER AND I named you boys and then put those names on a shelf for a couple of weeks," dad said to me once. "There was enough confusion going on."

There's going to be a lot of confusion over the next several months, but I haven't said anything to Mary Anne or Jonathan, although I think he's aware of it. He's already packed away most of the nice clothes he buys from the Gap, sporting less fussy choices now, T-shirts and sweats. The confusion won't be about figuring out which baby is which, but about keeping track of who got fed and who needs to be changed.

These are the stories our mother told Susan. "On more than one occasion, I'd put a clean diaper on a clean bum," she said, "or give one of them a second bottle by mistake. It was exhausting. We were both up all night, for months. Out of three babies, you'd think one would have slept through the night. Talbot came into our bedroom one evening, the boys were teething and had been fussing all evening. Nobody got any sleep. Talbot was only ten or eleven, standing at the foot of our bed, rubbing his eyes and crying. *Take them back*, he shouted, *take them back*. He wanted to crawl in between his father and me, but we didn't allow that."

"Why not?"

"We were afraid it would become a habit. And if the boys discovered their older brother sleeping between us some night later on, they would want to do the same thing. We'd never get any peace."

"Do you think Talbot remembers that night?"

"I doubt it. He's never said anything, even when we broke our own rule later on, letting one or two of the triplets sleep with us. You're always firm with the oldest child, but the younger ones have a way of breaking you down."

"Did you have anyone to help you with the triplets?" Susan asked.

"No, it was just me and the boys' father. All the women in the neighbourhood were either pregnant or had babies of their own to take care of."

"What about grandparents?"

"I'm from Newfoundland, so my folks were pretty far away. Besides, we tried that once before, it didn't work out. When Talbot was three, I came down with tuberculosis and spent almost a year in the annex. Talbot and his father moved in with the boys' grandparents.

"I didn't recognize that child when I got out of the annex. He was as bald as a bat and there were nicks on his scalp from the straight razor his grandmother used to cut off all his hair. She had a horrid fear of lice.

"And I knew she used to beat Talbot's father something wicked when he was a child, so the first thing I did when I got Talbot alone was strip off his clothes and look for welts on his skin."

"Did she beat him?" Susan asked.

"No, and we've never hit the boys or raised our voices at them. But we didn't coddle them either. Best way to raise a child is to let him figure things out on his own. Like we did with Cameron and his brothers."

Life with the triplets will be easier for Mary Anne and Jonathan. Susan spent the first couple of weeks in their guest room, helping them out during the nights. I pitched in during the afternoons, rehearsing in the mornings with the new choir I joined.

I must admit, after a few weeks I was looking forward to the festival in Venice for a break. There's something about that city that has always puzzled me. Since the city is built on water, are there trees in Venice? Anyway, aside from Susan and myself, Jonathan's family are always on call for the weekends to help out with the babies. Between all of us, food is cooked, laundry washed, floors swept, and babies burped.

VENICE WAS A BLAST, boys. Standing alongside the canal, the three of us enjoying a good jaw before my concert, inspired by the beauty of the church, our talk peppered with effortless confession.

"I didn't tell either of you that I was going to marry Susan," I said. "Did you ever keep anything to yourself, Rory?"

"Nothing."

"I don't believe you. Look at his face, Adrian. He's keeping something from us now."

"Or someone."

You waited a minute or two, Rory, canny as usual. "Well,

there is someone. A widow. She lives in Torremolinos. That's in Spain, Cameron. She owns a bar."

"How old is she?" I asked.

"Ouch."

"It's okay. She's thirty-four."

"I do like Spanish women," I said, arching my eyebrow, a trick, it seems, that neither of you has ever mastered.

"Your turn, Adrian."

"I have something to admit. It happened a long time ago." You raised your voice, and then waited for the din of the water taxi to die out as it passed La Pieta, the church where my concert would start in fifteen minutes.

"I don't have all day, Adrian. Out with it."

"I ate the pie. You know, when we were kids?"

Silence.

"The lemon meringue pie. Two pieces."

We were on you in a flash, Adrian. I had you in a choke-hold while Rory gave you a knuckle rub on your freshly cropped hair. I still can't believe both of you decided to get crewcuts in honour of my big day, waltzing to the barber a couple of days earlier, we three, three sheets to the wind.

The water taxi continued to belch as it motored down the canal. We released you, and straightened our clothes.

"There's something I don't understand, Adrian," Rory said, watching the boat disappear. "All this water, everywhere you look, and not once have you complained about getting on one of those contraptions. Do you wear a seasickness patch when you're here?"

"No. It never occurred to me." You grinned. "Maybe I'm cured."

The choirmaster popped his head out the side door of the church. "Ten minutes," he barked.

"I keep forgetting to show you these," I said, removing an envelope from the inside pocket of my tuxedo jacket and passing it over.

"Eve is on her left, Ruth to the right, and Faith is on her lap."

"Is that your dog?"

"That's Surefoot," I said. The dog is suckling a litter of pups.

"Are those her puppies?"

"Don't ask," I whispered. "Mary Anne and I were out for a walk in Stanley Park and I let Surefoot off her leash for a run. I watch this babe jog by and before you know it, some German shepherd is giving Surefoot his Johnson."

"His what?" Adrian asked.

"His Tallywhacker."

"We have to teach you some *English*, Adrian," I offered.

The choirmaster reappeared. "Places, Cameron. Now."

"Straighten your tie, Cameron, and roll down your shirt-sleeves."

"How do I look?" I asked.

And you said it together. "You look like us."

THE COLLECTION OF Mario Lanza records has found a place of honour on a table in my rehearsal studio. When Kalim's dad passed away last year, he gave them to me. I've stripped the floors. Kalim's meditation mat is below my bare feet, anchored by the podium holding my sheet music. On my left, a gallery of his framed Borneo photos graces the east wall of the room. I still haven't heard from him, other than one postcard, so I guess he isn't hooked up to an email account yet.

On the wall opposite, to the west, I've hung one of your *Red on Red* paintings, Rory. The one you gave me the year after you returned from your apprenticeship in Venice, before you created any of your exhibits. That was the last year you came home for the summer, the last summer any of us spent in Cape Breton. I went on that awful make-work project in Ontario and Manitoba, abandoning Susan and Mary Anne for almost a year.

"Your parents were very good to me, Cameron," Susan told me, years later, during one of her trips home to visit her mother, staying overnight with me in Halifax. When her father died, Susan's mother remarried within a year, and it was many years before Susan forgave her, which is why she stayed on with the folks after I left Sydney.

"Things settled down after you left, after you all left," Susan said. "Even Talbot stayed away most of the time. Your parents spoiled me. Your dad used to drive Mary Anne and me everywhere. Sometimes he even let me borrow the car, when I asked."

"Without a fight?"

"We never fought. Did you know that your mother knew you used to sneak me into the house for the night?"

I was blushing.

"I think they knew more than they let on," she said, the memories of those months evoking a wistfulness in her voice.

"Your mother always knew what to do when I had problems with Mary Anne. She put an ice cube in a facecloth one night, and rubbed it on her gums to soothe her, insisting that I go back to bed. I think she sat up all night with Mary Anne that time. They had all the answers."

I've also built bookshelves in my studio. They line the French doors leading out to the backyard. All of Mary Anne's children's books are there, waiting to be opened, read again, when the babies get a little bigger. It's my insurance policy, if they want a bedtime story they'll have to bunk down at my place for the night. I'm going to fill the shelves with enough books to keep them reading here until they're at least twenty!

I seem to have the grandfather thing under my belt, and the girls are growing like crazy. And strong! Eve likes to lie on her stomach and lift herself off the bed with her arms. Faith is the kick-boxer. Those chubby little legs can be lethal if you get too close during a diaper change. And Ruth seems to like blowing bubbles. Don't knock it, it's an art. Any day now they're all going to start crawling, probably in different directions, just like their granddad and grand-uncles did.

After I got back from Venice last month, I discovered that Mary Anne's been asking Susan if I've been dating anyone. Mary Anne, my foot! I saw that one coming a mile away. It was *Susan* doing the asking, using Mary Anne as a decoy.

"Mary Anne's asked me if I thought you'd ever get married again."

"Just like that," I said, feigning surprise at the question, "out of the blue?"

Jonathan and Mary Anne were putting two of the babies down for the night. Ruth was still fussing, so I was giving her a bottle in the living room. It didn't leave Susan with anything to do for the moment, other than to ask her question.

"Anyway, the answer is no," I said. "I don't want to get married again."

"Why not?"

"There's no one available at the present time."

Bad choice of words.

"What do you mean there's no one available? Do you have a girlfriend? Cameron, is she married? Is that why she isn't available right now?"

Ruth came to my rescue by refusing her bottle and starting to wail. I held her out to Susan.

"Do you mind? I have to take a piss. Ruth's been pressing on my bladder for the last ten minutes." I waited in the bathroom until I heard Jonathan's voice in the living room before I return, safe from any more ambushes.

Below your painting in my rehearsal studio, Rory, there's a long, low table. There are four or five framed photos on it, among them one of Mary Anne at your cottage on Georgian Bay. Beside her, Tenderfoot is staring into the camera.

I spent the afternoon with Mary Anne and the babies today, playing yet another game of tug-of-war with Surefoot, knocking over a plastic glass of water. It splashed the dog and she scampered off to the kitchen with a yelp.

"Be warned, Daddy, this one's a keeper."

Unlike Tenderfoot, this one doesn't like water, not even at the beach. When the waves wash ashore, Surefoot scampers away. She's adapted well to the addition of the babies. Mary Anne takes her for a walk every day, more to keep her primed than for exercise, although I think she enjoys the break. Surefoot has a basket with stuffed toys in the living room and has an uncanny knack for knowing which toys are hers and which ones belong to the babies.

As Mary Anne powdered the baby's bums earlier this evening, she was humming "Down in the Valley to Pray," a gospel tune I heard somewhere a long time ago and sang to her when she was a baby.

> *As I went down in the valley to pray*
> *Studying about that good old way*
> *And who shall wear the starry crown*
> *Good Lord, show me the way!*
> *O brothers let's go down, Let's go down, come on down,*
> *O brothers let's go down, Down in the valley to pray.*

I've sung that song a hundred times, lulled by its melody and the richness of the refrain. Mary Anne and Jonathan are going to have the girls baptized, and have asked me to sing.

"Anything in particular?" I asked.

"The baptism song," Mary Anne said, as if I was stunned.

"I don't know any baptism songs."

"Your *favourite* hymn," she said. I don't think of the songs I sing as hymns, psalms, or requiems. The religious elements don't interest me. Sometimes I think that's the reason I always find the sound the choirmaster wants. For me, the song has to bounce off the walls of the church in just the right timbre. When it's there, I know we've arrived.

Speaking of baptism, I told Mary Anne, Jonathan, and Susan a joke. There were polite chuckles from Mary Anne and Jonathan, but Susan hooted with abandon.

"And that's what attracted you to Daddy in the first place?" Mary Anne asks, in a deadpan voice.

"Among other things," Susan said, giggling.

I think we're both still getting used to Mary Anne's new fondness for the church, joining Jonathan's Methodist congregation.

Susan wiped her eyes. "Your father is a very funny man."

I love Mary Anne, with all of my heart, but I'm also glad Susan and I can still connect about things beyond our devotion to our daughter.

In case you're feeling left out, Adrian, don't worry, I have a picture of you on the wall in my studio. It's from *En Route* magazine, the time they did a feature on fine dining in Montreal. You're standing outside a restaurant, leaning against the stone wall, legs casually crossed in a *nonchalant* pose, dressed all in white with a starched apron around your waist, three black buttons on your chef's jacket and one of your trademark smiles splashed across your face. We can't be more than twenty-one or twenty-two. Rory and I were barely starting out in life and you were already a chef at a fancy restaurant in Montreal. Not too shabby, not too shabby at all. Don't blush, I'm not trying to embarrass you.

But speaking of embarrassment, do you remember the time the three of us whipped out our dicks to see who had the longest? I knew I was going to lose, because I didn't have any foreskin to stretch. I was the only one the doctor snipped at our birth. You and Rory were making fun of the little cherry at the end of my dick. Then we started comparing our bells and we discovered Rory was missing one. He was all in a panic and started crying. It hadn't descended yet. Even the folks seemed at a loss as to what was wrong. I'm assuming it finally did fall in place, Rory, as we haven't really got back to that conversation, to find out how the story ended.

Acknowledgements

I WOULD LIKE TO THANK Sheldon and Dawn Currie for their
encouragement, and Peggy MacDonald for generously listening to four years of updates on the other end of the line without ever once yawning. I am grateful to Jane Buss and the
Writers' Federation of Nova Scotia, and the Nova Scotia
Department of Tourism, Culture and Heritage for their financial support; and Clare McKeon, Mom and Dad, and Lars, all
for allowing me to explore.